# STONE OF DESTINY

BOOK ONE IN THE IRISH CYCLE

# ALSO BY DAVID MILLER

NOVELS

*Gateway to Sheol*

*Daughter of Darkness*

*Through the Ages*

*Stone of Destiny*

# STONE OF DESTINY

## BOOK ONE IN THE IRISH CYCLE

# DAVID MILLER

# COPYRIGHT

## STONE OF DESTINY

For exclusive content, information about upcoming new releases and other deals,

please join our mailing list here:
https://www.subscribepage.com/irishcycleseries

For Kage,
This man's best friend
Miss you, little mister

# STONE OF DESTINY

# CHAPTER 1

THE LOUD BANG on the cruiser's hood snapped him awake.

Patrolman Sean Regan sat bolt upright behind the wheel of his patrol car. He pushed his cap back off his eyes as he blinked away sleep and looked around. "What the…"

"Officer! Hey, wake up, man!"

A wiry young man wearing an Army field jacket, an Indiana Jones-like fedora, and carrying a backpack slung over one shoulder stood at the front of the car. A light snow had fallen, leaving a scrim of glistening flakes on the windshield, distorting the young man's image.

Regan wiped at the corner of his mouth with the back of his hand. He twisted the key in the ignition, starting the car, then lowered the side window and stuck his head out as the young man was about to slam his fist down on the hood again.

"Hey! Quit it. What do you want?"

An hour ago Regan had backed the cruiser into a tight alley off 8th Street, just a few blocks from Old Harbor. It was one of his favorite napping spots. Dark, and just wide enough to accommodate the width of a vehicle, so no one could sneak up alongside.

"You've gotta come," the young man said excitedly, glancing

furtively west down the street. "There's a fight. You've gotta see it to believe it."

Regan waved him away from the front of the car and pulled out. When the driver's side door cleared the sidewalk, Regan stomped on the brake. "What the hell does that mean?"

"It means it's like crazy. There's this Amazon chick on a great big horse and some little midget dude."

"This some kind of joke, kid?" Regan thought if it was, he'd run the skinny punk in. "Or are you high on something?"

"No." He held his left hand up. "Scout's honor, man. It's a woman on a horse. And she's got a sword!"

*Damn it.* Regan looked at the dashboard clock. *My shift's barely started and I've gotta deal with crap like…this.*

"All right. Get in." He hooked his thumb toward the back door.

"What?" The young man backed up a step. "No friggin' way, man. I almost didn't get out of there alive the first time. I ain't going back there."

The snow flurries were getting heavier—it was three days before Halloween—who'd ever heard of it snowing in October? At least not in Boston. Flakes landed lightly on the young man's shoulders and the brim of his stupid fedora, melting into dark wet circles. He rearranged the backpack draped over his shoulder, clutching at the straps with two hands, and licked the snow from his lips.

After eleven years of police work, Regan recognized fear when he saw it. The question was, was he scared by what he'd seen or because he was participating in some kind of college prank? "If you're messing with me, son…"

"I'm not, man. I swear. There's this horse, and a woman yelling and waving a sword around. I got the hell out of there, man, and I'm not going back."

*Swords. Horses. Midgets. Yeah, right.* Regan could hear it

now back at the station house. Like he didn't have it bad enough already...

"Okay. Where's this supposedly going down?"

"On William Day Boulevard. Right off I Street, man. You can't miss it."

Regan took the kid's personal information and waved him away. "All right, get out of here. If I see you around again..." He let the threat hang.

The kid was already high-tailing it down the block. His shoulders hunched against the snow as he shook his head, mumbling, "Ain't nobody gonna believe this when I tell 'em. Nobody."

Regan flipped on the emergency lights and turned onto 8th Street. At the corner he turned left, leaving the side window open, trying to ignore the cold, and listening. The cruiser's tires rolled wetly over the pavement. The air was heavy with moisture and smelled of salt water this close to the harbor. Snow clung to the blades of grass along the sidewalks, coating them white, and the slick roadway shimmered from the amber splashes of light from the curbside streetlamps.

Regan rolled through the intersection ahead, I Street and Columbia Road, and spun the steering wheel to the left. He slowed to a stop, blinked, and waited for the windshield wipers to clear the falling snow from the glass, hoping they would swish away what it was he thought he saw. They didn't.

*No. Frigging. Way.*

The kid hadn't been lying, nor had he been tripping on drugs. Maybe it was Regan who was tripping. Maybe he hadn't really woken up and this was all a dream.

Up ahead, his headlights illuminated a huge white horse. It stood at nineteen hands, at least. Its mane was hogged. Not something you saw very often nowadays. He marveled, recognizing the breed. An

Irish sport horse. But bigger than any horse he'd ever seen.

There was a rider, but too high above the glow of the headlights for him to see anything but a shadow, even after Regan flashed the high beams.

On the road facing the horse and rider stood a man, or a boy, squat and no more than three and a half feet tall. He wore a red coat with tails and a ridiculous red top hat. In one hand, he held a lantern high. Its flame flickered green and bright, giving him the appearance of a lawn gnome. Caught in the penumbra of the intense halogen light, he twisted around and snarled a sinister, sharp-toothed sneer. The odd lantern glow gave his misshapen face a jaundiced look.

Regan snapped his jaw shut, shivered, and stepped from the cruiser.

"Do not interfere," a voice warned from atop the restless horse. Steam billowed from the equine's nostrils as it snorted angrily.

Lightning flashed in the sky behind them, giving Regan a millisecond glimpse of the rider.

It *was* a woman, as the kid had reported to him. She wore a vest of chain-mail armor, an animal skin kilt and a cloak of brown fur. Regan guessed it had been fashioned from animal pelts. A metal band encased her upper right arm. Auburn hair, highlighted with red, flowed in waves over her shoulders and down her back. It billowed in the wind. In her gloved left hand, she held a sword. Its blade gleamed menacingly in the pulsing light of the cruiser, its honed tip aimed at the lawn gnome's chest.

*You have got to be kidding me.*

Regan drew his service gun. "Put the sword down."

"Do not interfere," she repeated. "You know not what transpires here, nor what troubles you might cause if you do."

"You're right, lady. I don't have a clue what's going on here, but I do know this. There's going to be a whole lot of trouble if you don't put that sword down. Now." Regan stepped out from behind the open door, keeping an eye on both the woman and the living lawn gnome as best he could. "Don't you think about moving either," he warned the red-clad midget.

"I cannot protect you if you persist," the warrior woman said.

"You've got it backwards, lady. I'm the one here to serve and protect. Put the sword down so nobody gets hurt. Then we can talk about what's going on."

In his peripheral vision, Regan noticed a few people had gathered to watch, curious residents from the middle-class homes lining Columbia Road, the strobe of police lights having roused them from their beds or away from their flickering late-night television shows. They congregated in small groups of twos, threes, and fours, clutching parkas and thick robes and murmuring at the spectacle.

*Great. Now I've got civilians to worry about, too.*

The woman swung her leg over the horse's withers and slid from its leather saddle. The horse pawed at the road with one hoof and snorted. The woman patted his neck, calming him.

"Easy, Enbarr." With her sword still pointed at the lawn gnome, she said to Regan, "You are a protector of the people in this Otherworld?"

Regan scowled. *Otherworld?* Maybe it was this woman who's tripping on something. "Yes. I am the police."

"I am Plor na mBan, daughter of Oisin and Niamh." She said it as if that explained everything.

*At least I have her talking,* Regan thought. "That's a mouthful. Can I just call you Plor?"

"As you wish."

"Okay. Good. Plor, I need you to put the sword down on the ground and step away from it."

"That would be a most unwise thing to do."

"Why is that?" Regan asked.

She indicated the red-coated gnome. "Because he will tear off."

Regan scowled again. Her brogue was thick, and her word choices odd, as if English were strange to her. "I won't let that happen."

"You cannot stop him."

"You'd be surprised what I can do."

"Sean, what's going on?"

Hearing a familiar voice, a voice he knew as well as his own, Regan spun around. It belonged to his wife, Deidre. What the hell was she doing here? He scanned the faces in the crowd. He didn't see her. Where was she? "Dee?"

Other than the few pedestrians who had come out, the animated lawn gnome and Plor, the street was empty. Perplexed, he called out his wife's name. "Deidre?"

"'Tis a mind trick of the fear darrig," Plor shouted. "Do not listen."

Regan whirled back around. His heart hammered inside his chest. *That voice was Deidre's.* Before he could question Plor about it, about what she said, the air split with a loud, sudden cawing.

"Look out!" The warning came from a cluster of pedestrians hunkered down behind the row of cars parked on the street. An older man pointed into the air.

Regan spun.

Overhead, a bird of incredible size swooped out of the dark, snow-filled sky. Brown-winged with a plume of white around its crooked neck, it was a species of vulture, but one with a wingspan of over twenty-five feet, twice that of any normal-size bird.

The creature dived with missile-like precision, straight at Plor na mBan.

Again it cawed, its black talons splayed.

14

The horse reared.

Regan tracked the large bird with his gun but feared taking a shot. The damn thing was too close to Plor and the horse. If he missed, he risked shooting one of them.

"Keep Ciag from tearing off," Plor shouted, raising her sword, prepared to face the attacking vulture. "The fear darrig! Do not allow his escape."

The gnome put his lantern down at his feet, bared a sharp, snaggletoothed grin, and hopped, dancing a jig, and clapped, watching the vulture descend on Plor. His bloodshot eyes beamed from under the brim of his ridiculous top hat.

Regan rushed at the little man.

Ciag, as Plor had called him, stood his ground. His grin widened.

As Regan made a grab for him, he retrieved the lantern he'd put down and held it high over his head. He tapped the top of his hat with his free hand, three times. It made a hollow popping sound. And then, incredibly, the fiendish little gnome vanished. Just poof. Gone.

Regan came up short, slack-jawed and blinking. He twisted and turned, scanning the area around him. *How the ...! That's impossible.*

The clang of metal on pavement captured Regan's attention.

Plor had somehow avoided the vulture's first attack and retaliated by swinging her sword at the darting giant bird, but she missed. She stood with the tip of her blade embedded in the pavement. Cracks in the asphalt radiated outward from the broadsword's strike.

The vulture shrieked and circled, diving toward her again.

Unable to free the blade of her sword in time, Plor abandoned it, ducked, and spun, but too late.

The vulture's talons raked deeply across her cheek, neck, and arm. She cried out.

Enbarr reared up and snorted, angrily thrashing his hoofs at the departing bird, and quite possibly saved his rider's life. A hoof clipped the vulture, knocking it off-kilter. It screeched, flapped, and cawed, circling up and away from the horse and Plor, and gave Regan a clear shot at it for the first time.

He took it. His Glock boomed once, twice, thrice. The muzzle flash coruscated yellow in the snow-filled air.

Each shot hit its mark. Hardly a surprise, since Regan was an expert shot...and the damn bird was as big as a barn. The vulture convulsed, cartwheeled, and flapped its wings, emitting a god-awful squawk as it plummeted to the wet pavement and skidded across the street in a flurry of fluttering dark feathers.

Breathless, Regan approached the unmoving bird. Awkwardly, it struggled to get up. Regan marveled at its size, almost unable to comprehend what he was seeing, what he had just seen. The bird faltered and fell. Its claws clicked across the pavement as it tried to stand. Regan drew his baton and bashed the creature's head in, putting it out of its misery.

In the distance, sirens wailed. Someone had called in the disturbance. Police were responding.

Regan started to turn away, but a movement caught his eye. He turned back to the dead, gigantically oversized bird. Could the damn thing still be alive? As he approached, the carcass burst into a wraith of black smoke. He jumped. "What the..."

The smoke quickly dissipated in the heavy, snowy air, leaving behind nothing but an acrid smell and a smudge of soot on the pavement.

"'Twas," Plor said from behind him, "a conjuring. Meant to distract us."

He turned to see her leaning heavily against Enbarr's flank. The horse snorted great plumes of steam, his large eyes on Plor. In them, Regan saw concern, but that was crazy.

The sword she'd swung with such ease earlier lay on the

16

pavement at her feet. Blood from the talon wounds covered her arm and neck and coursed down her chain-mail vest.

"You're hurt," Regan said.

"'Tis truth you speak." Plor looked around. "That sound. What is it?"

"Sirens. More police."

"Police. Protectors like you?"

"Yes."

"What is to happen when the other…police arrive?"

Regan shrugged. Standing directly under a streetlamp, he was getting his first good look at her. Her features were strong and angular, sharp with high, well-defined cheekbones. Her arms and legs were muscular, well sculpted, but not overly developed. At six feet tall, she matched Regan's own height. If he could use just one word to describe her, it would be *statuesque.*

"First, we'll take you to the hospital where we'll get you patched up." He pointed at the bloody diagonal claw marks raking her arm, neck, and cheek. "Then, it'll be down to the station house where we can talk about"—waved a hand around—"all this."

"I am to be your prisoner?"

He hesitated. "No."

"A lie."

She said it without accusation. A simple statement. Nothing more, nothing less. And it was spot on. He sensed there was no point in arguing with her.

"I will tell you my tale," she said. "But I will not be your prisoner."

The sirens were louder now.

"You've broken the law. I don't think you'll have a choice."

She didn't answer; she simply nodded. Then she reached down and picked up the sword with her uninjured arm. It appeared to be very heavy for her now. She set the reins over Enbarr's saddle. "What has been wrought here this night, what you have witnessed with thine own eyes, you consider unusual. Do you not?"

"Yes I do. I very much do." What else could he say?

She held him with a steely stare, one filled with passion and intensity, yet the emerald green of her eyes sparkled with mirth and depth and excitement. "Then chance me to tell you my tale. Others who have not seen, who have not battled a conjuring or witnessed the trickery of the fear darrig will not believe. Once you've heard my tale, then you may decide what is to become of me. If prisoner it be, then so be it."

Several blocks away, two patrol units sped around the corner from L Street, their lights illuminating the night with strobes of blue and white.

A cold, bracing wind blew in from the harbor, swirled the flakes of snow, coming down in faster, heavier waves. He'd have to decide fast. Coming up on the scene without having been here, what would he think? Would he believe stories about evaporating giant birds and disappearing lawn gnomes? He'd been there and seen them, and he was having trouble believing them himself.

He cocked his head, trying to evaluate her. He had only seconds to decide. "You won't resist? Whatever I decide?"

"You grant me a fair hearing. After which, I will abide your choice." She handed her sword to Regan. "Take *Claiomh Solais* as a sign of my good faith."

Regan took the sword—needing both hands to hold it—and laid it across the backseat of his cruiser. He glanced down the street and saw that the patrol cars were almost upon them. Holding the door open, thinking he was out of his cotton-picking mind, he said, "I don't know what to do about the horse."

"I can ride him."

"Is he as fast as a police car?"

Her full, beautiful mouth spread into a smile that lit up her whole face and made her emerald eyes twinkle with amusement. "The question is, is your police car as fast as Enbarr? Assist me."

He gave her a leg up. She mounted her horse with only the tiniest of grimaces tightening her sculpted face. Whoever she was, Regan thought, admiringly, she was drop-dead gorgeous and tough as nails.

With her settled in, he K-turned the cruiser and drove back up I Street, away from the scene, away from the approaching cruisers. He was leaving a crime scene with a woman who had committed any number of crimes. He'd discharged his weapon at…at what, a sooty smudge on the pavement? How could he explain that?

As they sped north, Plor drew Enbarr up even with the cruiser's driver's side door.

Regan powered down the window and shouted out into the wind, "Keep up."

She patted the horse's neck. He neighed, throwing his head forward, eager to run. Plor na mBan smiled, despite cradling her injured arm, and shouted down to Regan, "Enbarr says the same to you."

# CHAPTER 2

AT PRECISELY THE moment patrolman Sean Regan was racing Plor na mBan and her oversized horse Enbarr up I Street, Kurt Kegler sat at the bar in the Old Sea Dog Tavern, thinking he was the luckiest man on the planet.

Beside him sat a woman named Yuki, sipping an apple martini and watching him coyly over the rim of her glass. She had alabaster skin that creased into fine lines around her thin, red lips and radiated from the corners of her almond-shaped, sea-green eyes and straight black hair streaked with gray. More salt than pepper, as they say, but it took nothing away from her beauty.

Breaking eye contact, Kurt reached for his scotch, feeling his face flush. He hadn't felt this nervous since he asked Rebecca Lawton, his high school sweetheart, to marry him.

"How long has it been since your husband passed?" At his age, asking about recently departed spouses, family members, and old friends who had died was the fallback position for all his conversations lately.

"Several years," Yuki replied, carefully setting her glass on the bar. She'd barely touched it.

"Rebecca, too. Cancer." He took another large gulp, finishing his drink. His second. He waved to Tom, the bartender and owner of the old joint. "Another round."

"Heart attack." Yuki raised her fresh glass. "To the spouses we loved, and lost."

They drank. Kurt said, "I know it'll sound lame, but what brings a beautiful gal like you to a dump like this?"

He waved a hand around the Old Sea Dog. It was his favorite watering hole: a single room roughly the size of a doublewide trailer, with enough room for two pool tables, a couple of tables and chairs, and a dance floor nobody ever used. The bar ran along the length of one dingy, beige-colored wall under a few casement windows aglow with neon beer signs. Not exactly the dictionary definition of a classy joint.

Kurt and Yuki were the only ones there, besides old Tom who sat at the far end of the bar—to give them privacy—reading that day's edition of the *Boston Globe*.

Yuki looked away, demurely, and though it was hard to see in the low light, seemed to blush. "You flatter me, sir."

So taken by this woman, Kurt didn't notice she'd completely avoided answering his question. Her beauty, her demeanor, her interest in him captivated him and distracted him from everything else, making Kurt all the more self-conscious about his basketball-like gut, his weak, aged muscles, and his wispy, thinning white hair. At sixty-eight years old, he was hardly the catch of the day, especially for a woman like…this.

Though she was no spring chicken herself, Yuki patted his liver-spotted hand and glanced past Kurt to where Tom sat, pretending not to watch them. "Perhaps there is someplace more…private we could go."

Kurt gulped down the last of his drink, again not believing his luck. He cleared his throat. "So, yeah, sure." He deposited his glass on the Boston Lager coaster on the bar and leaped to his feet. "Tom," he called out, "we're outta here."

Yuki slipped gracefully from her barstool and stooped, quite ladylike, to retrieve her purse from the floor. "Are you okay to drive?"

He stood up straight and tall. "Steady as a sailor on dry land. I am German after all. If nothing else, we know how to hold our liquor."

Kurt placed his hand on the small of her back and steered her toward the door. "Good night, Tom." Behind Yuki's back, he gave his old friend a thumbs-up sign.

Tom smiled and waved back before folding up the newspaper and climbing off his seat, going about closing down the bar now that his last patrons had left.

Kurt Kegler stiff-armed the door and led Yuki outside. There, they carefully navigated the three concrete steps to the sidewalk below, white from the sudden snow flurries that had begun to fall.

*Really. It ain't even Halloween yet.*

He unlocked the passenger side door of his battered, ten-year-old Toyota Tundra, his service vehicle for his fledgling handyman business, wistful for the days when he tooled around town in his '62 Corvette, bought at auction and painstakingly restored and refurbished over more weekends than he cared to remember. Where had the time gone, he wondered as he stiffly pulled himself into the driver's seat of the old truck, wishing his muscles didn't ache the way they did. It was a chronic complaint, but especially tonight with the cold and snow.

Yuki put her hand on his arm and sent an electricity-charged chill through him. "Let's go down to the bay. I love looking out over the water at night. It reminds me of my childhood home in Japan."

"Hell," he said with a smile. "Sure." He knew just the spot

and it was only a block away, down at Marine Park, overlooking Pleasure Bay.

They parked in a row of spaces facing the water, all of them empty. It was near two in the morning and too cold for anyone in their right mind to be out, not with the sudden wind gusts whipped up along the beach with an icy fury. Snowflakes blew past his windshield, too cold to stick.

Only October, Kurt groused again, in awe.

"You don't want to get out, do you?" He hoped not. He didn't take to the cold the way he used to, shivering just thinking about it. With the engine still running, he turned the heater up a notch.

"No. Let's just sit here and watch."

He wanted to ask, watch what? But he didn't.

After a time, Yuki asked, "When was the last time you parked with a girl, Kurt?"

She placed a hand on his thigh.

He stammered, feeling like a kid on his first date. Well, it was— his first in thirty-five years. "A long time."

Yuki shifted in her seat. The amber glow of the nearby streetlamp caressed her features, casting the side of her face in shadow, masking it. "It makes me feel like a young girl again. All this." She waved a hand at the sidewalk and the empty beach and the flat, dark water, looking more ominous and black than it should, Kurt thought.

Yuki reached out and caressed his white-stubbled cheek. He shivered from the touch of her icy fingers, realizing for the first time how cold she felt. She leaned into him and kissed him on the mouth. He tasted the apple martini on her tongue, her lips feeling like shaved ice, even as her kiss ignited a fire within him.

Then the incredible happened; even without those damn blue pills, he got a woody!

He sucked in a breath and his heart raced in his chest.

Panting, he reached out for her, pulled her in close, returning her kiss, probing her mouth with his tongue. Could this really be happening? At his age? In his mind he heard all those medical warnings from TV: *Be sure you are healthy enough for sexual activities before taking...*

And with that thought, he noticed the first inkling of trouble. His stomach churned, roiling like the waves they'd been watching out on the bay, stirred into a frothy cauldron. *Lord, please, don't let me throw up.* He hadn't had that much to drink, had he? Short of breath, he tried to push Yuki away. *I need to breathe.*

But she climbed over him, straddling him, pressing his body hard into the split, plastic-covered bench seat. Her icy lips sealed around his mouth, so cold they burned like dry ice. It was then that Kurt suddenly smelled something rancid, like bad meat left out too long. He wanted to gag. His esophagus became tight and raw. The taste of bile rose up in his throat.

He felt clammy. Sweat dotted his forehead even as he shivered. He felt drained, too weak to struggle against the iron grip Yuki had on him. Still she kept her lips locked over his mouth. Her hands were like icy claws grasping the sides of his face. Her tongue lashed wetly about inside his mouth, thick, but flickering fast, darting this way and that, the way a snake's tongue would flit. He gagged.

*What is going on?* An icy fear chilled him as his skin grew cold. His insides churned, tearing, ripping, pulling, until he felt as if his viscera were being sucked out of him. A howling, deafening whistle filled the cab of the truck, like a rushing wind filling his ears.

Frantic, Kurt thrashed about under Yuki. He pushed desperately at her shoulders, kicked at the truck pedals, the dashboard. His eyes were open wide, filled with something beyond fear, filled with terror. But his ability to escape, to fight, quickly ebbed away. Drained, he felt too old, too tired, too worn out. More tired than even his normally fatigued sixty-eight-year-old body should be, he felt more like he was one hundred and sixty-eight. The last essence of energy now drained from him.

His body went limp, and when Kurt Kegler knew he couldn't survive another minute, sure this woman's kiss had finished him, killed him off, Yuki released her grip. She sat back, away from him. She wiped at the corners of her mouth with her long delicate fingers, her nails shiny and blood red in the ghostly glow of light. The skin around her mouth and her almond-shaped eyes was less wrinkled, supple now with a healthy, warmer sheen than before. But it was her hair that frightened him the most. Gone were the streaks of gray. Now, her hair shimmered black and glossy, with only a single, thick highlight of white, like a solitary lightning bolt against a black night sky. Yuki appeared to be twenty years younger. How could that possibly be?

Kurt remained wedged between the door and the bench seat, too weak to move, too spent to try, too tired to even draw a breath. Left like that, he was sure of two things: first, he was dying, and second, Yuki *was* younger, more energized, more beautiful than she'd been before.

Gasping, he asked, "What have you done to me? Why?"

Kurt Kegler never got his answer. His head lolled to the side, catching a glimpse of his face in the rearview mirror. It was the final thing Kurt Kegler saw in this world, and it made him scream.

# CHAPTER 3

SEAN REGAN DROVE hard and fast up I Street in his cruiser. Plor and the horse, Enbarr, kept pace easily. The animal's hoofs struck the gleaming pavement with thundering clops, kicking up fantails of bright sparks. He snorted, eyeing the front bumper of the cruiser, as if to make sure he stayed just that far ahead of it. The sport horse was fast and unfazed by the wet pavement, the blue and white emergency lights, and the swirling snow.

The same could not be said for the few pedestrians and motorists they passed. None failed to do a double take at the near-glowing white sport horse galloping along, sparking the pavement and snorting steam from his nose like a locomotive, and the warrior woman atop him, her cape and auburn hair billowing freely behind her as she clutched the reins and held on tight.

They arrived at Regan's condo apartment off Dixfield Street in short order. His was an end unit that came with a two-car garage. There he helped Plor lead Enbarr into the empty bay. By the time he returned from the kitchen with a plastic bag full of apples and carrots, Plor had the animal untacked and was wiping down his flank with an old towel.

"Come on," he said, feeding the horse some carrots before taking the towel from her and leading her to the apartment door. "I'll take care of the horse after I get you patched up."

"You have a knowledge of horses, yes?"

"Some. My grandmother ran a riding stable not far from here. I spent a lot of summers there, mucking stalls, cleaning tack, and lunging horses."

His one-bedroom apartment was long and narrow. They came through a short hall that led to the combined living room-dining room. The kitchen was to their right, the bedroom and bath off to the left. Glass panel French doors opened out from both the living room and bedroom onto a single balcony overlooking a courtyard pond and fountain—the geysers of water ablaze with multicolored, alternating lights—and Boston Harbor beyond.

Regan guided Plor to the far end of the living room to a red leather couch set along the interior wall. She sat, gazing around the room, with a look of awe on her face, as if she'd never seen anything as magnificent as his modest apartment before in her life.

"I've got a first-aid kit in the kitchen," he said. "Sit tight."

When he returned with it, a bowl of warm water, and a wet washcloth, he found Plor gripping the arm of the couch and the cushion under her with a talon-like death grip.

"Is everything all right?"

She said, "It would appear so. Isn't it?"

Confused, he set the bowl and other things down on the coffee table. "I ask because…the way you're holding the couch…" He pointed at her hands.

"You requested I 'sit tight.' Was I doing it wrong?"

Regan felt his forehead furrow. *This is one strange chick.* "It's okay. I meant relax."

With the curtains open over the French doors, the fountain lights splashed a kaleidoscope of warm color over the room's boring beige walls and sand-brown carpet. He turned on one lamp. At its lowest setting, it provided sufficient light to see by.

Plor jumped away from the lamp, staring, then, guardedly, she leaned over to look up under the shade, awestruck. "I was told to expect such wonders, but how is there light with no flame? What manner of sorcery is this?"

"It's not sorcery. It's electricity." Regan shook his head, annoyed at himself for getting sucked into whatever delusional fantasy this woman was indulging in. "Never mind that now." He wiped at the drying blood on her arm and neck with the warm, wet washcloth. "You said you have a story to tell."

"One of grave importance."

Regan hoped so, thinking about all the departmental regulations he'd broken, and the common sense ones: not waiting for the officer-involved-shooting detectives; leaving a crime scene; harboring a... what was this woman...a criminal? A fugitive? An escaped psychotic mental patient?

What had he been thinking?

"Well, let's hear it. You can start with that giant vulture. Where'd it come from and why'd it attack you? And how in the hell did it disappear into a puff of smoke?"

The wounds to her neck and cheek were superficial; a good cleaning with warm water, a little hydrogen peroxide, and they'd be fine. The three claw marks on her arm were another story. They were deeper and must have been very painful, though Plor sat with her hands in her lap without complaint and gave no indication of any discomfort at all.

"As I told you earlier, 'twas a conjuring. A creature created by Ciag—"

"This may sting a little," he said before applying the antiseptic to her wounds. "So you're saying it wasn't real?"

"Nay. 'Twas quite real." Plor glanced down at her injured arm, as if to indicate just how real it had been. "And very dangerous."

After he was done cleaning the wounds, Regan placed two large bandages over the lacerations in her arm, held them in place while he wound an Ace bandage around her bicep, then secured the Velcro ends. A less than professional effort, but it would do the job for now.

"What you're trying to say is this Ciag...conjured up this creature from nowhere. How?"

"Nay. Not from nowhere. From energy. Energy that is all around. It is an...ability of the fear darrig."

"You're serious?"

"I am."

Regan plopped the bloody washcloth into the now tepid bowl of water and took it back to the kitchen. *We're approaching looney-tune central now*, he thought, putting the bowl in the sink and wanting to grab a beer from the refrigerator. He didn't. He was still on duty after all.

"You deny what your own eyes reveal to you?" Plor asked, coming up behind him.

He whirled. "No." He stepped around her and back into the living room. "I deny...your explanation of what I saw. I reject conjured-up creatures from energy and dancing little leprechauns disappearing into the night. Things like that don't happen."

"They do, and they did," she countered.

Regan nodded, agreeing but still not believing. "Yes they did."

For a reflective moment neither one spoke. Then Plor said, "A fear darrig."

Regan scowled. He felt a headache coming on. "Excuse me?"

"Ciag is not a leprechaun, though I understand your confusion. 'Tis a relation to the wee folk they have, yes, but the fear darrig are a far nastier bit of business."

He waved that away. "Okay, whatever. Let's get back to why you were menacing this fear darrig...with a sword?"

"I am here to stop Ciag."

"Stop him from what?"

"In honesty, I do not know." Plor began to pace the length of the living room. "I have been sent to this Otherworld because he is here. Is that not enough?"

Regan blinked as he tried to sort out what she was saying. "No, it's not enough. Why do you care if he's here?"

Now it was Plor's turn to look confused. "A fear darrig brings mischief wherever it goes. They can do nothing else. It is their nature. Ciag should not be in this world. He does not belong here. He belongs...where he belongs."

Plor began to get agitated, so rather than push her further for an answer to why she was after him, Regan changed direction. "Where is that?"

"Where he came from. Same as I. *Tir na nÓg.*"

*Okay, this broad's a few bricks shy of a load.* Regan clapped his hands, done. "On that note, let's say—"

"Wait," Plor pleaded, somehow anticipating what he was about to say and do. "You made a bond to listen. You have not yet heard my full tale."

"No," Regan said, "but I've heard enough."

"Why are you afraid to hear what must be told?"

"I'm not afraid. I'm a cop, been one for eleven years. I listen to crackpot stories from people all the time. They're a dime a dozen."

"I do not know what these dimes and dozens are you speak of, nor why you mention broken pottery, but you made an oath to listen. I implore you, honor thy word and fulfill the oath you freely entered into."

"All right. All right," Regan said, about to add, *in for a penny, in for a pound.* He refrained, in no mood to explain that saying too. "I'll listen to your tale, all of it, but make it snappy."

"Snappy?"

Regan glanced at his watch. "Just get on with it. I need to get back on patrol."

She smiled, satisfied. "I am Plor na mBan, daughter of Oisin and Niamh. I am of the divine people Tuatha Dé Danann, from *Tir na nÓg.*"

A blast of earsplitting static caused Plor to stop and jump to her feet while reaching for her empty scabbard. Her sword remained safely locked in the backseat of Regan's patrol car. "What is that shrilling noise?"

It was a call coming in over the radio strapped to Regan's belt. *Oh, man, no. Not now.*

"There's been a report of a dead body found in Marine Park. Please respond."

*Crap!* He keyed the shoulder mic. "This is Officer Regan. I'm en route."

# CHAPTER 4

SEAN REGAN ROLLED slowly up to the parked ten year old Toyota Tundra. It was three eighteen in the morning. Just seven minutes after the 911 call had come in. The vehicle was parked head-on, facing the combined sidewalk and boardwalk overlooking Pleasure Bay Beach. Whoever had made the anonymous call was already long gone. No surprise, Regan thought, zipping up his uniform bomber jacket and dreading having to get out of the warm cruiser.

Regan grabbed his hat, not liking the cold or the snow, and climbed out.

The snow had fallen heavier in the last half hour, having already dumped an inch of the white stuff on the ground. It being two nights before Halloween, Regan expected craziness, but having to deal with the likes of Plor na mBan and her whole warrior-woman act, and Ciag the leprechaun—excuse me, fear darrig—and a conjured-up giant vulture thing, that was beyond the pale. And now a full-blown October snowstorm?

The 911 call reported that the dead body had been seen inside the parked Tundra.

Regan flicked on his heavy Maglite and approached the vehicle, following the fading footprints in the snow, his other hand on the butt of his service Glock. The light reflected back off the wet metal of the truck chassis, then the beaded glass in the back of the cab, blinding him. Regan turned away and blinked, trying to clear the bright spots from his eyes and regain some of his lost night vision.

Moving up along the driver's side, Regan reached the truck's door and shined the light into the interior, this time at an angle. Inside the cab he saw what looked like an old man slumped in an awkward position behind the wheel.

The top of his head—it was almost certainly a male—was covered in wispy, snowy-white hair.

Regan stepped out, faced the door straight on, and gasped. The old man's face was pressed up against the interior glass. His flesh was dark, mottled purple and brown, and sagging. His eyes were wide and his mouth was open in a silent death scream.

One withered, brown, skeletal-shaped hand pressed against the window, cupped and with split fingertips, like the poor bastard had been clawing at the glass to get out.

The corpse's skin was shriveled and drooped loose in jowly folds, as if the skull underneath had been shrunken, leaving the dry flesh nothing to cling to, so it hung slack. But it was the eyes that were the most disturbing. They were open, wide and bulging. Each sclera was bloodshot and the once blue irises were now cloudy behind a milky gray film. Blood had burst forth from beneath the eyes, staining the old man's face with drying red tears.

Regan tried the door handle. It opened. Despite his best effort to stop it, the corpse tumbled out. Its legs, tangled up in the well under the dash, caught, so the body's fall was arrested, leaving it draped headfirst out of the side of the vehicle. Its arms flopped across the cold, snowy pavement.

Pointlessly, Regan checked for a pulse. There wasn't one.

Regan pulled his hand back, shivering. The flesh on the corpse's neck was dry, paper-thin and as cold as touching a block of dry ice. Regan took a step back, trying to catch his breath. Eleven years a cop, six as a detective investigating homicides, and he'd never seen anything like this before.

Nor could anything in his experience account for the bloody tears marking the dead man's face.

Regan keyed his shoulder mic and called for a forensic team, the ME, and the detective on duty catching calls. While he waited, he secured the quiet crime scene under the penumbra of a single ghostly yellow streetlight from across Shore Road. A lone figure in the gusting cold, snowy wind, he spooled out the crime scene tape, looping it around the corner streetlamp, a garbage can, then a beach restriction signpost. He listened to the storm-stirred waves lapping against the sandy shoreline. Regan's thoughts turned to Plor, the warrior woman with a sword and her crazy story about the fear darrig and a strange place called *Tir na nÓg*.

That name sounded hauntingly familiar to him, but for the life of him he couldn't place it.

Detective Mike Hall was the first to arrive. Regan was relieved to see it was Mike because he was one of the few cops left who would give him the time of day.

The detective parked his unmarked Crown Vic behind Regan's cruiser. Hall was a big, linebacker-size cop with nearly twenty years in as a cop. He was old school, hard-nosed, and competent. At one time he and Regan had been friends. Now their relationship was strictly professional. Which was more than Regan could say for how the rest of the detectives on the force felt about him, and forget about the patrolmen he worked with. *Can you say pariah, boys and girls?*

"What'd ya got, Regan?" Hall asked, getting out of the car and snapping on a pair of blue latex gloves. Before Regan could answer,

Hall asked, "You got booties in your cruiser?"

Regan nodded. "Yeah." He already had his own booties and gloves on, old habits from his detective days. Hall leaned against the front of the cruiser, putting his booties on while Regan brought him up to speed. "Patrol's sending two more units over to start a canvass." Regan looked around the desolate area. "Not that we'll find anyone out here at this time of night."

Hall nodded in agreement, but they had to do it. "Good. Any sign of our 911 caller?"

"Gone by the time I got here."

"Okay," Hall said. "Let's take a look."

Regan held up the crime scene tape, then followed Hall over to the body.

"Jesus. You found him like this?"

"No. He fell out of the door when I opened it up to check on him."

"You had to establish there was no need for emergency aid." It was a statement. Hall's words held no recrimination. Regulations required preservation of life above all else. Regan had acted properly. Yet, he silently thanked Hall for the consideration. That was something Regan wasn't used to in recent months.

"Obviously no pulse, not breathing."

"Dead a long time if you ask me." Hall pointed at the corpse. "Looks like there's a wallet in his pants pocket."

The victim—which was how Regan thought of anyone who'd died in a manner like this—wore loose blue jeans with paint and spackle stains on them and a red, black, and white plaid flannel shirt. Working class, Regan thought, as were many of the people who lived here in Southie.

Regan carefully extracted the billfold from the man's back pants pocket. Thick with papers, receipts mostly, a few credit cards, and about a hundred dollars in twenties, tens, and singles. Regan also found an AARP membership card, a AAA card, and a driver's license, all in the name of Kurt Kegler. He told Hall, adding, "According to his license, Kegler's sixty-eight years old."

Hall squatted by the victim. He cocked his head to get a look at the exposed side of Kegler's face. "You ever see a body look like this one, Regan?"

"Nope."

"I did. Once." Hall shook his head. "But not on the job. At a museum. Some mummified king they found. Came from a long-forgotten tribe in sub-Saharan Africa, I think."

*A mummy.* Regan shivered and turned, hearing the approach of another vehicle. A dark SUV pulled up to the crime scene tape. The headlights went out and a petite woman slipped out of the vehicle. She moved quickly and with confident efficiency strolled toward them, carrying what looked to Regan like a fishing tackle box.

Hall came to his feet to stand beside Regan.

The woman wore black slacks, boots, and a dark, wool-trimmed jacket. She had her black hair pulled severely back and tied in a long braided ponytail. In the pale streetlight, Regan saw she was Asian. She walked with purposeful, athletic strides. When she reached Regan and Hall, she confidently extended her hand. "I'm Dr. Saito Izumi, the new assistant medical examiner."

"Patrolman Regan." He shook her hand, then waved toward Mike Hall. "This is Detective Hall."

"Pleasure," she said. She put her kit down, snapped on a pair of latex gloves, and put booties on her feet. Glancing up at the snow falling heavily through the orange glow from the streetlamp, she gave it a look of annoyance. "We certainly could do without *that.* Let's take a look at what we have."

While Saito Izumi quietly and methodically examined the

corpse, Regan and Hall busied themselves with giving directions to the responding patrolmen who had arrived, starting them on a canvass of the neighborhood, while also directing the arriving forensic team, who set up powerful halogen work lamps to illuminate the area—now as bright as a night game at Fenway Park. They began the job of photographing, sketching, and documenting the crime scene.

When the photographer was done taking pictures of the body, Saito asked Regan and Hall to give her a hand untangling Kegler's legs and removing him from his truck. They laid the corpse faceup on a blue tarp put out by the forensic team to catch any particulates that might drop off the body or from his clothing.

Regan noted the corpse was light as a feather, barely a hundred pounds he guessed, though he figured the man to be at least six feet tall. His mouth remained open in a silent scream. Regan noticed his tongue had turned black and his teeth were discolored—yellow and green—and rotted.

Hall asked, "What do you think, Doc? Natural, right?"

In the detective's tone, Regan heard his former friend's hope for death by natural causes. If it was, he could wrap up the incident with a simple written report. But a homicide meant a new case, one added to the already overburdened cop's workload.

"Too early to tell," she said. "Though I see no obvious cause of death, there's so much here that makes no sense—"

"Like what?" Hall asked, not liking the sound of that, his notebook out.

"First, I can't begin to guess what caused the eyes to bleed like that. A rupture of some kind certainly, but from what? As you can see, the victim urinated prior to his death." She pointed at the poor man's stained crotch. "He experienced a tremendous fright prior to death."

"Good to know," Hall said, "'cause I wouldn't have guessed that from the expression on his face."

Dr. Izumi leveled him with a steely, sour look.

"By victim, you're suggesting foul play?" Regan asked.

"Come on, Doc," Hall said. "You're not suggesting he was scared to death, are you?"

Saito narrowed her eyes to a point where Regan shivered, even though she was staring at Hall. "Clinically, a person cannot be scared to death, detective. So no, of course not."

Saito Izumi elaborated no further.

Regan glanced at the driver's license photo. It had been taken only two years earlier, when Kegler was sixty-six. It also registered his height and weight at a respectable six feet and one hundred and ninety-five pounds. He looked down at the corpse. This guy wasn't even close to that weight.

"Doctor, take a look at this." He handed the license to her. "Check out the recorded weight. This corpse can't be half that. What would cause a person to deteriorate like that in so short a time? Drugs? Disease?"

Saito shrugged, agreeing, maybe, maybe not. "Cancer, certainly. Extreme and advanced rheumatoid arthritis. Osteoporosis. Any number of progressive, degenerative illnesses. I won't know for certain until I've completed the autopsy. All I can confirm, for now, is the body is unusually cold and appears be in a very advanced stage of aging and deterioration."

"Looks damn near mummified to me," Hall offered. "Can you give us a time of death at least?"

"Not out here in the field,"—she squinted up at the falling snow— "in these conditions. Not without a more detailed examination, detective," Saito said. When Hall sighed, Saito explained. "Body temperature will be useless. I've no idea how warm the cab of the truck might have been before the body got tumbled out onto the ground, or how long the corpse was in there, or what other kind of atmospheric exposure there might have been since he died. Also, whatever's caused this body to become this cold isn't natural."

"What do you mean, not natural?" Regan asked.

It was Saito's turn to sigh. "Again, without a thorough examination I'm only speculating. Which I shouldn't be doing, but the body is not in rigor. Under normal conditions, that means the body is less than three hours dead or over three days old. And since there's no sign of livor mortis—"

"No way a body goes unnoticed out here for three days," Hall said. "So you're putting time of death at three hours?"

"No. I said under normal conditions."

"So the guy's been dead for awhile and dumped here," Regan said, thinking out loud but immediately rejecting that scenario. "When I arrived on the scene there was only one set of footprints in the snow near the car. They lead up to the driver's side door." He pointed. "Then go back off that way. I'm guessing they were from the anonymous 911 caller who discovered the body in the first place."

"Maybe something was on the passenger side?" Hall suggested. "Covered over by more snow?"

"Nope. I checked."

"Gentlemen," Saito interrupted, coming up to her feet. "Let me complete my field examination. Then, after I get the body to the morgue and conduct my autopsy, including a full toxicology screen and panels for diseases, I'll give you a complete report of my findings. Until then it does no good to go on speculating like this."

Regan disagreed. Brainstorming, speculating, tossing about what-ifs was what cops did. It was how they solved cases, but he kept that to himself.

"How long?" Hall asked.

"Twenty-four hours. Now leave me so I can do my work. Please..." Saito turned her back on them and set about cataloging her findings on an open tablet.

Regan and Hall stepped out of earshot of Saito Izumi.

"Well," Hall said, huffy as he took a cigar out of his pocket, careful to return its cellophane wrapper to his coat pocket. "This is some kind of weirdo case, ain't it?"

"Sure is," Regan agreed. "Makes me glad I'm not a detective anymore."

Through the blue hue of cigar smoke, Hall considered him with a squinted eye. "Bull hockey."

*Yeah. Bull hockey.* Regan agreed but didn't admit it. He had no one else to blame for torpedoing his career except himself. He was the one who'd gallantly taken on a two-and-a-half-year, undercover, department-wide IA investigation. His investigation. One that ended with several cops being arrested and indicted. Many of them were currently awaiting trial on corruption, theft, assault, and organized murder charges, while several others had been fired, suspended, demoted, or reassigned.

One of them had ended up eating his own gun. It happened to be Sean Regan's best friend since childhood, Patrolman Dale Brandigan.

Hall puffed mightily on his cigar, the red tip glowing brightly as they stood outside the pool of harsh white light from the forensic team's work lamps. "Guess we'll have to see what the canvass turns up."

"Not to be pessimistic, Mike, but except maybe from that rundown old dive." Regan pointed through the football field and baseball diamond in Marine Park to the Old Sea Dog Tavern on the corner of Farragut Road and 2nd Street. "Where do you think you're going to find witnesses at this time of night?"

Hall shrugged. "Gotta try. Aw, hell!"

Regan saw what caught Hall's attention and spiked his ire. A Fox 25 news van roared down Shore Road, heeding the perimeter officer's raised hand, his command to stop, which they did. Regan and Hall watched as the side door opened and two people leaped out, a man and a woman. The man was young with wild, '60s-style long brown hair; he hefted a large camera up to his shoulder. The woman was dressed smartly in a gray pantsuit and white blouse, and her hair was long, wavy, and fire-engine red.

Regan's stomach soured. How the hell did she do it? he wanted to know.

"Reporters," Hall groused.

The woman thrust a microphone into the startled uniformed cop's face, suddenly lit in harsh white detail by the cameraman's light. The reporter, beautiful and determined, immediately pelted the young officer with rapid-fire questions.

Hall puffed a thick curl of blue-gray smoke into the cold night air. "Am I mistaken or is that your soon-to-be ex?"

Regan rubbed his eyes, suddenly feeling very tired. "Yeah, that's Deidre."

Hall slapped him on the shoulder. "Since you're patrol and securing the crime scene is your responsibility, I'll leave you to handle the press." Hall sneered. "I'm sure you still have the magic touch with her."

"Mike, you're a dick," Regan grumbled as Hall walked away. He sighed and headed over to rescue his subordinate from his wife and her cameraman. He called out. "Dee. Dee! Listen, you guys know you can't be here. Both of you. Back in the van. Now."

# CHAPTER 5

DEIDRE O'DELL STOOD with her hands on her hips, her microphone clutched tightly in one fist. "We're outside the crime scene tape, Sean. You have no right to make us leave."

She was right and they both knew it.

The snow had started to lighten up, more a rainy-wintery mix now. About an inch lay on the grass, less on the streets and sidewalks where it melted faster even though the pavement hadn't been treated. Snow clung to the trees, many still heavy with leaves that had not yet fallen.

Crazy weather, he thought.

Regan remained on the police side of the yellow tape that snapped in the strong breeze. His line in the sand. The officer Deidre had been grilling for information retreated quickly, leaving Regan to deal with her.

"You should have a coat on, Dee. It's freezing out here."

"That's what *I* told her, dude," the cameraman said, leaning his head out away from the viewfinder. His name was Todd, Regan remembered. "She don't listen."

*Tell me about it,* Regan thought. He said, to Deidre, not Todd, "You look good."

And she did. The snow coated her shoulders like dandruff, glistening in her flaming red hair where it melted. Her green eyes shimmered in the white glare of the work lights, and he remembered how high her cheekbones got when she smiled. A smile he saw infrequently these days.

Nor was she smiling now. Her beautiful lips were set in a firm straight line.

He remembered that expression too, and he shivered.

"Thank you," she said tightly, in that southern drawl he remembered all too well also. "What's going on over there you don't want me to see, Sean?"

"There?" Regan pointed over his shoulder, back toward the Tundra and Kurt Kegler's corpse. "Over there? Nothing."

"If it's nothing, Officer Regan, why not give us a statement?" she said officially, meaning she was speaking for the camera now. Todd was filming and everything caught on tape would be subject to possible public airing, after editing of course. A process that would put Dee in the most favorable light, Sean knew. And if she could make him look like an idiot—bonus!

Sean cleared his throat, practiced at speaking to the press, which was how he and Deidre met in the first place. "Earlier tonight, Boston police received a 911 call reporting the discovery of a deceased individual in a vehicle parked near Shore Road at Pleasure Bay."

"Who was the caller?"

"Anonymous."

"You were the responding officer?"

"I was."

When Regan wasn't forthcoming, Deidre asked, "What did you find?"

"A body."

Deidre sighed. "Can you describe what condition the body was in?"

"Deceased."

She lowered her microphone. "Damn you, Sean. Give me something."

"There's nothing to give you, Dee. Honest."

Deidre waved her hand across her throat, signaling Todd to stop filming. He lowered his camera and, appearing grateful, headed back to the van where it was warm inside.

"You're doing this on purpose," Deidre said. "To get back at me."

Regan shot back, "To get back at you for what?"

"For going forward with the divorce, for not reconciling," she said.

A thousand things shot through Regan's head: questions, recriminations, angry retorts. Finally, he asked the one question he wanted the answer to, one she never answered, not to his satisfaction. "Why are you going ahead with the divorce?"

He saw the hurt in her eyes, the pain, because of him. He knew that, wished he could change it, but he couldn't. It was the past. He wanted to move on, together. Why didn't she?

"No time for that now, hotshot." Mike Hall came up beside Regan at a hurried clip, grabbed his arm, and propelled him away from Deidre. "Interview's over, sunshine." Over his shoulder, he called out, "Cross the tape and the officers have my permission to shoot to kill. Ta ta for now."

Behind them, in frustration, Deidre growled and stomped her feet. "Oooohh!"

Hall flipped the crime scene tape up and over their heads, leading Regan through Marine Park. When they were a safe distance from Deidre, Regan said, "Where are we going?"

"I followed your advice. Surprisingly, it panned out. I put a call into the Old Sea Dog Tavern—found their number on the Internet—the web, it's a wonderful thing. Anyway, the owner of the joint, a Tom Casico, lives in a room in the back. He tells me he knows our corpse, says he's willing to talk to us. Our lucky day,"—he waved at the dark, snowy sky—"or night as the case may be."

Hall climbed the concrete steps to the darkened door of the Old Sea Dog Tavern and pounded his meaty fist against the peeling wood. The overhead light popped on and a gray, elder face appeared in the window beside the door. Regan stood where his uniform would be plainly visible and Hall held up his badge. "Detective Hall and Patrolman Regan," he shouted to be heard through the heavy door. "Thank you for seeing us, Mr. Casico."

The door was yanked open, then lights flickered on inside the bar. Fluorescents that buzzed like trapped bees in a jar. With a large metal flashlight in hand, Tom Casico stood off to one side, giving them room to come in. He shut the door behind them.

"Nice place you've got here," Hall said, looking around the single room with its two pool tables, its few tables, and its scuffed linoleum floor.

Regan couldn't tell if he meant it or was being sarcastic.

Casico shrugged. "Saves me spending all my money at somebody else's place."

"Makes sense," Hall agreed. "You said on the phone you knew Kurt Kegler."

"I do." Casico went behind the bar, selected a bottle of Wild Turkey, and set out three glasses. "Going on thirty years. You sure he's dead?"

"We're sure," Hall said, watching Casico pour three fingers in each glass. "You told me Mr. Kegler was here tonight?"

"He was." Casico pushed two of the glasses across the bar,

46

then downed his in one gulp. Hall followed suit. Casico looked expectantly at Regan, who shook his head. The old man shrugged, took the glass, and downed that shot, too. "You didn't say how he died. Heart attack?"

"We don't know yet."

Casico's expression was a portrait of sudden suspicion. "It was natural, wasn't it? He wasn't...killed?"

Regan opened his mouth to reply, but Hall cut him off. "The medical examiner needs time to fully examine the body before she'll know for sure."

"I understand." Casico held a hand on the bottle, clearly contemplating another drink.

"How was Mr. Kegler's health?" Regan asked.

"Fine. Healthy as a horse, as far as I know. And he would have told me if he wasn't. We were close that way. Damn shame. He was just in here a few hours ago. Happy as a clam."

"He was in good spirits?" Regan asked.

Casico gave a hearty laugh. "I'll say. He left here with this hot dame on his arm. Never would've guessed a chick like that picking up Kegs, but damn if she didn't. He went out of here happier than I've seen him since his Rebecca passed on a few years back."

Regan and Hall exchanged glances, then together asked, "He left with someone?"

"Yeah. I just said that." Casico chose to take that next drink after all.

"I don't mean to be insensitive about your friend, Mr. Casico, but could this woman have been a...pro?" Hall asked.

"A prostitute? Girl like that in a place like this? Sure, I suppose. Don't get working girls in here much though." He drank his drink. "Not that I'm opposed to them morally, mind you, just ain't much of a call for 'em in here. My place,"—he waved his arms around—"ain't a bar, not really, though the government taxes me like it is. It's more a place for my friends to drop in and have a drink, shoot some pool. Friends. And regulars. Don't get a lot of strangers dropping in."

"This girl then," Regan asked. "You've never seen her before?"

"Nope. Classy-looking chick though. Nicely dressed. Polite. She had kind eyes. I would've probably made a move on her myself if she hadn't set her sights on Kegs."

"Can you describe her?"

"Drank an apple martini," Casico said, pouring the last of the bourbon from the bottle into his glass. "Guess that don't help you out much, does it?"

Hall shook his head.

Casico furrowed his forehead. He leaned on the bar. His bushy white eyebrows came together over his eyes as he concentrated. "Kinda tall. Couldn't say about her clothes. Didn't see them other than the long white leather trench coat she wore. She had long black hair with gray streaks in it. You know, like the kids do today, to make fashion statements, but hers looked natural, you know, where it had gone gray."

"So she was older?" Regan asked. He had his notebook out and was taking notes.

"Depends on your perspective, sonny."

"Approximate age then?" Hall asked.

"Hard to say. Older than you two. Younger than me and Kegs by a fair amount. Fifty. Fifty-five. Whichever, she looked damn good, even being an Oriental." He downed the last of the bourbon. "Not usually my cup of tea, but this one…"

"She was Asian?"

Casico gave Hall a hard look. "I just said that, didn't I?"

Regan and Hall exchanged a glance. Neither one of them could

48

think of anything else to ask, so Hall handed Casico one of his business cards. "If you think of anything else or if the woman returns, give me a call. My cell's on the back."

Hall moved toward the door and Regan fell in step to follow but stopped, thinking about the driver's license picture of Kurt Kegler and how different he looked in it from how he looked in death.

"There is one more thing." At the scene Regan had snapped a picture of Kegler with his cell phone. He pulled the photograph up and handed it to Casico. "This is Kurt Kegler, isn't it?"

Casico recoiled at the sight of his friend. "Jesus, Mary, and Joseph! What happened to 'im?"

Regan pressed. "Mr. Casico, is that Kurt Kegler or not?"

"Yeah, yeah, Jesus Christ, it's him. But he looks like he's had the life sucked out of him. What in holy hell can do that to a man?"

# CHAPTER 6

BY THE TIME Sean Regan arrived back home, it was after ten in the morning. He'd been stuck at the Kegler crime scene, coordinating the canvass of the neighborhood, overseeing the removal of the body, arranging the transport of the truck to the impound yard, and securing the area not only from his soon-to-be ex-wife, darling of the morning television news, Deidre O'Dell—who'd already dropped the hyphenated Regan—but a dozen other television, Internet, and print newshounds who'd shown up, and the ever-increasing number of lookie-loos who arrived with the sun.

Saito Izumi had taken charge of the body, had it removed to the city morgue, and had left just before daybreak, leaving behind the forensic team, Regan and his uniformed officers, and an increasingly grouchy Mike Hall, who was fielding calls from the captain of detectives and the deputy supervisor. Regan didn't miss that part of being a detective, the pressure of the politics.

Once the body and the vehicle had been removed, there was little more to see, so the lookie-loos drifted away, too.

Soon after, Hall released the crime scene.

Regan closed his apartment door and moved into the kitchen,

where he dropped his keys on the counter, unhooked his gun belt and looped it around the back of a kitchen chair, then grabbed a Boston Lager from the refrigerator. Sure, it wasn't even the middle of the day yet, but for Regan it was the end of a long, weird, tiring shift. He leaned against the counter, bone weary and glad to be home. He twisted the beer cap off with a *phizztt* and flung it into the kitchen sink—a rim shot—and took a long, cold pull.

"'Tis high time you returned, Officer Regan."

Plor na mBan stood at the archway leading into the living room, looking none too happy, with her arms folded across her chest.

Startled, Regan gulped down his beer to keep from spitting it out, wiping at his mouth with the back of his hand. "Hell's bells. I thought you'd be sleeping or something."

Actually, a part of him had even hoped she'd packed up and left. It would have made his life so much simpler if she had...but here she was.

Plor had on a white terrycloth robe. One of a matching pair he and Deidre had appropriated from the Key Biscayne Ritz-Carlton when they stayed there a few years back, before his life and his marriage had gone straight to hell. Plor was barefoot, and the robe—short on her tall, slender frame—revealed a lot of strikingly beautiful leg. Her long, auburn hair was damp from a recent shower and cascaded in waves over her shoulders and down her back. The light behind her highlighted the red accents, made them glow like gold-spun fire.

Really, there wasn't much not to like about the strange woman's appearance, and Regan took the moment to appreciate the sight.

"I did not mean to frighten you," she said.

"You didn't frighten me," Regan said defensively. "Just... surprised me is all."

All business, Plor said, "I have wasted time enough. Will you listen to what you have sworn to hear or shall I simply depart and resume my hunt for the fear darrig on my own?"

"Whoa. Hold on, lady. No one's going out hunting…anything."

A smile twitched at the corner of her mouth. "And if I refuse to…conform? Are you prepared to stop me?"

"Yes. No. I mean, look…I don't see a need to go there. I'm here. Let's talk."

He stepped over to Plor and, admittedly cautious, took her by the arm and guided her into the living room. It was sound police protocol to keep a situation calm, to do anything to not instigate a confrontation. But, if he were being completely honest, the woman intimidated him, just a little bit. "Let's talk in the living room."

"That would be acceptable." Plor took a seat in the club chair beside the couch, facing out toward the balcony doors. She pulled the flaps of the robe over her statuesque legs, which she had crossed.

Reluctantly, Regan pulled his eyes away from the sight and sat opposite her on the edge of the couch. He drank his beer and wondered again what exactly had compelled him to bring this woman here, to put his career, and for all he knew his life, in jeopardy. For what?

Regan finished his beer. It tasted good. The perfect counterbalance to the gallons of bad, acidic coffee he'd drunk all night. He excused himself and returned to the kitchen. He had a feeling he'd need another…at least one more.

Plor called out. "Is that ale you are consuming?"

"It is. You want one?" he asked, figuring she wouldn't take him up on it.

"I would."

Regan shrugged and withdrew two bottles, giving one to Plor as he returned to the couch.

Plor took a tentative sip. "'Tis colder than it should be." Then she downed the rest of it in one full, unstopping draught. "But, 'tis good ale. Do you have more?"

Regan raised an eyebrow. "Yeah. Sure."

He got her another.

After settling back on the couch, Regan said, "Okay. Time to tell your tale, Ms. Na mBan."

"As I have told you, I am Plor na mBan, daughter of Oisin and Niamh."

"Right," Regan interrupted. "Of the divine people of *Tir na nÓg*. We covered that earlier." Plor gave him a withering look and Regan put up a hand, stop-sign style. "Sorry." He sat back, tamping down his impatience with a sip of his beer.

"*Tir na nÓg* 'tis my home, yet it is only one of many Otherworlds, and all of them are in danger."

"In danger from what?" he asked, even as he wondered why he was listening to any of this in the first place.

"To explain that, I must tell you of the ancient times, of wars fought long ago, of battles won and lost. Battles fought by my people, the Tuatha Dé Danann, against the Fir Bolg, then a race of misshapen giants called Fomorians, and finally the invading Milesians."

"Giants, you said?" Regan asked with a raised eyebrow. "Okay, I think this is gonna take another beer after all."

When he returned, Plor went on with her story. "Many years ago, years before my birth, my people, the Tuatha Dé Danann, lived in this, your world. They arrived in great ships to a land that came to be known as Ériu."

"Wait. Do you mean Éire? That's a place, Ireland. It's been called Éire. You're from Ireland?"

"If that 'tis your name for it, I am not from there. I was born in *Tir na nÓg*, but the Tuatha Dé Danann ruled this land you call Ireland for many generations, back before the mists shrouded our home, our existence, from this Otherworld. When this was our home, my people were forced to defend their right of sovereignty many times. It was during one such struggle, in what my people call the Second Battle of Magh Tuireadh, High King Lugh defeated Balor of the Evil Eye in battle and drove the Fomorians evermore from this land, from this world."

"Drove them out. To where?"

"To a land of their own, an Otherworld called Magh Meall. There, and forevermore, the Fomorians have lived, but their leader, King Tethra, has grown restless. He is not content to rule over only Magh Meall."

Listening, and caught up in what she was saying, Regan wondered if he was as nuts as she was to believe such hogwash. In an attempt to rein in the craziness, Regan asked, "What does any of that have to do with you and the crazy little leprechaun you were menacing?"

"Fear darrig."

Regan closed his eyes and pinched the bridge of his nose. "Right. They're not leprechauns."

"It is King Tethra who sent Ciag to this world."

"Okay. Why?"

"His exact purpose is unknown to me. Only that King Tethra wishes to extend his rule beyond Magh Meall, and he will stop at nothing to achieve that goal."

"Why? What's so bad about this Magh Meall?" he asked, completely mangling Plor's pronunciation. "It some demonic hellhole or something?"

"Quite the opposite, it has been called the Plain of Joy, a vast kingdom of beauty and plenty, said to be located beneath the ocean floor."

"Said to be?"

"Magh Meall, like all Otherworlds, exists beyond mystical barriers. None are accessible to those from realms not their own, except in rare, special circumstances. Magh Meall 'tis separate from *Tir na nÓg* as *Tir na nÓg* 'tis separate from this world, and all others."

"Of course it is," Regan said, like that explained everything. It didn't. "Look."

Regan opened his mouth to follow up but snapped it shut when he heard a rattle of keys followed by his front door flying open. He jumped to his feet, as did Plor, in time to see Deidre O'Dell storming through the front hall. Rage burned in her eyes as brightly as the light shimmered through her flowing red hair. She had on the same pantsuit she'd worn earlier at the crime scene, now with a tan belted raincoat over it. Her shoulders were wet from melting snow, and water droplets dotted her hair and glistened like fairy dust.

"What were you thinking, Sean Cassidy Regan!"

Regan noticed Plor stood with her feet planted in what he recognized as a defensive fighting posture. Her fists were balled and her eyes narrowed, no doubt evaluating the threat level—and finding it very high—of this crazed woman charging through the apartment.

*Aw, crap!*

# CHAPTER 7

"DEE! WHAT ARE you doing here?"

Deidre O'Dell stopped short. Her eyes shifted quickly from Regan and locked in on Plor na mBan. Her mouth dropped open. After what seemed to take a lifetime, she regained her composure and snapped her jaw shut. Her milk-white face darkened to a crimson shade. Regan knew it to be a combination of embarrassment and anger. Maybe a little bit of jealousy, too.

He could hope.

"Who is this?" Deidre demanded, pointing at Plor. "And why is she wearing my robe? Damn it, Sean. We're not even divorced yet, for God's sake!"

Regan looked at Plor then back at Dee. "What? No. This is… Plor." He added quickly, "It's not what you think. She's a…an acquaintance."

Deidre fisted her hands and planted them on her hips, exactly as she had earlier at the crime scene. She stood tapping her toe, trying to retain or regain some sense of decorum. "An acquaintance? I'm listening."

"From work." Regan winced. That was a stupid thing to say.

"Oh, really?" Deidre raised a single eyebrow and shifted her attention to Plor, defiantly. "I know every single person who works for the BPD. I don't know her. What kind of name is Plor anyway?"

"It's…um…Gaelic," Regan stammered. Her people were from Ireland after all, he reasoned. "She comes…from…um…" Then he gave up. "Oh, hell. I don't know. I'm getting a beer."

As Regan headed for the kitchen, Plor said, "My name means 'the flower of women.'"

"I bet it does." Deidre turned away sharply and darted into the kitchen. There she started in on Regan again. "Sean Regan, you tell me what is going on here, right this instant." She pointed toward the living room but lowered her voice. "Who is that woman and why is she wearing my robe?"

"It's not your…it's complicated." Regan shut the refrigerator door and offered a bottle to her. "Wanna beer?"

"It's eleven o'clock in the morning. And no, it's not complicated. You're still married and you're carrying on with this, this tramp." As she spoke her eyes locked in on Regan's beer, watching him drink. "Oh hell."

She snatched the bottle from him and took a swig.

Regan let her keep it. He got another one for himself and, seeing Plor standing at the kitchen archway, grabbed two. At this rate, he'd need to resupply before the day was out. He walked around Deidre and handed Plor the beer.

"I am no tramp," Plor said to Regan. "Nor shall I allow this wench to call me one. I demand an apology from this trollop of yours."

"Trollop!" Deidre slammed her beer bottle down on the table. "I'll show you trollop!"

Regan caught her around the waist as she charged Plor—who stood still, ready to engage in battle—and swung Deidre back around. "Ho-kay. Everybody just calm down. No need to get physical. Why don't we all relax and go into the living room where we can discuss this like civilized people."

Deidre stopped struggling in his arms, but neither she nor Plor made a move to leave the kitchen. Regan waved at them. "Go!"

The two women moved toward the living room; like cats, they kept a wary eye on each other.

Regan returned to his place on the couch, relieved that Plor wasn't wearing her chain armor and animal pelts. That would have been impossible to explain. Plor stood before the club chair and waited for Deidre to walk around the coffee table and position herself next to Regan in front of the couch. Deidre stood, waiting for Plor to sit. Plor did the same. Neither woman would sit first.

*Oh, for Christ's sake.* "Sit down. The both of you."

Plor sat down. Deidre started to sit, then straightened up again. "No."

"Excuse me?" Regan asked.

"I didn't come here for some meet and greet with your...your girlfriend."

Regan had reached his limit. He leaped to his feet. "Plor is not my girlfriend. I only just met her this morning."

Deidre raised an eyebrow at that.

"Oh, come on, Dee. Plor's helping me...on a police matter."

"I'm sure she is," Deidre said mockingly. "In my bathrobe?"

"She is," Regan demanded. "She's got...information. She got hurt—"

Without demonstrating an ounce of inhibition, Plor flipped back her hair and pulled the robe to one side and dropped it off her shoulder to show off the long, ragged claw marks along her face, neck, and arm—and revealing a generous amount of other things as well.

Dee turned her head away. "Please."

Regan found he had the opposite desire and didn't turn away until Plor covered up again. "I needed to take her somewhere safe. She's a material witness in a case I'm working on."

"What case, Sean? You're not a detective anymore. Remember?"

"Thank you for that," Regan said, letting the anger and hurt into his voice. "I need you to remind me. It keeps slipping my mind."

"I'm sorry. I shouldn't have—"

Plor interrupted them both, standing up. "Patrolman Regan is truthful in what he is telling you. I am looking for someone, a fear—"

"A missing person," Regan shouted, jumping in.

"Yes. He is assisting me in finding this person missing."

Deidre knotted her brow again. Regan wasn't sure if it was in disbelief of what Plor was saying or the strange way the self-proclaimed warrior woman spoke.

"Why exactly *are* you here, Dee? This is my place. The condo I had to buy after you threw me out of our house. Remember?"

She clamped her jaw shut, taken aback. Before she could reply, Regan pressed on. "You came here to get some kind of inside information. To get something from me about that dead body in Southie, didn't you? So you could scoop the other stations, get an exclusive none of them had. To use me."

"No," she snapped. "You made it perfectly clear this morning that I wasn't getting any preferential treatment." Then her shoulders slumped as she came clean. "Okay, so what if I did?"

"You know I can't do that, Dee."

"You used to."

"We used to be married."

"We still are." Deidre looked at Plor. "Technically."

"We're separated, Dee. You served me with papers."

"Come on, Sean. Something hokey was going on down there

this morning. What was it?"

"There was nothing…hokey. An old man died. Nothing more."

She stood, searching his face. Her green eyes were like twin probes trying to read his thoughts. "You're lying. Whatever happened out there upset you. It frightened you."

"It did not," Sean said too forcefully.

"Tell me, Sean. You don't scare easily. What was it?"

"Nothing. Stop. I can't help you."

A silence settled over the room, thick, cloying, until it was broken by the sound of Deidre's phone pinging an incoming text. A second later, Regan's phone rang, the opening theme song from an old '80s TV cop show.

As she read her text, he turned away to take the call. "Regan."

To his surprise, the voice on the phone said, "Officer Regan, this is Dr. Saito Izumi. We met this morning."

"Yes. Of course."

"I was wondering if you'd come down to the morgue. There's something I'd like to discuss with you."

"Is this about Kurt Kegler?" Even though he'd kept his voice low, Deidre spun around at hearing the victim's name. Regan turned his back to her.

"It is," Izumi said.

"Now's not a great time. Can you tell me what it is over the phone?" Regan asked, curious about what she had to say, but even more curious why she called him. He wasn't the detective on the case. Hell, as Deidre so recently reminded him, he wasn't a detective at all.

"It would be better if I showed you," the woman said.

He thought about it for a minute. "All right. I'll be there as soon as I can."

He ended the call as Deidre returned her phone to her purse.

"That was work," they said simultaneously.

Deidre actually smiled at that, maybe remembering, as he was, all the times when they were married and living together, when they got calls like that, and they both had to suddenly go out.

"There's another story they want me to cover. I've got to go." To her credit, she didn't add, *Since you won't give me anything on the Southie body so I can scoop the other networks.*

"Yeah, me too." Regan pointed at his phone. "Work."

Deidre headed for the door. There she stopped with her hand on the knob and turned. She looked from Regan to Plor, then back again. "We need to talk. Straighten some things out."

"Yeah," Regan said. "We do. I'll call you."

Deidre nodded. "Do that." She gave Plor another once-over and left.

The door closed with a quiet click.

That bothered Regan more than if she'd slammed the darn thing shut.

# CHAPTER 8

SEAN REGAN ARRIVED at the Office of the Chief Medical Examiner of the Commonwealth of Massachusetts, located on Albany Street in the South End, a little past lunchtime.

Conflicted, he'd left Plor in the apartment watching the plasmascreen TV hung over the fireplace, but only after securing a promise from her not to leave except to tend to Enbarr until he returned. Reluctantly, she'd agreed, using the remote to thumb through the channels the way he'd showed her. She seemed both fascinated and puzzled by it, as if she were a child deprived of TV her whole life and seeing it for the first time.

He'd changed into civvies, so now Regan flashed his badge to the security personnel manning the metal detectors at the front entrance, allowing him access without them taking his off-duty gun from him. When he arrived at the autopsy room it was empty, except for a body—presumably Kurt Kegler—on the stainless-steel examination table. A pale blue sheet covered him from head to ankle, his feet exposed. They were bone-thin, dark, and an ugly, greenish-purple color. A toe tag hung off the right big toe.

Regan went through to the back where he knew the staff offices were and nearly bumped into Saito Izumi coming out of an office, her nose buried in a medical folder. Startled, she looked up. "Oh, Officer Regan. I'm sorry."

"No," he said. "My fault. You wanted to see me?"

"Yes." She smiled. "Thank you for coming. This is turning out to be a fascinating case."

"How so?"

Saito waved for him to follow her back into the operating room. "Well, for starters," she said, laying the file folder on Kegler's chest cavity and flipping it open, "I have no clue about COD yet, and we can forget about establishing a time of death, too."

"Why's that?"

"I don't know how familiar you are—"

"I was a detective for six years, Doctor. I've worked a homicide or two in my time."

"Oh, yes. Right. Of course." She seemed flustered. Regan wondered why. Had she heard about him? Knew what he'd done? "Then you know time of death calculations are always tricky and can be affected by any number of factors, both external, like weather conditions, air temperature—"

Regan interrupted. "Whatever it is you're trying to say, Doctor, just say it."

She cast her gaze away from him for a second, clearly uncomfortable with whatever it was she had to say. "The corpse has already begun to skeletonize. Meaning the bones have reached a stage of decomposition called diagenesis. There is significant skin shrinkage and slippage, and a complete absence of moisture."

"Mummification?"

She nodded. "Yes, but…"

"How long would something like that take?"

"Nearly impossible to tell. Once again it depends on conditions: temperatures, air quality, exposure to the elements. We're talking from several weeks to two years."

"Two years!" Regan thought for a moment. "That's impossible. Kegler was alive and in a bar called the Old Sea Dog just hours before his body was discovered. Is it possible it's not Kegler?"

"No, but let me continue, because that's not all," Saito said. "There are established stages of decomposition, as you might know—"

"Sure. Rigor, livor mortis, decomp…"

Saito nodded. "And in each of those stages things happen, consistent, expected things, within accepted variations, of course, but occurrences of scientific certainty: putrefaction, insect activity; autolysis." Noticing Regan's arched eyebrow, Saito explained. "Autolysis is the liquefaction of cells and tissue. Adipocere should have formed—it's when fatty tissues decay into a waxy, yellow-white, oily substance."

Regan held up his hand to stop her. His stomach, empty except for the beers he'd consumed earlier, started to roil as he noticed the overly sweet smell in the autopsy room, masked by the stronger scents of formaldehyde and ammonia and bleach. "Please. I get it."

Undeterred and, he was sure, amused by Regan's discomfort, Saito went on. "These stages take set amounts of time to occur, determined by external conditions, of course, and leave telltale signs. But, in this case, there is no sign any of that took place. It is as if Mr. Kegler's body decomposed at an accelerated rate, so rapidly none of the external factors normally affecting a dead body had time to take effect. This body went from death to complete mummification in less than an hour's time."

Regan shook his head. "How do you explain that?"

"I can't." She sighed, as if she were angry the science she relied on had failed her. "And there's more. The internal organs…"

Saito moved to take off the blue shroud covering the dead Kurt

Kegler, but Regan put his hand over hers, stopping her. Her hand was dry and soft, and ice cold. An occupational hazard, he assumed, from pulling cadavers in and out of the freezer drawers all day.

"It's okay. I don't need to see," he said. "Just tell me."

"Internally, the organs—the heart, liver, intestines, the bladder, the stomach, they were all,"—here she had to search for the words—"withered, shriveled, as if all the moisture they should have contained was gone. Every single organ inside this man looked like a cardboard juice box…sucked dry."

"What does that? Disease? Poison?"

"Nothing I've encountered, certainly, and nothing I've ever heard of." Saito flipped open the patient chart still on the corpse's chest, as if looking for the answer. Apparently not finding it, she closed the file again.

"So, Doctor," Regan said, broaching the question he'd had since she called him. "Why did you call me?"

"To give you these results," she said, avoiding the real question. "To tell you I'm no closer to figuring out what killed this man than I was when I first laid eyes on him."

"No, Doctor," Regan insisted. "Why did you call *me?* I'm not the detective on the case. Hell, I'm not even *a* detective."

Saito Izumi picked up the brown folder and walked over to a stainless steel counter. She laid it down, clearly doing it for no other reason than to have something to do. She turned around.

She was petite, barely five two and small framed, as Regan had assessed last night, but now, in the harsh fluorescent lights of the autopsy room, he could see and appreciate for the first time her flawless, smooth skin, her exotic, almond-shaped brown eyes, her thin, dark-red lips, and the long, silken black hair tied in a ponytail, now draped over her left shoulder.

"I called you because I felt you might be more…receptive to my thoughts about my findings."

Regan cocked his head. "How do you mean?"

She jutted her chin toward Kurt Kegler, toward the body lying on the chrome table. "What happened to him…the condition of these remains…isn't natural."

Regan opened his mouth to speak—

"What ain't natural, Doc?" Mike Hall asked, coming through the autopsy room door and dropping his hat on a stainless steel table covered in sterilized scalpels, probes, and other cutting utensils. "What are you doing here, Regan? You're on nights, ain't you?"

Saito frowned. Regan knew she'd have to re-sterilize the instruments before she could use them. Though why pathologists needed to use sterile equipment on the dead he never quite understood.

"It appears, detective," Saito said sharply, diverting Hall's attention away from Regan, "that your victim has suffered from accelerated decomposition."

"What exactly does that mean?"

"Time of death will be almost impossible to pin down."

"I ain't worried about TOD, Doc. We've got that established to within like two hours. Our guy was seen, alive and well, drinking like a fish in the bar down the street." Hall looked at Regan. "Tell me again why you're here?"

She gave Regan a quick, pleading glance, like a child caught in a lie and looking for someone to keep her out of trouble. Her expression said, *Play along. Please.*

"I couldn't sleep."

"So you came down to the morgue?" Hall waved a hand around the autopsy room. "This place's like propofol to you?"

"I was curious," he said. "That's all."

"Whatever." Hall rubbed at his bloodshot eyes and pulled out a small, spiral-bound notebook from his overcoat pocket. "So, bottom line. You got anything for me or not, Doc?"

"Not without more tests, extensive tests."

"You know, without a cause of death, Doc, I've got to investigate this as a suspicious death. That's more work for me. I don't need more work than I've already got."

Saito made a noise and moved away from Hall. It was not a sound anyone would confuse with sympathy.

Hall waved his arm in the air, slapping it exasperatedly against his Columbo-style rumpled overcoat. "You see the kind of cooperation you get from this office. Tell me it's a heart attack and we're both done."

Saito whirled and her dark eyes flared with anger. "I will do no such thing, detective. Not ever. You will get a cause of death when I have determined it. To my satisfaction. Is that clear?"

"Hey," Hall said, backing up and putting his hands up in surrender, "I'm just saying."

"Well, don't." Saito turned her back to Hall and Regan, went over to the sink, and turned on the water. "You now know what I know, detective. I've sent fingerprints to latent, ordered a toxicology report, and we're running DNA as a matter of routine." She shut off the tap with her elbow, drying her hands. "When I get the results, I'll call you. Now, if you'll excuse me, I've got another autopsy to perform."

The way she said it, Regan was sure she wouldn't have minded if the autopsy to be performed had been Mike Hall's.

"Fine," Hall said. He flipped his notebook shut and snatched his hat from the stainless steel cart. He put it forcefully on his head. Under his breath, he said, "Thanks for nothing, Doc."

Saito had already pushed through the swinging door and was in the next autopsy room by the time Hall finished mumbling. Yet she called out, "I heard that."

Hall blinked, mouthing, "How the…?"

Regan shrugged, trying not to laugh.

"You got any bright ideas for me, Regan? Or just more smartass crap to spew at me like her?"

"You know the drill, Mike. Sounds like you need to find Kurt's mystery woman."

"Yeah!" he said, faking excitement, then let his disappointment in Regan show. "Thanks, Sherlock. As if I wouldn't have thought of *that* on my own." He banged open the swinging door.

"Glad I could help."

Hall flipped him the bird but said, "I'll see you later."

"Yeah. Later."

Regan started to follow Hall out but stopped. When he was sure the big cop was gone and not coming back, Regan crossed the room and popped open the door into the next autopsy room. "Dr. Izumi, may I ask you a question?"

Saito stood facing an autopsy table. The body she was about to dissect was uncovered, a young woman, but she hadn't begun the examination yet. "Is Detective Hall gone?"

"Yes."

She turned, wearing a warm smile on her face. "Then yes, you may ask, and please, call me Saito."

"Saito. Great. I know you don't know what happened to Kegler to cause the accelerated decomposition."

"I don't. And believe me, Officer Regan, I've been doing this for longer than you can imagine. It's not often I'm stumped."

He nodded, wondering just how long had she been doing this. Judging from the way she looked, he doubted that the young woman had yet to reach her twenty-fifth birthday. He had to be wrong. She must have been older than that.

At his silence, she said, "You had a question?"

He was unable to shake her earlier comment. *The condition of these remains...isn't natural.* "Right. Yes. My question." She had been about to tell him something, confide in him just before Mike Hall showed up. He wanted to know what it was. "In cases like this, what do you do? You know, to figure out what happened?"

"Under normal circumstances, I'd probably solicit professional consultations. I might send cell and tissue samples to the research center at Tufts University. I'd think about sending samples to a friend of mine down at John Hopkins in Maryland, maybe even to the CDC in Atlanta."

Regan arched an eyebrow at that. "The CDC?" Regan thought about that. "Wait. You don't think it's something contagious, do you?"

"No, officer, I don't." Saito shrugged. "As I said before..." Then she stopped, as if reconsidering what it was she'd been about to say. "I don't know what it is. The sad truth is we might never know. Some deaths just can't be classified. It happens."

*Isn't natural.* He shivered. She'd called him down there, had wanted to tell him...something, but, for some reason, she'd changed her mind about opening up to him. "You're sure there isn't anything else you want to tell me, Doctor?"

She looked up, seeming to consider him for a moment, then shook her head. "No. That's it."

"Oh, well, okay, thanks. Call me if you find anything more or there's something else you want to tell me." He backed out of the room. "And, by the way, it's Sean."

"I'm sorry?"

"It's Sean. You said earlier, 'Call me Saito.' I'm Sean." Regan waved a hand.

"It's a pleasure meeting you, Sean," Saito said with a smile. It was a nice smile.

Regan said, "Yeah, you, too."

Once he was out of the autopsy theater, he let the door swing shut. There he stood and wondered again what it was she might have wanted to tell him. It didn't escape him that when he asked her what she would do under normal circumstances, Saito Izumi had said, "I'd probably," "I might," and "I'd think about" sending cell and tissue samples out, about getting second opinions.

Classic avoidance. She never said she would.

Regan wondered why.

# CHAPTER 9

IT HAD BEEN long past an hour since Sean Regan left Plor to wait. "'Tis approaching the noon hour," she said out loud, pacing the empty apartment, worrying at the time now slipping away. She feared she'd lose Ciag's trail while waiting, but she also saw wisdom in pairing herself with Sean Regan, a protector of this world, someone familiar to guide her. Yet she was conflicted.

"What good is a guide who is always tearing off, who leaves me caged to accomplish nothing?"

Suddenly, loud, sharp music blared from the sorcery window in the wall over the fire box Regan called a *teevee*. The noise caught her attention. Words and numbers and bright colors spun confusingly around the glass surface. Plor stepped back, fearful they would fly from the window, but they did not. When the images settled, inside the window appeared a little man and little woman, seated, smiling at Plor. They introduced themselves and said, "Thank you for joining us."

"You are welcome," Plor said, but they didn't reply back. The woman just began talking. *Rude.*

"First up," the woman said, "we have late-breaking word of a brazen, overnight burglary at the famed Museum of Antiquities and

Early History in Boston's South End. Morning news correspondent Deidre O'Dell is on the scene. Deidre, what can you tell us?"

Plor gasped. Inside the window was the woman who'd been in Regan's apartment only a few short hours before. A woman known to him and for whom he had obvious affections. She had been shrunk to a wee little size and trapped inside the window with a short, bulbous wand near her mouth.

"Deidre O'Dell, are you hurt?" Plor asked.

The woman ignored Plor's inquiry. Instead, Deidre said, "Hi, Elizabeth. As you can see, I'm standing in front of the Museum of Antiquities and Early History's south entrance on the corner of Harrison Avenue and East Brookline, where police tell us nighttime burglars broke in and vandalized several exhibit rooms and damaged an as-yet-undetermined number of irreplaceable, artifacts of both historical and high monetary value."

"Do we know if anything was actually stolen, Deidre, or was vandalism the motive?"

"We don't know, Elizabeth, not yet. According to police, museum officials are now conducting a detailed inventory to determine just what, if anything, is missing. They also tell us they have no significant leads, except for this blurry image from the security camera footage. Can you play that now, Jim?"

On the darkened TV screen, Plor watched as meaningless numbers flickered along the bottom before shadowy movement could be seen along what appeared to be a chamber corridor. It was a figure, dark and impossible to see in detail, but Plor knew instantly who it was from his awkward, seesaw gait, from his funny tailed coat and top hat, and from the ghostly glowing lantern in his hand. It was Ciag!

"Is that a...lantern in his hand?" Elizabeth's voice asked.

"It appears to be," Deidre confirmed, appearing once more on the TV window. "Police tell us they think it is, adding just one more bizarre element to an already unbelievable story. Live from the South End, this is Deidre O'Dell. Now back to you in the studio, Elizabeth."

"Thank you, Deidre," Elizabeth said, her smiling face again back on the window.

Plor dropped the robe she wore and went into the bedroom where she began to dress, putting on her chemise, then the burnt-orange doublet. Over that, she donned her byrnie—a sleeveless, waist-length chain-mail shirt—her short, pleated, leather bliaut, her chausses, her black bear-hide boots, and her left-handed chain-mail glove, before securing her half cape around her throat and grabbing *Claiomh Solais* from the closet where Regan had insisted she keep it after he left. They had argued long and loud. She refused to let him leave until he had retrieved the sword from his police cruiser. The forged blade gleamed brilliantly, reflecting the apartment light.

In the large room Regan called a garage, Plor quickly saddled Enbarr and left—losing precious minutes trying to activate the magic door to make it rumble up the way she'd seen Regan raise it. Finally, she'd found the hidden button and succeeded. Freedom was hers.

There were many things Plor na mBan had found wondrous and fascinating in this new, strange world, but the one thing she found most distasteful was the level of noise. It came at her from every direction as Plor walked Enbarr at a fast clip, moving the steed toward the large blue-toned buildings of glass and gray stone she saw over the trees in the distance north of Regan's domicile.

Officer Regan had explained to her that what she saw in the *teevee* box was not really *in* it, but images—sort of like how Ciag conjured the great vulture—of real places in the great city of Boston. Plor remembered where Deidre O'Dell said she was: *in front of the Museum of Antiquities and Early History's south entrance on the corner of Harrison Avenue and East Brookline.*

Plor winced as the metal horseless carriages traveled past her, emitting loud, offensive siren blasts, many of them releasing a jarring, booming racket Plor came to assume was music in this Otherworld. She didn't like it. There was nary a harp's chord or flute heard in the ear-pounding blaring. And the carriages—like Regan's police cruiser—produced foul, cloying smoke.

When she and Enbarr got too near, those inside shook their fists at them and shouted. What did the terms *freak* and *crazy-ass bitch* mean? She had no inkling, and so she continued on her way, doing her best to ignore the increasing commotion she and Enbarr stirred as they drew closer to the strange city.

The snow and cold from the previous night had given way to a splendid day of bright sunshine, clear blue skies, and a cool westerly breeze that gently caressed the bare skin of her arms, raising prickly goose bumps as she rode. A glorious day for a ride, she thought, if not for the strangeness of her surroundings and her urgent business.

As she neared the city, Plor was amazed at the number of people she found there. Crowds clustered in chaotic groupings, rushing along the narrow paths—wisely stopping for the horseless carriages that seemed to speed past with little regard for pedestrians—pausing at the larger cross sections before surging forward as if pushed by a giant, invisible force. Flameless lights flashed in different colors, and more lights glowed from within the impossibly tall—so tall Plor nearly fell from Enbarr's back trying to look up high enough into the sky to see where they ended—smooth walled towers.

At a cross section, Plor urged the frightened horse forward while carriages behind her came to sudden, screeching stops, emitting yet more blasts of noise.

"Hey, lady!" someone cried out. "Stop at the light. Can't you see it's red?"

Plor pulled Enbarr's reins back, stopping him as several carriages roared past them in the cross path, nary slowing down a bit. "I see it now," she said to the man standing beside her. He had almost no hair and wore dark, odd-looking clothes with a white undertunic, and a thin red strip of cloth hung around his neck, much like a severed noose. "What is the significance of the light?"

Someone shouted, "Watch out, ya crazy broad. What're'ya bringing a horse downtown for anyway?"

A small crowd had started to gather around her. "They must be shooting a TV show or a commercial," one woman said.

"I don't see no cameras, you?"

"Whatever," another man said. "Just get your stupid horse outta my way. I only get forty minutes for lunch."

"I am sorry," Plor said, put off by the crowd circling, while she worked to keep a nervous Enbarr steady. The horse was getting agitated by the closeness of the people. "I did not mean to cause a rouse."

"Can I pet her?" a young girl asked, putting her hand on Enbarr's flank.

"All right, all right, break it up. Break it up. What's going on here?" The voice came from somewhere within the throng, where people had begun to move, parting for a man in the same sort of uniform Sean Regan had worn.

He made his way up to Plor.

Plor brightened. "A protector of the people, excellent. Sir—"

The officer shielded his eyes with his hand as he looked up at Plor. "Lady, what in the world do you think you're doing here? If this is some sort of publicity stunt, let me tell you…"

"Your words are strange to me, sir, but, please, I am in need of your help."

"I'm sure you are. Now, I know it's Halloween tomorrow, but you're creating a disturbance, so why don't ya just slip off the back of that nag and tell me what it is you think you're doing."

"Alas, there is little time for me to engage in idle conversation. If you would, instead, please tell me where I might find the Museum of Antiquities and Early History. I am told it is located at Harrison Avenue and East Brookline. Then I shall be on my way."

"I don't think so, sweetie." The officer's voice turned stern. "Come down off that horse. Now."

Concerned this protector would not assist her after all, Plor thought about what she should do. This city was too large for her to search for the museum by herself. She needed help. If this police officer would not be the one to—

"Hey, lady. The place you're looking for? The museum?" The voice came from a tall, young man with long, brown woman's hair draped over his shoulders like curtains. "It's just a few blocks up." He pointed northeast. "Follow Atlantic up about a mile or so. It's on the left near the aquarium. Off Milk Street. You can't miss it."

"Much gratitude." Plor nodded her thanks and snapped the reins, urging Enbarr to the right. Her trusted friend whinnied, warning those around him to move as he picked up the trot.

"Hold it," the officer called out again.

Plor knotted her forehead and called back, but did not stop. "Hold what? Please specify."

"I'm saying, stay put," the officer said, walking along beside her. "Don't you think about going anywhere." He had his hand on a piece of metal hooked to a belt on his hip. From her earlier encounter with Sean Regan, Plor knew it to be a weapon. A loud, projectile-firing weapon.

"I am sorry, but I must go. Someone I know may be in mortal danger." She spurred Enbarr's sides with the heels of her boots. Enbarr snorted and threw his head down, relieved to be on the move.

The officer shouted, "Lady, I'm warning you!"

Plor cast a glance over her shoulder. "Please, do not try to stop me." By now the crowd ahead of her had pushed back out of her way. Plor clicked. "Go, Enbarr."

Enbarr nickered, warning any who still stood too close to get out of the way, but not waiting. He charged into a canter. The officer shouted and pointed the forged weapon, but he did not use it. Angry, he returned it to its place on his hip. "Son of a…!"

Plor saw him grasp a small black knob affixed to his shoulder, attached there by a coiled black wire. She had seen this before. It was similar to one Officer Regan wore.

"Dispatch," he said into it. "I've got some crazy broad on a horse. She's escaping up Atlantic toward the aquarium. Yes, that's what I said, a goddamn horse. And she's got a friggin' sword, too, okay! Send units."

Enbarr galloped away, taking Plor the mile or so up the road in the direction she'd been told. A few minutes later, at a corner where a glass enclosure angled into the ground, Plor brought Enbarr to a halt. Again, people stopped and stared, crowding around her. "Please, I am trying to find the Museum of Antiquities and Early History. Can anyone tell me its location?"

"Why, they having a costume party there?"

"Love the getup, toots, but aren't you a little chilly?"

*Strange denizens occupy this world,* Plor thought, ignoring their barbs and wishing Sean Regan was there to assist her. Plor shook her head. She was unsure what to do next. Then a plump woman glanced up at her from under a floppy hat. She wore several layers of clothing and looked unbathed and disheveled.

She said, "You've gotta go back a block. Make a left across from the fountain. Down the street, you'll see a building with a big IMAX sign on it. The museum's behind that."

Plor looked back and then down to thank the woman, but she was already walking away, dragging a wire basket on wheels behind her, grumbling to herself as she shambled away.

Strange folks, indeed, Plor thought again. But following the shabby woman's directions, she found the museum. Its name was in large letters affixed to the building wall. Here it appeared the fast, noisy carriages were prohibited. Crowds larger than any she'd encountered yet—how many people lived in this Otherworld?—mingled between the buildings and ate meals from little metal wheeled carts placed in haphazard locations under brightly covered canopies.

Plor dismounted and tied Enbarr to a metal post embedded in the cobblestone ground.

"What in the hell do you think you're doing, lady?"

Plor turned to encounter a short, rotund woman with oil-black skin and a white version of Regan's protector uniform. She wore a rectangular, brass jewel that had written on it: Naomi Johnson. Regan wore a similar plate on his officer's uniform.

"I am tying my horse—"

"Not here you ain't, honey." The woman's voice was low and threatening. Plor did not care for it, or for her. "We's got laws against"—she glared at Enbarr and waved a book of some kind at him—"against…this."

"I do not understand. You have laws against horses?"

"Not horses, honey, parking horses. You simply can't do it. Not here."

"What then am I to do with Enbarr?"

The woman flipped open the cover of her book. "Far as I'm concerned, you can get right back on him and ride the hell on outta here, you feel me?"

Frustrated, Plor said, "You wish for me to feel you? I am sorry but I do not wish to."

The large woman sighed. "Lady, you gonna get your horse outta here!" She had a thin, tubular object in her hand. With her thumb she made it make a clicking noise. "Or am I gonna ta write you up?"

"Write me up?" Plor shook her head. She didn't have time for this. She started to walk away. "I must go to the museum."

The white-shirted woman called out, "Wait. What? You can't. What about your horse?"

Plor walked over to Naomi Johnson and looked down at her. While the woman was many times wider than Plor, the Celtic warrior towered menacingly over the shorter woman. "I am placing Enbarr in your care. Should any harm come to him..." Plor half drew her sword from its scabbard. "...the vengeance I would have would be...worse."

Wide-eyed, Naomi Johnson swallowed hard.

Plor pushed her sword back into place, turned, and ran off, waving over her shoulder. "Thank you."

Naomi Johnson reached for Enbarr's reins. "Damn, crazy bitch."

Enbarr snorted, angry and forceful.

Naomi Johnson snatched her hand back and jumped away.

"Damn, lord, they don't pay me enough to be dealing with this crap." She yelled out after Plor, "I'm calling animal control. You hear me?"

Plor had already reached the doors to the museum. She worried little about Enbarr; the steed could more than take care of himself.

It was Deidre O'Dell who occupied her thoughts now. If Regan's woman faced Ciag alone...

Inside, the building was cold and dark with lots of little glowing colored lights: blue and yellow and green and red. Several men, wearing similar uniforms to Regan and Naomi Johnson outside, except these were gray and the emblems on the shoulders said security, not police, stood talking, but they stopped when Plor walked through the metal archway entrance.

Suddenly there was an ear-screeching blare of alarms and lightning-like flashes of light all around her. Plor crouched into a defensive stance and drew *Claiomh Solais*.

The men all turned, drawing their small, black, metal weapons as one, facing her.

"What the hell..." one said.

"Who the..." said another.

A third one shouted, "Drop the sword, lady."

"I am Plor na mBan," she announced with authority. "I am here to rescue the woman Deidre O'Dell."

# CHAPTER 10

SEAN REGAN ARRIVED at the museum in record time. He'd just finished up with Saito Izumi at the morgue and was getting back into his car, a five-year-old silver Camaro convertible, when his cell phone rang. He didn't recognize the number. He answered, surprised when the caller identified himself as Wade Dixon, the security director for the Museum of Antiquities and Early History. Regan loved that place. His mom and grandma used to take him there all the time when he was a kid.

"There's been a disturbance," the security director said over the phone. "Your name was given to us."

"What kind of disturbance?" Regan wanted to know.

"It would be best if you came down here and saw for yourself."

Regan told the man he was on his way. En route he flipped on his police scanner and suddenly Director Dixon's cryptic message made perfect sense. Over the scanner he heard about the call regarding "some crazy broad on a horse with a sword". Everyone else laughed it off as a Halloween prank, accusing the poor patrolman of drinking on the job.

Regan knew better. He wished he didn't. He arrived at the museum and, dressed in his civvies, badged his way through the metal detectors, wondering if this day could get any worse.

"You Officer Regan?" a uniformed guard asked. His face was tight with concern.

"I am. Where is she?"

"This way," he said, leading Regan to the right, through the lobby.

"Looks like the museum's closed. Not because of this, I hope."

"No," the security guard said. "We had a break-in last night, early this morning, actually. The museum personnel and police are going through the scene now to determine what's been taken, inventorying the damage. Follow me, please."

"That sucks," Regan said.

They rounded a corner, walking past a large stone statue of what looked to Regan like a winged lion. The withers on the thing were eight feet high. It was called a griffin, Regan dredged up from his childhood memories, wondering who'd sculpted the massive likeness. It was marvelous. But his curiosity about the mystical creature or its artisan was short-lived when the security guard stopped.

There stood Plor na mBan in full warrior regalia, including her sword, surrounded by seven armed security officers. Their service weapons were pointed at her. She in turn held *Claiomh Solais* raised in a two-handed defensive posture, poised to strike.

"Oh, for Pete's sake," Regan groaned.

Among the guards encircling Plor stood an African American man with short-cropped hair graying at the temples and a flat nose, one that looked like it had taken a punch or two in its day. He wore a business suit, and though he had a boxer's stance, he appeared as comfortable in the suit as Regan imagined he'd be in boxing shorts and gloves. Broad-shouldered, he carried himself with authority. He also held a small black automatic in his hand, but he kept it pointed at the ground.

At Regan's arrival, the man glanced over. "Patrolman Regan?"

"Yes." Regan walked over. "You must be Wade Dixon." The man nodded. They shook hands, and Regan said, "This is all a big misunderstanding."

"I'm sure it is," Dixon said.

"I can explain…" Regan waved at Plor. "Hey, Plor."

He wanted her to know he was there, to make sure she knew he was handling things, to keep her from slicing anybody's head off.

"Sean Regan," Plor said, without lowering her sword, "it pleases me you have arrived. Perhaps now we can carry on with our business."

Dixon followed the exchange, his head turning from Regan to Plor then back again. "About that explanation, patrolman, I think now would be a good time for me to hear it."

Regan blinked. "What? Oh, yeah. Right. Well, it's kind of embarrassing." He called out to Plor, "You can put the sword down now. None of these nice men are going to hurt you. Are they, Mr. Dixon?"

Regan waved at Plor to lower her sword. As she did, Dixon signaled for his men to lower their weapons as well. *Good,* Regan thought, relieved, while he frantically tried to come up with a way out of this mess, one that hopefully wouldn't involve gunshots and severed limbs.

"That explanation, patrolman?" Dixon prompted.

"Right. Of course." Regan took Dixon by the arm and guided him away from the others. "As I said, it's embarrassing. That"—he pointed over his shoulder at Plor—"she's my sister."

"Your sister?"

"That's right. And she…suffers from…she's not really right…" Regan tapped two fingers to his temple for emphasis. "…in the head."

Dixon knotted his eyebrows. "What's wrong with her?"

"What's wrong with her? Um, she suffers from delusions. She thinks...she's got this crazy idea she's a warrior woman from ancient—"

"Like Xena, the Warrior Princess."

Feigning excitement that Dixon was getting it, while his heart galloped at what felt like a thousand beats per minute, Regan said, "Yes. Exactly. And the doctors...they've told us, as part of her therapy, to help her work through her...issues, we should play along. In an attempt to identify what's...she hasn't always been like this...what triggered this condition. Get to the root cause..."

Dixon nodded. "It just came over her? One day she decided she was Xena?"

Regan nodded. "Uh-huh. That's right. Well, not Xena specifically but—" He snapped his fingers. "Like that. Sudden."

"So how come she's down here? All alone?"

"A renaissance festival," Regan blurted out, the idea suddenly occurring to him. "I was actually buying the tickets—"

"To the renaissance festival?"

"Yes. And Plor, she wandered off. I was looking for her. That's why I was so close when you called. I've told her over and over. If she ever got lost she's to have someone get ahold of me, tell 'em I'm a Boston police officer."

"Well that part worked," Dixon said slowly.

Regan studied the man, trying to determine if Dixon was buying the crap he was shoveling or not. He couldn't tell, which made him glad he wasn't playing poker against the man. Regan glanced over at Plor, still surrounded by the seven security officers, but with her sword sheathed at her side. Regan gave her a thumbs-up. "Good job, sis. Having them call me. Just like we practiced." He nodded and made a phone hand sign, his thumb to his ear, his pinky pointed toward his mouth.

"What about the sword?" Dixon pressed. "That's a deadly weapon. That makes her guilty of menacing."

Regan shrugged and soured his face, like *That's ridiculous.* "It's fake. A Hollywood prop. It's retractable. The blade?" He harrumphed. "That thing couldn't cut through butter on a hot summer day."

Dixon raised one eyebrow. "Really?"

"Really." An idea struck Regan. "I'd be happy to show you, but I'm sure you've got your hands full, what with this break-in you're dealing with. Cops, crime scene people, reporters. Jeez, I bet the museum muckety-mucks are going crazy, making your life miserable right about now."

Dixon nodded, carrying a harried expression on his dark face. "You don't know the half of it." Then, as if to emphasize the point, Dixon's radio squawked, followed by a female voice asking for his location, then telling him he was needed on the second floor.

Regan seized on the distraction. "You're retired PD, aren't you?"

"FBI. Thirty-one years."

Regan smiled. He knew how to play an overworked cop in a difficult situation: a combination of flattery and an opportunity to lighten the poor man's overburdened workload.

"I thought so. I could tell. The way your men are trained, they look sharp, well disciplined. You've done a fine job with them. So look, no one's been hurt, right? You don't need one more problem on your plate, do you? You call the cops on my sister, you need to have someone hold her until BPD frees up a unit to come swear out a complaint, wait to get her transported. All your guys will be needed to give statements—"

Dixon held up a hand. "Fine, fine. Look, take your crazy sister and get out of here. But don't ever come back here, you hear me? You or your sister."

Inwardly, Regan grinned. *Works every time.*

Excited, Regan nodded. "You got it. Yes, sir. Loud and clear. Never hear from us again." To Plor, he called out, "Come on...sis. Let's get out of here. We're free to go."

Tentatively, she joined him, but her furrowed forehead told Regan she wasn't happy about it. "Go? But we haven't—"

"Shush, not now, sis. We'll talk about it at home." He raised an arm to put over her shoulder and steer her back toward the museum entrance. "Come on now, let's let these fine gentlemen get back to work." He propelled her toward the main entrance, waving behind him. "Goodbye, Mr. Dixon. Thank you. Good luck with your break-in."

Outside, and away from the museum's front entrance, Regan grabbed Plor by the arm and laid into her. "What were you thinking? What are you doing down here? How'd you get here? Why?"

Plor folded her arms over her chest. She gave him a steely stare. "Do you wish me to answer your questions one at a time or all at once?"

Regan sighed in frustration. "Whichever. Whatever. Just tell me what's going on."

"After you left me alone...again," Plor said.

Regan opened his mouth to protest, thought better of it, and snapped his jaw shut again.

"I saw on the window box you call *teevee*, that woman from your domicile, from this morning—"

"Deidre? You're talking about my wife, Deidre?"

Plor furrowed her brow. "I believe that is what I said. She told me she was here, at this place. She told me about the...burglary. How did she know to tell me about that?"

Regan pinched the bridge of his nose. *Has this woman really never seen TV?* "She wasn't telling you, Plor, not specifically. That broadcast goes out to hundreds of thousands of…magic window boxes. She's a reporter. It's her job to tell the public, the people, about things that happen. We call it getting the news. Anyway, what was it about this burglary that so interested you, that made you decide to come down here?"

"Ciag."

"The fear darrig," Regan said. "What about him?"

"It was his doing, this burglary. Deidre saw him do it. She showed me him. He was inside the magic window but here at this… this museum."

"She…saw him?" Regan stammered. The conversation was beginning to make his head hurt. "She said that? On TV?"

"No. She showed it. Through the window I saw him, sneaking around in the corridors with his lantern held high."

Regan needed to sit down. He led Plor over to where tiers of concrete circled a fountain, shut off now and the water drained for the upcoming winter season. Regan sat. The concrete was cold, but he didn't care. His world was spinning out of control, and he didn't have a clue on how to get on top of it. "Ciag was here?"

"I could have stopped him if it were not for those men. If not for you."

"Plor, Ciag was not here when you saw him on TV. I'm sure that was a recording, an image from last night when the burglary occurred."

"I do not understand."

Regan waved her confusion away. "I'll explain it to you later. Right now, we need to figure out why Ciag was here."

# CHAPTER 11

THIS IS A *really bad idea,* Regan told himself. *Really bad.*

After they checked on Enbarr and assured parking enforcement officer Naomi Johnson they would return shortly, he badged himself through the metal detectors once again, this time with Plor in tow— without *Claiomh Solais,* her metal arm bands, or her chain-mail— wearing an old London Fog raincoat he had in the trunk of his Camaro.

Regan told the security guard downstairs he'd forgotten to give Security Director Dixon important information…about the burglary. That got them admitted and directions to the *Ancient Celtic Exhibit* on the third floor.

So far, they'd made it onto the elevator and were on their way up to the crime scene. "Now," Regan said to Plor, "when we get upstairs, let me do all the talking."

She nodded. "As you wish."

The elevator pinged and jerked to a stop. Plor held tight to the handrail and instinctively reached for her sword. Regan was glad it was locked in the trunk of his car.

The doors opened onto a dark, unoccupied corridor. Tense, Regan stepped out, not looking forward to running into Dixon again but thinking he had no choice. He needed to know why Ciag had broken in and what the creepy little gnome was after.

The corridor was lined with rectangular pedestals with small, round-bottom cooking cauldrons, plates, cups, iron rings, leather pouches, corroded pieces of chain-mail and iron, and bronze tools, buckles and brooches, knives, and rusted weaponry. An acrylic sign pointed them toward the *Ancient Celtic Exhibit* down the hall.

At the opening to the exhibit, Regan and Plor ran into a uniform BPD cop, someone he didn't know, there to control access to the crime scene. Regan flashed his badge—quickly—and said, "Detective Mike Hall, homicide unit." He nodded nonchalantly toward Plor. "This is…she's an investigator from the museum's insurance company."

"Homicide? What's homicide got to do with a simple smash-and-grab?"

As Regan forged Hall's signature on the entry log, he said, "Don't know yet. Might be connected to something we're working on." Regan put a hand to the small of Plor's back and scooted her away from the cop to discourage any further discussion.

Walking inside the exhibit was like stepping back in time a thousand years.

The large exhibition hall had been transformed into a gigantic Celtic village, with three wattle-and-daub circular huts, complete with conical thatched roofs, wooden carts, troughs, and mannequins wearing wool *bracae*—trousers—sleeveless shirts fastened with fibulae fasteners, long-skirted gowns and colorful shawls, and what Regan swore had to be taxidermy cattle, chickens, roosters, and dogs. The ceiling was domed and had been painted midnight blue; it glowed from concealed mood lighting and twinkling yellow-white stars. Orange lights flickered from inside the huts to represent cooking fires, complete with curls of smoke—most likely steam—escaping from the hatched roof vents.

Awed, Regan said, "What is this place?"

"Conmaicne Mara," Plor replied.

"I'm impressed," a voice behind them said. "You know your ancient Irish history."

In unison, Plor and Regan turned to find a woman standing beside them. She reminded Regan of every librarian he had ever met, except maybe not the old ones. She was scarecrow thin, wearing a nondescript dark skirt-suit combination with a shimmering purple blouse underneath the jacket. She had her dark hair pulled up into a tight bun on the back of her head. She wore dark-rimmed glasses and had green eyes and what Regan regarded as avian-like features: a narrow nose, hollow cheeks, a jutting chin, and thin lips.

"I'm Dr. Abigail Buckley." She stuck out her hand to shake. "I'm curator for this exhibit."

"Detective Hall," Regan said, shaking the skeletal-like hand without making reference to Plor at all.

Dr. Buckley said, "You're here about the break-in?"

"We are." Regan looked around, relieved he didn't see Dixon anywhere. "Can you tell us what happened?"

"A real shame. Come on, I'll show you." She led them between two of the huts toward a secondary domed room. This one wasn't set up as part of the replicated village, but was rather a straightforward display area, filled with shelves, stands, and display cases, many of which had been smashed to smithereens. The wreckage was extensive; there were even scorch marks on the walls and the acrid smell of smoke, melted plastic, and burnt rubber.

Like some of the display cases out front, these contained—or had contained—similar items of bronze, iron, and silver jewelry, tools, weaponry, cutlery, and plates and bowls and cauldrons. Display cases were smashed, tripod sign holders were broken and tipped over, and signage had been destroyed. The wholesale destruction had been committed in what looked like a willful act of rage.

A crime scene team was busy at work, taking pictures, jotting down notes, filling out forms, taking measurements, and talking with people Regan assumed to be museum personnel.

"What is your interest here, detective? Are you with the burglary squad, because they were already here—"

"Homicide."

"Homicide? Oh, my."

To explain, Regan said, "Viewing the surveillance video, we believe the man seen on it may be linked to another crime."

"That strange little man with the lantern, do you know who he is?"

Plor opened her mouth to respond, but Regan cleared his throat. "We can't say at this time."

A particular, rather large cauldron set on a low table caught Plor's attention. She drifted over to it. Regan and Dr. Buckley followed. The cauldron appeared to be made of bronze with crude but intricate reliefs carved along its sides of faces and animals like antelope or deer.

Plor stared down at it. "'Tis *Coire Dagdae*, from the island city of Muirias. How did you come in possession of it?"

Delighted, Dr. Buckley seemed almost ready to clap. "It is indeed. You know your Celtic artifacts, detective…"

But, Plor had already moved on to the next display. "And the Spear of Lugh."

"Tell me," Dr. Buckley said, somewhat suspiciously, "how does a police detective know so much about ancient Celtic antiquity?"

"Oh, she isn't with the police department, Dr. Buckley," Regan said quickly. "She's from the…the bureau's Art Crime Unit."

"The FBI," Dr. Buckley said, her mistrust turned once more into excitement. "Fabulous. We were concerned this matter might not get the…attention it deserved. To answer your earlier question, the *Coire Dagdae*, the Cauldron of Dagda, was acquired from a private collection in Denmark several years ago, by the National Museum of Ireland. As for the spear…" Dr. Buckley led Plor to yet another area of the room. "Here, you must see this."

Plor gasped. "*Lia Fáil*."

"That's right," Dr. Buckley said, pleased, the way a teacher or a parent would praise a child for getting a difficult problem solved. "It *is* the Stone of Destiny."

Regan came up to the source of their astonishment and glanced down, expecting to be amazed. He wasn't. "It's a rock. A very big rock, but just a rock."

The phallus-shaped stone stood on one end. It measured eleven feet high and was as thick around as the trunk of a hundred-year-old tree. Pitted and scarred, it was sandstone in color.

"Oh, Detective Hall, it is so much more," Dr. Buckley told him. "*Lia Fáil* is magical. It is said when the claimant to the Irish throne touched upon the stone, it roared with joy, thus proclaiming the possessor the celestial lordship over Éire, conferring to the new high king ancient powers—"

"The power to endow him with a long reign," Plor said.

"Okay, well, that's great and all," Regan said. Acutely aware of how much time they'd taken and how little they'd actually learned—they still had no idea why Ciag had broken in and what he had stolen or why he'd vandalized the exhibit—Regan was eager to skedaddle out of there before Dixon returned. "But, Doctor, can you tell us what's missing? What did the thief come here to steal?"

Dr. Buckley turned away from the display and glanced around at the destruction around her, the bent, twisted, and broken shards of countless artifacts. The place looked like it had been trashed by a two-year-old having a temper tantrum.

"That's just it," she said. "We've just about finished our inventory and as near as we can tell, nothing is missing. Many, many irreplaceable items have been destroyed, but nothing has been taken."

"Then vandalism appears to be the motive?"

"So it would seem." She shook her head. "What sort of sick, sick person would do such a thing?"

Plor stood staring down at a sword. It was beneath a glass display case and undisturbed by the violence wreaked upon nearly everything else in the room. Regan wondered why.

"Doctor," Regan said. "Can you tell me—"

Plor interrupted him. She had a puzzled look on her face. "This appears to be King Núadu's sword."

"It is the Sword of Light. Yes," Buckley said. She took her glasses off and wiped the lenses clean. "The fourth and final item in the Four Treasures of the Tuatha Dé Danann collection."

Regan blinked. Tuatha Dé Danann. That was what Plor had called her people.

As if someone had activated a hidden switch, Dr. Abigail Buckley launched into full lecture mode, monotone voice and all. "The Tuatha Dé Danann were a race of deities, schooled in the arts of sorcery before migrating across the seas, riding in upon dark clouds, or maybe ships—the ancient texts are unclear about that—to Connaught in Ireland."

"Conmaicne Mara," Plor corrected.

"That's correct, the region was originally known as Conmaicne Mara."

"When the Tuatha Dé Danann arrived, they brought with them four magical treasures: the Cauldron of Dagda, from which no one would ever go away unsatisfied; the Spear of Lugh, which guaranteed victory for the man who held it; *Lia Fáil*, as we discussed, which would cry out beneath the king who took the sovereignty of Ireland; and finally, Núadu's sacred sword, from which no enemy escaped once it was drawn from its sheath. These are some of the most significant items related to the Celtic mythological cycle and among some of the exhibit's most valuable pieces."

"But…" Plor protested, pointing at the sword in the case.

"So why do you suppose, Doctor," Regan interrupted, "if these items are so valuable, they are the only pieces not disturbed?" Regan waved a hand around at the wreckage around them.

"I cannot answer that, detective. These items are part of a traveling exhibit hosted by the Natural Museum of Ireland and part of their Irish archaeological collection, on loan to us until the end of the month. They do not belong to us. As for how the vandals chose which pieces to destroy and which to leave alone? I have no idea."

Plor stepped between them. "That sword…" She pointed at Núadu's sacred sword, "…it is a—"

Regan grabbed her by the hand, cutting her off. Wade Dixon's deep voice growled from inside the replica village exhibit, just next door. "Where are they?"

In reply, Regan heard the cop posted at the entrance, stammering, "In there. But I'm telling you, his name's not Regan. It's Detective Hall. He's with some insurance lady."

*Damn. Overstayed our welcome.*

"But the Núadu Sword," Plor said. "How may they possess the Sword of Light when *Claiomh Solais* 'tis secured in your vehicle?"

"I don't know." He pulled Plor's arm. "We can sort it out later."

"But—"

"Come on, I think it's time we let Dr. Buckley return to her cataloging." Regan nodded to the woman. "Thank you, Doctor, you've been most helpful." He pulled at Plor's arm. "Any chance there's a back way out of here?"

# CHAPTER 12

**AS LUCK WOULD** have it, there was a back way out, a fire exit to the street below. Regan and Plor charged down the stairs and burst out into the plaza. Having barely escaped being caught by ex-FBI agent and current museum security director Wade Dixon, Regan and Plor retrieved Enbarr (where parking enforcement officer Naomi Johnson was busy feeding him apples) and they returned to Regan's condo, Plor on horseback and Regan in his Camaro.

Once home, Regan untacked Enbarr and rubbed him down while Plor went inside to change clothes. Regan told her she could find some of his wife's stuff in the bedroom closet, something a little more appropriate for being out and about in the twenty-first century.

Brushing the large stallion's coat with long, hard strokes, Regan was determined to unravel the mystery that was Plor na mBan. Enbarr whinnied, content to stand there in Regan's garage and be pampered, his belly full of apples after an exhilarating run through downtown Boston.

"It's a shame you can't talk, big fella." Regan stroked Enbarr's nose, impressed with the magnificence of the animal. In response,

Enbarr threw his head down, seemingly nodding in agreement. "I'd love to hear the truth behind this one."

"To whom are you speaking, Sean Regan?"

Hearing Plor behind him, Regan spun around. On seeing her, Regan was speechless.

Plor stood at the doorway leading into the condo. She wore a purple, form-fitting, mid-thigh-length dress, something Regan remembered Deidre called a sheath dress. It was shorter on Plor's statuesque figure and hugged her body, revealing an eye-popping amount of bare leg, more than he remembered it ever being on Dee. She wore it with black, high heeled Vince Camuto "Dira" half-boots.

"Tell me," Plor said, and he swore she struck a pose. "Is this a more appropriate attire for your world?"

"It 'tis." Regan cleared his throat. "I mean it is. You won't go unnoticed, but yeah, that'll work. You look fabulous."

"It pleases me you approve."

"I'm pleased that you're pleased," Regan babbled, then tossed the horse brush he held into a nearby bucket. He had to remind himself that this woman was still looney-tunes, regardless of how sexy she looked. "Come on. Let's get something to eat. I'm starving."

Plor came down the two wooden steps. "Agreed. So long as the meal will include ale."

"Oh, believe me, I wouldn't have it any other way."

Regan drove them back downtown—to SkipJack's in the heart of the Back Bay and with a magnificent view of the John Hancock tower and St. Elias Church. Over pints of Guinness, Plor marveled at the downtown buildings, their size and construction, the congestion on the streets, the speed and noise of the traffic as it sped by.

All as if they were sights she'd never seen before.

Regan ordered a Caesar salad and the Wasabi-crusted salmon, while Plor asked for the steamed clams and mussels from the appetizer menu and the seafood platter—a generous portion of scallops, shrimp, clams, haddock, and calamari—the Baja fish tacos, and the teriyaki steak and jumbo shrimp surf and turf.

When the food arrived, along with two more large beers, Plor dug into her food with relish.

Regan ate too, but kept his meal at human proportions. Between bites, he said, "Okay, now that we've got a breather, it's time we got to the bottom of a few things."

She gave him a quizzical look, with her cheeks puffed with food.

"I have questions, Plor. I need answers."

Plor swallowed, took a gulp of her Guinness—when was the last time this girl had eaten—and smiled. "'Tis the moment I've been waiting for since a moon and one-half sun cycle ago."

Regan settled back with a full beer mug. "Then start at the beginning and I'll jump in with questions as they come to me."

"My mother is Niamh, queen of *Tir na nÓg*, of the Tuatha Dé Danann."

"The same people Dr. Buckley talked about, who brought those magical whatchamacallits, the four treasures, from some islands somewhere."

"That is correct. To understand, I must go to the beginnings, before even my time. The Tuatha De Danann came to live in Éire, having travelled from four faraway islands: Murias, Falias, Gorias and Findias. With them, they brought the four treasures; Dagda's Cauldron, the Spear of Lugh, Núadu's sword and *Lia Fáil*, the Stone of Destiny."

"The items we saw at the museum?"

"That is correct." Plor went on. "My people are skilled in the sorcery arts, witchcraft, and magicks, guided by our four druids: Morfesa, Esras, Uiscias, and Semias. When we lived in Éire, a beautiful land of fertile ground, lush woods, peat bogs, and coastal regions, ours was not always a peaceful existence. The Tuatha Dé Danann fought for our homes many times, in many great battles."

Regan signaled their server for another round of drinks.

*On the assumption I believe all this hogwash,* Regan thought, he asked, "What does that have to do with last night, with the fear darrig?"

She gave him a reproachful look. "The telling of a tale should not be rushed. The Tuatha Dé Danann fought against an invading force of a misshapen, gigantic race called the Fomorians, who rose up out of the sea to claim Éire as their own in the Second Battle of Magh Tuireadh."

"Against misshapen giants? The Fomorians?" *Here we go again.*

"Aye, led in combat by King Balor of the Evil Eye. A fervent and brutal battle was fought, so savage and indomitable the mountains of Éire shook and fire rain fell from the skies, pelting the lands. The two mighty forces clashed with a sound like rumbling thunder, muting the harsh cries of fierce warriors, whose shields and helmets, armor and flesh were struck with spears and swords until the rivers ran red and the gorged earth filled with blood. Then all seemed lost when King Huadu was slain by Balor, struck down by the Fomorian king's poisonous eye."

Despite himself, Regan leaned forward, engaged in the tale, more than he was willing to admit. "Then what happened?"

"Lugh, son of Ethlinn, a youthful and handsome warrior and grandson to Balor himself, slayed the misshapen cyclops by piercing his terrible eye with a sling-stone, killing him. Defeated, the Fomorians were driven back into the sea where they have been banished ever since."

"I take it by 'driven into the sea' you don't mean just under the ocean but into yet another Otherworld."

"Indeed. The one called Magh Meall, ruled ever since the First

Battle of Magh Tuireadh by King Tethra."

"That's all well and good, Plor, and very interesting. It really is, but it doesn't tell me how the Tuatha Dé Danann ended up in *Tir na nÓg*, or what any of that has to do with you and Ciag and the smoked vulture of death."

"Patience, Sean Regan. I told you, the tale is a long and complex one. May I have another Guinness?"

"Sure." Regan waved for another round. Plor had finished her meal. All of her plates were cleared, down to the china cleared, and now they sat drinking their third round of ale and waiting for the check.

"After the Fomorians were defeated, the Tuatha Dé Danann were attacked again, this time by a race known as Milesians. After many fierce battles, the three Tuatha Dé kings—MacCuill, MacCecht, and MacGreine—were killed in conflicts, and thus the divine rulers of Éire were defeated. The Milesian poet, Amergin Glúingel, was called upon to divide the land. He did so by use of trickery, allotting the land above ground to the Milesians and the land below to the Tuatha Dé Danann, driving my people to the sidhe mound under the earth."

"So, *Tir na nÓg* is underground, but like Tethra's Magh Meall, it's really an Otherworld, its own place."

"Yes. Each Otherworld exists where it is, there but not there, shrouded beyond the barrier veils and impossible to access or leave."

"Then how did this Ciag, and you and Enbarr for that matter, slip through?"

"The veils over time, millennium, have begun to weaken. There are areas where at certain times of the year and with the assistance of very powerful druids the—"

"Druids? What's a druid?"

"They are priestesses skilled in the ways of magicks and

sorcery."

"And they can breech these barriers, these magical veils?"

"At certain times and under certain circumstances. The Samhain for example."

"This Samhain"—a word that sounded vaguely familiar but Regan could not place it at the moment—"is happening now and that's how you and Ciag slipped through."

"Correct."

He'd finished his beer, as had she. They both sat back, each contemplating the other. "Okay, Plor, I'm just going to say it. This all sounds kind of fantastic. Giants, cycloped monsters, Otherworlds existing under the sea and below ground, but they don't exist here. It's all pretty hard for me to take in, you know, to believe."

"Harder to accept as true than the fear darrig who vanished before your eyes or a conjured bird of prey that turned into smoke upon being slain? Do you believe they did not, do not exist?"

"You've got a point there." Regan contemplated his empty mug, desperately wanting another beer, but he was scheduled to work at midnight that night. Being half in the bag wouldn't go over well at roll call.

He took a moment to consider Plor. She stared out the window at people passing, things, just watching with this wide-eyed and rapt fascination over everything she saw. Like all of it was shiny and new. He saw an innocence in her expression, a naïveté that he found downright adorable.

To hell with it. *It's still early,* he justified and ordered another round for the two of them. After the waitress delivered their drinks, Regan said, "Okay, get to the part about Ciag and the dusted bird."

"The fear darrig has been sent to this world for a purpose.

My mother's druidess, Birog, learned of this from Cethlenn, a Fomorian prophetess and wife to the defeated and deceased Balor. Cethlenn foretold of an impending invasion, one schemed by King Tethra. This invasion, her envisage told us, is dependent upon the achievement of Ciag's mission here to this world."

"So, stop the gnome, stop an invasion."

Regan's head throbbed from all the information he was taking in, and again he questioned not only this woman's sanity but his own for putting up with all this nonsense for this long. What was it that kept him from dropping her off at the nearest mental health facility for a full psych-eval and putting this all behind him?

He had no answer to that.

"That is my purpose, correct," Plor confirmed.

To clarify, Regan said, "To stop him from doing something, but you don't know what?"

"That was true, until this day."

"Oh, and what changed this day?" Regan struggled to keep his mocking tone under wraps.

"The exhibits. At the museum," she said.

"What about them?"

"There I discovered what Ciag is here for." She downed the last of her Guinness.

"Well, don't keep me in suspense. What is it? Why is the freaky little leprechaun here?"

"The fear darrig is not—"

Regan held up a surrendering hand. "I know. He's not a leprechaun. Why is he here, Plor?"

"To get *Lia Fáil*. Ciag's purpose is to steal the Stone of Destiny."

# CHAPTER 13

COULD THIS NIGHT *get any worse?* Brad Dumas wondered as he watched his fiancée storm out of the bar on Lansdowne Street, across the street from Fenway Park. He glanced at his watch. It was one o'clock in the morning. And it had started out being such a great night, too.

He and Leslie had scored bleacher tickets for game six of the World Series: Red Sox against the Atlanta Braves. His beloved BoSox had nearly blown their chance for the postseason, having lost the division to the hated New York Yankees only to secure the wild card slot and then defeat the Yankees in six games in postseason play. Now, going into tonight's game the Red Sox were up three games to two. He could have been there to witness history, the Red Sox winning the World Series again.

But, it wasn't to be. Fate was too cruel a mistress to allow that to happen.

No. The Red Sox had lost, sending the series back to Atlanta for a game seven. Bummed, the Boston fans filed out of Fenway and with them, Brad and Leslie. Many of them flocked to the crowded bars across the street to prolong their commiseration over even more alcohol.

Now Brad was alone with his half-finished beer, going over in his head the fight he and Leslie had just—very publicly—had. He'd just come clean with her, confessing he'd lost a good chunk of cash betting on tonight's game. It was supposed to have been a sure thing, he argued.

"It's never a sure thing," Leslie retorted. "That's why they call it gambling."

In fairness, Leslie had a right to be angry. The money he'd lost was savings they'd set aside for their wedding next spring, savings that had taken them two years to amass.

And so Leslie stormed out of the bar, her eyes shimmering with tears, her sobbing, *"How could you?"* echoing in his ears.

Brad didn't think he could feel any lower than he had after the final out of tonight's game, but he did. "Damn it."

He grabbed his coat from the back of his barstool, downed the last of his beer, and made sure there was money enough left on the bar for a tip he could no longer afford. Brad pushed his way through the crowd and out into the snow, looking for Leslie.

Outside, the cold braced him as he realized it was actually snowing. *In October? Really?*

He looked up and down Lansdowne Street. "Leslie," he called out, cupping his hands over his mouth. "Leslie. Where are you?"

Nothing.

"Come on, Leslie. I'm sorry."

Wind whistled down the desolate block, stirring crumpled newspapers, fast-food wrappers, and old ticket stubs in a cyclone of dust, dirt, and snow flurries. Brad shivered and with trembling fingers zipped up his coat and popped the collar around his neck.

"Jesus, it's cold." He started walking east toward Ipswich Street. "Leslie! Where are you?"

At the intersection, a single taxi drove by. Cars lined the streets parked at the curb, a scrim of snow dusting them. Hip-hop music blared from the Tequila Run, a nightclub at the corner. Two girls stood out by the entrance, wearing shorts and fishnet stockings. They huddled for warmth by the glass doors as they shared a cigarette.

She wouldn't have gone in there, would she? Brad had marked his thirty-fifth birthday last year, and Leslie was only two years younger than he was. Even in their best partying days, the Tequila Run was a little too fast-paced for their taste.

No. She'd have hailed a cab and was already halfway to their apartment by now. He'd call her and apologize—he envisioned a lot of apologizing over the next few days—telling her he'd see her later, maybe after he'd had a few more drinks and she'd had some time to cool off.

That sounded like a plan. He pulled out his phone. His fingers were already numb in the cold air. As he started to dial, he noticed the snow had really picked up, actually covering the sidewalk now. He looked around, squinting in the suddenly thickening swirl of white. "It's like a Halloween blizzard."

"Excuse me?" Soft and alluring, the voice was so close to Brad's ear he jumped with a start, fumbling the phone in his hand before it slipped out of his cold fingers and dropped to the ground. Just like Dustin Pedroia in the top of the ninth, letting two runs score.

His startled intake of breath and nervous scrabbling caused the woman who'd come up behind him to step back, with a sharp gasp of her own. Her spiked high heel came down on Brad's dropped phone, piercing the touch-screen glass with a pop and a spark.

"Oh, I'm so sorry," she said, crouching down to the ground, even as Brad did too. They bumped heads. "Owww." They each had pieces of the useless phone in their hands as they rubbed at their bruised foreheads. She tentatively smiled, straightened up, and tipped the broken pieces into his outstretched palm.

"It's my fault," Brad said, tongue-tied over her beauty. She was Asian with long, silky-fine black hair and smooth, flawless skin. She wore an unbuttoned, long, white leather trench coat and a black leather miniskirt, with dark hose and the aforementioned black spiked heels. She carried a black clutch purse.

A hooker, Brad initially surmised, and upon closer inspection he noticed she was older than he'd originally guessed. The fine lines crinkling around her perfectly shaped dark-brown eyes had him revising his age estimate upward by about ten years, putting the woman closer to forty-five than thirty-five.

He smiled, not caring if she was a hooker or not, as he'd always been okay with older women, finding her both exotic and alluring. Leslie and his fight with her were completely gone from his mind.

"I shouldn't have jumped like that." Brad took the bits of his phone and threw them into the trash bin at the corner. Returning to her, he said, "So do you like need help or something?"

She had her hands buried deep in unseen pockets of her jacket, her clutch purse dangling from her wrist. "Oh, yes. I'm so embarrassed really. I've managed to somehow lock my keys inside my car. The window is open a bit and I managed to find a wire hanger, but I can't seem to hook it…" She crooked a finger and made a pulling motion, then gave him a helpless doe-in-distress expression. "Would you please help me?"

Brad melted right there, despite the freezing temperature and the swirling, lashing snow. He was putty. "Of course. Show me the way." He kept his hands in his coat pockets while the woman snaked a hand through the crook of his arm and led him down Ipswich toward Van Ness Street.

"I'm Brad Dumas, by the way," he said.

"Yuki." She didn't offer her last name, and Brad didn't think to ask.

They squinted against the whirling, whistling wind, their heads bowed. The snow had turned icy and stung as it hit his cheeks. "Crazy weather, isn't it?"

"I like it," she said.

Brad had to admit he liked how the snow settled on her lush, black hair, shiny and sparkling like tiny starbursts reflecting the orange sodium streetlights that bathed the area in an ethereal glow.

"Sort of surreal though," he said, "this early in the year. It's nuts."

As they walked along the snow-blanketed sidewalk, along the brick wall of Fenway past Gate B, Brad sensed Yuki slowing her pace. Here the shadows of the stadium, closed up for hours now—and for the season, he thought miserably—made the cold, odd night feel even colder. They stopped under the red banner for Lefty Grove, who played for the team from 1934 until he retired in 1941.

"So where's your car?" Brad asked. Where they had stopped there were no vehicles.

"I have a confession," Yuki said, stepping in close to Brad. Her breath fogged the air in cold, crisp puffs. "I do not have a car. I wanted, instead, privacy."

*Yup. A hooker for sure.*

"I...um, have a fiancée," he stammered, nervous now that the fantasy was rapidly becoming a reality. Yuki pulled Brad against her and looked longingly into his eyes. Brad licked his lips and went on, "And I don't have any money. I don't, um, know what you charge. I'm guessing it's, I'd think you were worth a lot..."

"I'm not interested in money, Brad." She kissed him on the mouth. Her lips were thin and soft, but also icy cold. Brad tried to break her grip. She said, "I don't want to have sex with you, Brad."

She kissed him again. Brad shivered. She whispered, "I want your soul."

Yuki lashed out with a claw-like grip and grabbed Brad by the hair, yanking his head back. Brad yelped, sounding like a little girl. Yuki seized his mouth with her frigid lips, sealing his mouth with a kiss. Brad struggled to break free, feeling at first sick to his stomach then as if his insides were being sucked out of him through his esophagus. He felt his energy, his will to resist, his desire to live siphoned away, leaving him weak, tired, too frail to do anything but scream.

"Hey, what's going on down there?"

Yuki released the hold she had on Brad's mouth, snapping her head in a ferocious way toward the interruption. Her eyes glowed bright red.

Brad rolled his head in the same direction. He saw the two girls he'd seen earlier outside the Tequila Run. They'd been coming down the street behind him and Yuki. They stopped, frightened as they realized something was very, very wrong.

"Help me," Brad managed to croak. Too weak to stand on his own two feet, he began to slip from Yuki's grasp.

His plea and whatever they saw in Yuki scared the two women into action. The blonde shrieked and the brunette smacked her arm. "Stop screaming, Jozy. Call 911!"

"Ohmygod! I am! I am!" Jozy cried. She had a phone out and was frantically stabbing at it with long, orange-nailed fingers. "Now, run!"

And they ran.

# CHAPTER 14

BACK ON PATROL that night, Regan got the call when he was just three blocks away, on Park Drive near Peterborough Street. He activated the siren and lights and hit the gas.

A woman attacking a man outside Fenway Park? That wasn't a call one got every day.

Regan drove west on Peterborough and hooked a right onto Yawkey Way. He slowed at the intersection and turned right on squealing tires onto Van Ness. A row of cars lined the street to his right. The sidewalk to the left appeared abandoned until he got to Ipswich. There, in the shadows, he saw what looked like two people locked in an embrace. But something about it looked wrong, like one figure loomed over the other, overpowering him, or her.

Dry snow swirled across the windshield, obscuring his sight. He was too far away to tell what he saw for sure. He drove closer.

Nearly on top of the scene, he slammed the car to a stop, shut off the siren, but kept the emergency lights on and climbed out of the cruiser, his hand on the butt of his gun. As he approached the figures, he had his non-gun hand out, palm up, in the universal stop-sign fashion.

"Police! I just want everybody to stay calm. So no one gets

hurt."

Neither figure took notice. Regan continued his cautious approach. By the time he was six feet away, he could see the two figures were a man and a woman. The woman stood over the man, who appeared limp in her arms, his head thrown back, his arms hanging limply toward the ground.

Regan took quick notice of her spiked heels, her dark stockings, and her white leather trench coat. And her long, straight, black hair. The man had on jeans, sneakers, and a light coat. Too light for the sudden snow squall they found themselves in.

"What's going on here?" Regan demanded. "Let that man go!"

The woman whirled around, still clutching the man, who now hung from her one arm.

*How the hell could a little spit of a woman hold up a guy like that?* Thoughts of the strength Plor had demonstrated popped unpleasantly into Regan's mind. *Crap, don't tell me this is going to be more of that warrior woman hocus-pocus.*

The woman stared at Regan, but only for a second. He caught a glimpse of her eyes. They shone red, like an animal's caught in the light on a dark night. And her flesh was so pale, so white as to be translucent, at least that was the impression Regan had before she hissed. A terrifying, soul-rattling sound that froze Regan's blood even as it fogged the icy-cold air around her bluish-gray lips.

The woman dropped the body as a sudden cyclone of snow and pelting hail and wind swirled, whipping down the street so hard Regan had to put an arm up to shield his eyes. When he could see again, she was gone.

Amazingly, around where she'd stood, where she'd discarded her victim, and in the direction she'd fled, the snow—even though nearly a foot deep—was undisturbed. No footprints. No kicked-up piles of snow, no windswept depressions, nothing except virgin snow.

No indication anywhere someone had just run through the blanket of whiteness. And fast!

*How is that possible?*

Regan raced over to the body, left in a crumpled heap on the sidewalk. He turned the body over. "Hey, fella."

Regan recoiled, a gasp trapped in his throat. The man had the same frozen death stare as he'd seen on Kurt Kegler's face the night before. His flesh was blue-gray and frozen, hung in wrinkled layers, as if the skull underneath had been shrunk. Regan placed his fingers to the side of the man's neck. The skin was hard and cold, like touching ice. Sure there would be no pulse, Regan pulled back, shocked to have found one. It was faint, but it was there.

He keyed his shoulder mic. "This is Patrolman Sean Regan. I'm at the scene on Van Ness. I need an ambulance right away. And call Detective Hall. He'll want to see this."

While Regan settled in, prepared to wait for the ambulance, he saw two girls across the street. They stood huddled by the wall of Fenway, their arms around each other, clearly terrified. Regan called out to them. "You two the ones who called 911?"

Reluctantly, they nodded, saying they had.

"Good. Good job. Listen. I need to go after that..." He glanced down the street. He indicated the victim. "I've called for more units, for an ambulance. They'll come down here either from Peterborough..." He pointed. "...like I did, or from Ipswich." He pointed down the street in the opposite direction. "I just need you two to stay here, to flag them down and get them here, to this guy. Can you do that for me?"

The blonde looked dubious, but the other one nodded. "Yeah, sure. No sweat."

"Great. Thanks, girls."

Regan took a step away, then took another indecisive one in

the opposite direction. He turned back to the girls. "Either of you happen to see which way she went?"

The brunette nodded. "That way." She pointed toward the row of buildings across the street.

"Around those buildings?" Regan asked.

"Um, not around. Onto."

*Is that a joke?* "What do you mean, onto?"

"I know. Sounds crazy, right? But I swear, she rode that misty swirling cloud up onto the roof of those buildings." The brunette nodded insistently. "Don't look at me that way. I swear."

"Okay, okay. I believe you." Regan headed off toward the building, not believing a damn thing about anything that had happened tonight, or last night either, for that matter. As he trotted, he searched the snow ahead of him. Clear, clean, undisturbed.

While behind him, his path was plain as day, full of kicked-up snow, footprints, and patches of concrete showing through where he'd scuffed snow around. How had the woman not left any tracks?

The building ahead of him was three stories tall, all brick with large, wide windows, all dark at this time of night. He looked up, almost losing his hat. There were no fire escapes. No exterior way onto the roof. *How the hell am I...did she...*

He continued to walk the perimeter of the building, searching for a way up to the roof. He pulled out his cell phone. He punched in the speed dial number he'd programmed into it just hours earlier, placing a call to the burner cell he'd bought and spent two hours showing Plor how to use.

She'd insisted on returning to the Museum of Antiquities and Early History after it closed. She was convinced Ciag, the fear darrig, would return, and Regan had to admit, as much as he didn't want to, he agreed. He stayed with her as long as he could, until he had to leave for work.

The gnome had not shown up while he was there, so Regan explained and demonstrated for Plor how a cell phone worked. When he was sure she understood its functionality, he left her to watch, making her promise to not do anything except call him if anything happened. Reluctantly, she'd agreed.

He'd left her, wondering after that afternoon what her promise was worth.

Now, with the phone to his numb ear, he waited for her to answer. When she did, he said, "Plor, listen. I need your help with something."

He told her what he needed, gave her instructions, then hung up.

Sean Regan stepped into the alley behind the brick building the girls said they saw the woman arise to. Had he seriously just said, *arise?*

With a shake of his head he glanced upward, hoping for a glimpse of the woman the two girls said rode a swirling tornado of snow to the rooftop. He squinted against the falling snow that blurred his vision. The gray sky was swollen with drifting, dark clouds. They washed out the color of everything around him, creating a monochromatic landscape of stark whites, deep blacks, and shades of gunmetal grays.

Regan took off his hat, blinked melting snow from his eyes, then wiped them with his coat sleeve. He replaced his hat, about to give up and return to the victim and his witnesses when he noticed a shadowy movement by the building's cornerstone overhead. To Regan, it appeared to be someone leaning out over the parapet, watching him. Then just as quickly, it disappeared.

"Damn." Again Regan searched for access to the roof. This time, he thought he found it. "This is crazy," he told himself, eyeing the cast-iron drainpipe strapped to the corner of the brick façade.

The metal was cold to the touch, but he could get his hands

around the pipe, his fingers just fitting between the rough brick so he had a firm handhold. He pulled, testing the hold of the straps. They felt solid. Part of him was disappointed, wishing the pipe wouldn't hold his weight as he planted his feet on the brick wall and began to shimmy up the pipe. It the straps had failed, if he had managed to rip the cold metal pipe from the corner of the building, then he'd have had an excuse for not going up onto that roof.

But no, and now here he was. Hand over hand, climbing up the side of the building like he was Spider-Man. If he were still a kid, this might have been great. He glanced up, planted his foot again, then the other, and he climbed.

It was only two stories, he thought. Doable, he convinced himself. Until, after a time, he looked down and found himself twenty feet off the ground. Suddenly his shoulders ached and the strain in his arms made them quiver. He looked up and cursed when he saw the parapet above still looking very far away.

"What were you thinking, Regan?" he complained, climbing, now forcing himself not to look down. Finally, with cold, numb fingers, he grasped the concrete parapet and, breathing heavily, hauled himself over the edge, falling awkwardly onto the gravel and snow-covered rooftop.

"Made it," he said, panting, lying on his back, resting. A moment later he rolled over and clambered to his hands and knees, then stood up, rotating his shoulders, trying to relieve the tense muscle tension.

Regan saw across the rooftop a figure standing at the edge. Snow swirled around the woman—female as best Regan could guess—who wore a long white trench coat that billowed and snapped around her more like a cape than a coat. She had long black hair. It whipped in the air like living tendrils and she held her hands up to the skies, now alive with more snow, driving snow, and streaked with crackling lightning and booming thunder.

If he hadn't known better, while questioning his own sanity, he'd have sworn this woman—whoever she was—was conjuring the snow and calling down the lightning storm.

Regan shook that thought away. He drew his sidearm, held it in a two-handed grip, and approached her as he called out, "Step away from the edge of the roof and turn around."

*Put your hands in the air,* would be redundant, as she already had her hands up. Maybe he should tell her to put them down.

The figure did as he instructed. She stepped back off the parapet, but she didn't immediately turn around. She stood facing the gathering storm of snow and hail and wind. The roar of the storm got louder as the sky grew darker and more ominous. Before long the storm would be on top of them.

Regan needed to end this, to grab her and get them to shelter somewhere before the full brunt of the storm reached them. Regan shouted to be heard above the howling wind. "Turn around! I'm not going to tell you again!"

Still no response.

Regan moved closer. His thoughts returned to the condition of this woman's victims, the dehydrated faces, the pain their expressions revealed, reminding himself how deadly she was.

Then the woman began to turn.

She was petite in size, little more than five feet tall. Her long black hair snapped wildly across her face, revealing to Regan only snatches of flawless alabaster skin. Her almond-shaped eyes glowed ghostly and red—like a wolf's in the dark.

The ice, snow, and hail struck furiously, pelting his skin. The wind howled and churned and swept in a gust so fierce Regan's hat was suddenly torn from his head. He squinted as he grabbed for it but missed. It was gone, lost to the wind.

"How the hell are you doing this?" Regan screamed through the howling wind, tears streaming from his eyes and blurring his vision.

The ghostly figure fixed him with a glowing, penetrating stare, her hair streaming in frantic waves across her face, her mouth twisted in an angry scowl. She brought her hands down in a gesture that appeared to focus the brunt of the entire storm directly at Regan.

Regan swallowed hard, suddenly gripped with a cold, hard reality: he was hopelessly outmatched. "Stop! Whatever you're doing, stop it!"

Fear tightened his throat as her sweeping gesture stirred the wind into a whipping fury, pelting him with hailstones and ice. His clothing rippled and flapped in the windstorm like flags snapping. "Stop it!"

He tightened his grip on his weapon and started to squeeze the Glock's trigger when he was suddenly brushed back. From seemingly nowhere, Enbarr suddenly appeared, skidding to a stop on the roof, his shimmering white flank between Regan and the… whatever it was he faced!

Enbarr whinnied and gave the entity threatening Regan an angry snort.

Astride the great steed, Plor na mBan rode, her auburn hair and great cape billowing out behind her, her sword slicing the air, forcing the figure in the flowing white coat to backpedal.

Plor leaped from Enbarr's back while the horse trotted around the roof in a tight circle, snorting, his breath fogging from his nostrils like steam from a locomotive. Plor took a defensive position before the other woman, her sword drawn back and ready to strike. "Stand down, whatever manner of foul being you may be. Stand down," she demanded. "Or *Claiomh Solais* will slay you where you stand."

"Plor, don't," Regan shouted, probably unheard in the howling wind, as his mind reeled, trying to figure out where she and Enbarr had come from in the first place.

Clearly the woman in white had no intention of giving up.

She gestured toward Plor with her hands, palms out, somehow summoning the full blast of the storm and throwing it in a concentrated ball at Plor. The force of the blast struck her in the chest. Unable to maintain her footing, Plor fell onto her back and skidded across the rooftop.

Caught in the hurricane-force blast, Enbarr slid across the snow and gravel roof, his giant hoofs digging for purchase but having little success. In the animal's large black eyes, Regan saw something that scared him; in those eyes, he saw panic.

Regan shouted, "No!"

The animal hit the parapet, its long legs folding up underneath him, collapsing as the great weight of the animal catapulted him over the edge of the building. Scratching at the roof in her own failed attempt to keep from following Enbarr over the edge, Plor dug at the roof with her sword, slamming the blade down to try to use it like an anchor, but she lost her hold. Her fingers slipped from the carefully wrapped hilt, and the relentless force propelled her toward the same fate as her horse.

Outside of the vortex, Regan ran for Plor and caught hold of her as she reached the roof's edge. She smashed hard into the parapet. Shards of concrete broke off with the force of the impact, before the wind lifted her and tossed her effortlessly over the side.

Desperately, Regan caught her by the arm. The forward velocity of her fall dragged him across the rooftop snow and gravel on his knees, ripping through his trousers and bloodying his skin. The worse rug burn he'd ever experienced. He slammed into the small half-wall parapet hard, but not hard enough to break his grip. He grunted from the sharp, agonizing pain of the impact, the torturous yank on his shoulder. He grabbed the loosening concrete with his free hand, arresting his own plunge over the side.

He looked over the edge. Plor dangled by one arm in his grasp.

He called out, "I've got you."

"For now," she shouted back cryptically. "But for how long?"

*Good question.* Mercifully, the wind, pelting ice, and hail had settled down, becoming less relentless. Regan glanced down at Plor, noting with surprise that Enbarr was nowhere to be seen. He realized not seeing the horse lying in the snow, wounded and in pain, or worse, dead, brought with it a sense of relief.

Somehow the animal had found a way to survive the fall. Regan was sure of it, and that hope surged through him and gave him strength, drawn from a reserve he didn't know he had.

Still, Plor was slipping from his grasp.

He reached over the parapet to grab her wrist with his other hand, but changing his position caused him to slip farther, raining concrete debris down on Plor and loosening his grip even more.

Plor gasped and Regan cursed. "Hold on!"

"'Twas my plan, but not for all night. Can you pull me up?"

"I'm not sure," Regan admitted. He shuffled his feet to get better purchase. Sweat beaded his forehead in spite of the cold around him. His breath fogged the air in front of his face. Then a sudden cold washed over him.

"Sean Regan! Watch thyself!" If Plor's warning had not been enough to frighten him into action, her expression was.

Regan twisted around to look up over his shoulder and gasped.

# CHAPTER 15

**THE WOMAN IN** white loomed over him, still concealed by a swirling tornado of snow, ice, and hail funneling around her. Regan squinted against the torrent of wind, but he could make out no more of her face than when she'd stood one hundred feet away.

Below him, his arm ached, feeling like it was being torn from its socket by the pendulum-swing dead weight of Plor na mBan. Prone and with his grip on Plor, Regan was powerless to stop the strange apparition from whatever she planned to do.

*Come to think of it,* Regan thought. *I've been powerless to stop her from the get-go.*

The woman brought her hands together and aimed her palms at him.

"Oh, man. Here it comes."

Suddenly, the figure was swept away!

Regan blinked away snow and tears, but he still wasn't sure what he saw. What looked like a second figure, this one all in black, had come from seemingly out of nowhere and body-tackled their white-coated adversary. The two figures rolled and skidded across the rooftop in a swirl of snow and gravel and snarls as animalistic as they were scary.

Regan couldn't tell anything else.

"Sean Regan!"

Plor's cry whipped his attention back to her (and his) precarious position. He felt her wrist slipping from his grasp. Once more he reached over to grab her arm with his other hand. With both hands wrapped tightly around her upper arm, he was sure he could keep her from slipping away, from falling, but for how long? He had neither the strength nor the footing he needed to haul her back up over the crumbling parapet.

"I've got you, but, I...I don't think I can pull you up."

With an unexpected but welcome whinny, holding onto Plor no longer was a problem.

Below Plor, Enbarr had appeared. Like a champion Grand Prix jumper, the horse was leaping toward her with a determined snort, even though they were two stories off the ground!

"Release me, Sean Regan...now!"

Regan snapped open both hands and Plor fell from his grasp. He watched in stricken stillness as Plor dropped, then landed with a whoosh of expelled air squarely on Enbarr's back. The equine took the impact of the sudden weight as if it were nothing, crested his leap, and began his nearly two-story descent.

Unable to contain himself while his stilled heart began to beat again, Regan let out a loud yelp. "Wahoo!" He fist-pumped the air and rolled back around, smiling, until he realized he was on the rooftop... alone.

Their white-coated adversary and his black-clad benefactor—whatever it had been that swept her away—were both gone. In the wind, as it were.

"Son of a gun. Can you believe that?"

As he got to his feet and brushed away gravel and wetness from his torn and bloodied uniform trousers, Plor returned to the roof, atop Enbarr, who once more had managed to leap tall buildings. The stallion skidded to a sure-footed stop. Plor pulled at his reins and looked around, bewildered, with her sword raised in anticipation of battle, only to be disappointed.

"They're gone."

"Gone where?"

"No clue," Regan said, crossing over to the far end of the roof and looking down. He hadn't expected to see anything down below, and he wasn't surprised. "They're just gone."

Plor silently contemplated that, then said, "Tell me about the second one."

Regan told her what he had seen, which wasn't much. After he finished describing the blazingly fast blur of black shadow that had probably saved both of their lives, Plor gave him a disapproving cock of her head. "That is all?"

"Yeah, that's all. In case you hadn't noticed, I had my hands full at the time."

"Yes, I was aware of what preoccupied you, Sean Regan. Thank you. Your efforts on my behalf are appreciated. Be sure to know, I would do the same for you, should the need arise."

"Good to know. Let's hope it doesn't come to that."

"Yes," she agreed. "'Twould be best if it did not."

"In the meantime, do you have any idea what that thing…those things…were?" His clothes were soaked with cold sweat and his pants wet from all the rolling around in the snow. Regan shivered and zipped the front of his bomber-style uniform coat higher. He jammed his ice-cold hands into his jacket pockets, fisting them to warm them up.

"I do not. The Otherworlds, and there are many of them, are filled with many mystical beings, some both wondrous and strange, some benign, while others are…well, best avoided if possible. As for these, I am not familiar with them, specifically."

"Terriffic." Regan looked around the rooftop, contemplating all he'd seen since first encountering Plor and Enbarr the night before. Christ, his world had been turned upside down. Regan always prided himself on being in control, with his ability to remain calm and objective, his ability to logically analyze a situation and understand it. It would be an understatement to suggest that was anywhere near the case lately.

Plor had returned to Enbarr's side. The animal stood with his front leg extended, rubbing his snout up and down the bony limb in an effort to satisfy an itch. Plor circled Enbarr and patted his flank here and there to assess the animal's condition, searching for any unseen injuries. Miraculously, the equine appeared to be in perfect health.

"Look," Regan said. "We can talk about this when I get home after my shift. In the meantime, I need to get back to the victim."

"Agreed," Plor said. "And I wish to return to the museum. One fear I have is that this has been an elaborate ruse."

"A distraction while Ciag steals *Lia Fáil*?"

"'Tis my fear, yes."

Regan was too tired to argue with her. "Fine." He stroked Enbarr's flank, grateful for the magnificent steed. "So he flies?"

Plor laughed. "Of course not. Horses do not fly. But Enbarr..." she said, patting his neck, "...is a superior jumper."

"You're telling me he jumped all the way up from the street."

"No." Holding his reins, she led the animal to edge of the building. There she pointed. "We jumped to the top of that metal container, then onto the low roof there across the road, and then across to the next one there." She pointed north, where the buildings were progressively higher in height. "And then, finally, here to this rooftop."

They'd hopscotched their way up to the rooftop. Regan whistled.

"Wow. That's…that's…unbelievable."

Plor patted Enbarr. "He is an extraordinary animal, yes."

"I'll see you at home, but call me if anything happens at the museum before then." He began to walk away, heading back to the drainpipe to climb back down.

"Where are you going?" Plor had already swung herself up and was sitting on Enbarr's back.

"I'm going to climb down," Regan said.

"That would be foolhardy and unnecessary."

"How else do you expect me…" He stopped, realizing what she had in mind. "Oh, no. I'm not—"

The horse snorted and nodded his head, as if enthusiastic over the idea.

Plor smiled. "Enbarr says it would be his pleasure."

"No. Absolutely not."

But already the horse was charging toward him. Plor reached down and effortlessly swooped Regan off his feet and deposited him on the animal's wide rump behind her.

"This isn't a very good idea," Regan said.

Plor spurred the animal on, and Enbarr trotted toward the edge and leaped off the roof.

Regan latched his arms around Plor's waist to keep from falling off and tried hard not to close his eyes. He only halfway succeeded. The wind and snow rushed into Regan's face, blowing his hair back and billowing Plor's cape trapped between their bodies. Sure his heart had stopped, Regan sucked at the wind, unable to catch his breath as the animal sailed through the air.

*Can't fly, my ass,* Regan thought and squeezed his eyes closed tight. But he couldn't resist peeking.

Enbarr landed perfectly and galloped to the end of first one roof then another until finally he landed on the snow-covered street below, slowing to a stop at the Brookline Avenue intersection.

Regan hopped down from behind Plor with his heart racing, and breathless. He patted the horse's warm hindquarters again. "Thanks, big fella. That was…incredible."

Plor asked, "Shall we go with you to see the body? I am curious."

"I'm thinking no," Regan said. "The scene'll be crawling with cops and paramedics, civilians and reporters, too, by now. You're still a little hard to explain."

"I understand." She sounded disappointed.

"Check out the museum. If you find anything unusual, call me. You remember how to use the cell phone, right?"

"I do and I will." She pulled at Enbarr's reins, turning him away from Regan to trot away.

Under his breath, Regan added, "And try and stay out of sight."

They reached Ipswich Street. Plor steered Enbarr to the left at the corner, heading north, before disappearing behind a row of buildings, and Regan, with a shake of his head—still wondering if this could all be a dream—returned to the initial crime scene.

There he found both ends of the street blocked off by yellow crime scene tape and the surrounding buildings awash with a kaleidoscope of red and blue and white emergency lights from two ambulances, three patrol cars, an unmarked sedan with a red revolving bubblegum light, and even a BFD fire truck.

A secondary perimeter had been set up around the body of the victim, and there stood several technicians from the crime scene unit in dark-blue windbreakers, two paramedics with a trauma board (waiting), and Mike Hall, chewing on an unlit cigar and looking down at the latest vic with a scowl of disgust on his face.

Regan wondered whether it was from the unsettling condition

the body had been left in or because this added even more work to his plate. He happened to look up as Regan approached.

"Oh. Great. Nice of you to join us, Officer Regan. I never pegged you as a union man. What's the matter, this poor guy's untimely demise not important enough to keep you from your coffee break?"

Not in the mood, Regan said, "And I never pegged you as being an insufferable jerk, Mike. I was the first on the scene. I'm the one who almost saved that poor man's life."

"How'd ya figure?" He pinched his cigar between his thumb and forefinger and used it to indicate the victim. "By the looks of that stiff, he's been dead for centuries, just like that Kegler fella."

"And just like that Kegler fella," Saito Izumi mimicked, looking up at Hall from where she knelt over the body, "this man has been dead for less than an hour."

"Less than that," Regan said. "He still had a pulse when I chased after the perp, not twenty minutes ago."

Saito came to her feet. "He was alive when you arrived?"

Out of the shadows of the cars parked around her, the flashing lights illuminated her face.

Regan sucked in a breath. Saito Izumi had a dark bruise under her eye. Her skin was purple and black and yellow. Then he noticed her hair was disheveled, though she'd made an attempt—apparently a hasty one—to tie it back into a thick ponytail. The way she'd worn it the night before. Yet then it had been pristine, not a hair out of place.

"That's some shiner. What happened?"

Saito timidly touched at the bruise with her fingertips. Her face blushed. "I slipped and fell. On the ice." She pointed toward where the ME's station wagon was parked. "Hit the bumper…" She fingered the bruise again. "…with my face."

"Wow. That's got to hurt. You should get it checked out."

"I will when I get back to the office." She held his gaze with hers. "Thank you for your concern."

"So, what can you tell us, Doc?" Mike Hall asked.

She took a moment to ensure she could speak without being overheard. "I need to get him back to the morgue. I'll rush the autopsy, get it done tonight, but I already know what I'll find. This victim died in the same manner as Kurt Kegler. Why and how they died is still a mystery, but I can tell you, whoever is responsible for this young man's death is also responsible for killing Mr. Kegler."

"You know what you're saying, Doc?"

She met Mike Hall's intense stare and gave it right back to him. "I do. You may well have a serial killer on your hands."

Hall waved his hands and put a finger to his lips. "Shush!" As if saying it made it real. He lowered his voice to a harsh whisper. "Don't say the S word. You're new in this town, Doc. So let me give you a bit of advice—"

"You mean a warning."

"Tomato, tamato. You start slinging around words like...like..."

"Serial killer," Regan offered helpfully.

Hall glared at him. "Yeah, you're the funny guy. It's not your ass in the hot seat."

*True,* Regan thought, as he remembered when his ass was in the hot seat not all that long ago, Mike Hall had been one of the few guys who didn't piss gasoline on the fire he'd built under his career. "You're right, Mike. Sorry."

Hall nodded, accepting the *mea culpa.* "Think what you want to think, Doc. All I'm saying is keep your mouth shut about things you're not ready to stake your job and reputation on, either in court or to the press. You hear what I'm saying?"

"Yes, detective, I do. And in that case, I cannot speculate on any aspect of this case. My full report will be available in twenty-four hours." Saito knelt back down beside the victim and clearly refused to say anything more.

After a moment, Hall took Regan by the elbow and guided him away from the medical examiner to the edge of the crime scene near the back of Saito Izumi's black station wagon. "That woman's gonna be a pain in our asses," he said when they were out of earshot of the diminutive Asian medical examiner.

"Maybe," Regan tentatively agreed. "But she's not wrong."

Hall shook his head, like the idea didn't agree with him. Regan was sure it didn't. "Yeah, I know it. But, Sean, if word leaks out we're dealing with a serial killer thing here..." He looked around at the gathering crowd of onlookers, at the uniformed officers holding them back, and at the crime scene techs moving mechanically around the scene, taking measurements, snapping pictures, picking up samples of this and that, particulates they hoped would break the case wide open like they did on *CSI*.

They'd be better off looking at *Buffy the Vampire Slayer* for a TV playbook, Regan was beginning to fear and questioning his own sanity at the thought. Shaking that away, Regan asked, "What do we know about the victim?"

Hall flipped open his notebook and began to read. "The uniforms and paramedics found a wallet on him. The driver's license found on him says the vic is Brad Dumas, lives in a condo development in the Back Bay. Witnesses at the bar where he was drinking say he had a fight with his girlfriend after the Sox game and she stormed off. He left a little later, probably to go after her. We found a busted-up cell phone a few blocks that way." He pointed.

Regan said, "On Ipswich."

"Yeah. We figure it was his because that's where the two girls saw him get picked up by some hooker."

"Girls? The ones that called 911?"

"Them two." Hall pointed toward a cluster of police cars. The girls Regan had seen when he first arrived were there, huddled under blankets, receiving the full attention of two young, overly attentive uniformed cops. Each girl held a cup of steaming liquid, coffee or hot cocoa maybe. "They'd just come out of the Tequila Run for a smoke when they saw Dumas, with what they assumed was a hooker. Dixie and Trixie—"

"Don't tell me those are their real names?"

"Naw. They told me. I can't remember what they were." He pointed over toward the uniformed officers with the girls. "You can bet Taylor and Finnegan have their names, addresses, numbers, and full life stories by now."

"No doubt."

"Anyway, The two chirpies decided rather than go back inside, they were gonna call it a night and go home. They started heading for their car when they ran into Dumas with his floozy over on Lansdowne."

That was where Regan had found them upon his arrival. "But they realized something was wrong?"

"Yeah. At first they thought maybe it was a shakedown. This experienced working girl had lured a naive kid into the dark, was rolling him for all he had without putting out herself. But when they saw him struggling in her arms…" He checked his notes again. "…*it looked like she was killing him,* they reported."

"Well, they called that right."

"They sure did." A minute passed, then Hall asked the question he'd brought Regan away from everyone else to ask. "So tell me what you saw. What happened down there?" He waved toward the far end of the street from where Regan had emerged after his rooftop fight with…

Well, he certainly wasn't going to tell Mike Hall about that!

"I got here to see just what the girls reported to you: some girl doing something to that guy." Regan pointed toward the corpse. He noticed Saito was watching them. She quickly looked down at her clipboard when he caught her eye. "I yelled at her to stop. She dropped the vic and took off...that way." If the girls hadn't said anything to Hall about the perp riding a swirling snow cyclone to the rooftop, Regan sure as hell wasn't going to mention it.

"And?"

"And," Regan said, shifting his feet and looking at the snow on the ground, "I lost her."

"You lost her?"

"Yeah, I lost her." He added, "She had a pretty big lead on me."

He couldn't tell if Hall was buying it or not. The detective wrote something in his notebook. "Where did you see her last?"

Here Regan was in trouble. Any direction he gave Hall, the detective would send uniforms to check it out. They would discover no footprints anywhere he told them to go except his own, and worse, Enbarr's hoofprints. And how could he explain that away?

About to answer, Regan was saved by the bell—a siren anyway. The night air erupted with the whoop of a police siren, hit on and off in quick succession. Regan and Hall turned toward the disturbance to see an unmarked police sedan making its way slowly down the street toward the edge of the crime scene, the driver tapping the siren to move the pedestrian lookie-loos out of his way.

"Christ! Just what I need," Hall complained. "It's the deputy superintendent."

"Sucks to be you," Regan said.

"Don't laugh, funny guy." Hall pointed to the car. It had stopped and both rear doors snapped open. "Isn't that the patrol captain with him?"

Hall knew damn well it was. And Regan knew he'd be stuck here all night.

Mike Hall wandered off, presumably to make it harder for the superintendent to find him. When he did, Hall would look productive.

Regan was too worn-out to play games. The patrol captain, an old-timer named Nichols, hated him anyway. Ever since Regan had gone undercover at the behest of Internal Affairs and he'd exposed a half dozen of Nichols's men in a crime-for-profit scheme, he had hated him for it. The scheme had been run by one of Nichols's lieutenants, and one of Regan's best friends since the second grade, Patrolman Dale Brandigan.

The investigation didn't implicate Nichols in anything more serious than being incompetent. Even so, Regan could be standing there having just collared the people responsible for the Jimmy Hoffa hit and it wouldn't make a difference. In Captain Nichols's eyes, Sean Regan was worse than pond scum.

While he waited for his verbal thrashing, Regan glanced down at the ground around Saito's station wagon. She'd said she slipped and fell and hit her cheek on the car bumper, but as Regan looked around, at first one and then the other bumper, he found no indication someone had fallen and scrambled around in the snow, slipping and sliding to get back up. The snow around the car—except where the back hatch had been opened and materials removed and set down on the ground—was completely undisturbed.

Regan thought back to when he circled the building where his quarry was eventually found—on the roof—and he remembered how odd it was to find that the snow had been completely without blemish, completely untouched. Just like the snow around each of the car's two bumpers. Undisturbed.

Regan glanced over at Saito, remembering the impression he had in the low visibility as snow and ice and hail pelted him, that the strange woman who seemingly controlled the storm with her gestures and wore a large flapping white leather coat was petite and Asian with wildly windblown long, black hair.

He glanced at the snow, then at Saito. She happened to look up at him, perhaps sensing his scrutiny, and even from that distance he could see the dark, angry bruise on her face. There was no way she'd done that on a car bumper, not here.

That meant, he had no doubt, she was lying.

# CHAPTER 16

FOR THE SECOND night in a row, Sean Regan spent his shift at a violent death crime scene. *Déjà vu,* he thought, while watching the body-bag-shrouded victim being wheeled into the coroner's wagon. By the time the uniformed canvass was done and the forensic team cleared the scene, it was after eleven in the morning. The sun was up, the snow had stopped, and Regan's toes were numb.

Once everyone was gone, he tore down the crime scene tape and was balling it up, throwing the mess into the backseat of his cruiser when a car pulled up behind his unit. He recognized the car as if it were his own—because it was. The registration might have been in Deidre's name, but the payments were his to make, at least until he signed the divorce papers.

As his soon-to-be-ex-wife stepped out of the Lexus ES, Regan slammed the back door of his cruiser. She was dressed in dark slacks and nice shoes with sensible heels, a heavy sweater, and a red leather jacket with a wool collar. She was off duty—if on-air reporters are ever really off duty, always chasing the story—which explained why she didn't have her cameraman Todd in tow.

As she approached, Regan said, "Give me a break, Dee. I've

been up all night. I don't have it in me to fight about what I'm doing in my private time."

"I'm not here about your girlfriend—"

"For the last time, she's not my girlfriend."

Deidre waved his protest away. "I'm not interested in your explanation. Not right now, but we will address it…soon."

Regan sighed. "Then what is it you do want?"

"Last night."

"No." He turned away from her and gave the scene a final once-over to make sure he'd cleaned up as much as he needed to clean up. He pulled his car door open.

Deidre did a run around him, careful not to slip in the slushy snow in the street. With the driver door between them she put a hand over his, where he held the doorframe. He looked down at it then up at her. "What do you want, Dee?"

"Just confirm some things I've heard, that's all. It'll be an unnamed police source close to the investigation sort of thing."

He snorted. "Like no one will know I'm the unnamed source. Your husband."

"Ex—" She cut herself off. "Sorry."

He waved it away. "Dee, I'm not even 'close to the investigation.'" He used air quotes around the phrase. "I just happened to be the guy on patrol that caught the call."

"Yeah. Right. It was a coincidence."

"That's right. A coincidence."

"You were the one who told me there's no such thing in police work."

"I was wrong." He started to climb into his cruiser.

"Sean, please. I know the two deaths were similar, that a suspect escaped this time. People are already talking about it being a serial killer."

"You need at least three murders to be a serial," he informed her, even though he had earlier agreed with Saito Izumi. Maybe you needed three to be a serial crime, but you had to have one and two before you had three. Despite what he told Dee now, he knew that whatever it was he'd chased away earlier, she—he—it—was responsible for both Dumas's and Kegler's deaths.

"These two men died in the same way, under very similar circumstances. How do you explain that?"

"I can't. Talk to the medical examiner on the case."

"I tried. She won't talk to us."

"Smart lady." He sat down in his front seat and tried to pull the door closed.

Deidre held it open. "Witnesses said you saw who did this. That you chased the guy down but that you lost him."

Regan sighed again. "Come on, Dee. It's late." He squinted up at the sun cresting the brick façade of Fenway Park. "Early," he amended. "I need to go home and get some sleep."

"Go home to that girl, you mean." Deidre stepped away from the car. "What's her name? Plor…flower of women? Please."

"Dee, it's not like that. I swear."

"Yeah, right." Her eyes filled with tears. In them he saw the hurt he'd caused. Again.

The same hurt he'd caused over the last few years. All the time he was working undercover to bust a ring of bad cops. All through the various trials and the departmental hearings that followed. The pain he'd caused her as he grew more short-tempered, ill-mannered, and withdrawn, impossible to be around.

And now here he was doing it again. With lies and secrets. Not the sort of secrets Dee suspected, but secrets nonetheless. But what else could he do? Tell her Plor was some kind of warrior woman from—what did she call the Otherworld she was from—and she was looking for a deranged leprechaun who was on a quest for some mystical artifact, and that whoever killed those two men was a witch that could control the weather—make it snow, and weaponized it?

Yeah, that would go over really well.

"Dee, please. Listen. I'm telling you. I'm not having an affair with that woman. I'm just trying to help her. It's completely on the up-and-up. You need to trust me."

"Why? Why should I trust you, Sean? I've been a reporter covering the police for over twenty years. I know how police operations work. I know how cops and the legal system work. I've never—in all that time—seen a cop bring someone home and give her a bath and fill her full of booze except for cops who were cheating. Cheating on their wives or cheating on their girlfriends, but always cheating. So no, Sean Regan, I do not need to believe you and I don't."

She slammed his car door closed and stormed back to her car.

But not before Sean saw the tears that had filled her eyes fall.

Regan watched her drive away, fishtailing the Lexus dangerously as she drove too fast for the road conditions. Long after she'd gone and only after the interior of the car began to feel like the inside of a freezer did Regan start the cruiser, drive to the station, and check out, noting the only good thing he had going for him at the moment was that he'd earned another three hours of overtime.

He came through his front door and hung his bomber-jacket-style uniform coat on the back of a chair in the kitchen. Then he unbuckled his gun belt and gingerly hung it over his coat. His body had taken a beating and his muscles were starting to stiffen up. All he wanted to do now was take a nice hot shower and let the water pelt him relentlessly to massage away every tightening and bruised muscle in his body, namely every single one of them.

"You want a beer?" he called out to Plor. She was standing out on his balcony, looking out over the fountain and parking lot below.

She stood in full warrior regalia, her arms folded across her chest and the sun glinting off the sword she wore at her side. A gentle, cold breeze billowed the heavy dark drapes on either side, along with her cape and her thick mane of auburn hair. The good news was anyone who happened to look up and saw her would figure she was dressed up for Halloween or in some cosplay costume. He thought that was what the kids called it these days, cosplay.

The cost of heating the place wasn't bad enough, he thought as he joined her. *She's got to leave the doors open and let me heat all of the outdoors, too.*

Since she hadn't answered him, he asked again when he was next to her. "Beer?"

She glanced at the bottle he held and then up at him, as if she'd just realized he was there. "No."

"Did you get any sleep?"

"Your bedding is too soft."

Was that a yes or a no? "Um, okay. Sorry about that."

"I returned to the museum. Ciag did not return."

Regan nodded. "I figured, since you didn't contact me. I also checked the overnight activity reports. Nothing suspicious was reported. Maybe we're wrong and he's not after this *Lia Fáil* thing."

She shook her head. "He's come for the Stone of Destiny. I am certain of it."

Several people walking to their parked cars had looked up and noticed Plor standing there, watching them. Regan stepped closer to the edge so he was sure he'd be seen too. He waved. "Happy Halloween."

One guy shouted back, "Rad costumes, man."

To address Plor's certainty, Regan asked, "Then why didn't he come back for it last night? For that matter, why didn't he simply take it the first night? No one was there to stop him."

"I do not know," Plor admitted.

"And what about our little adventure last night?" Regan shuddered at the ease with which the woman had blown them across the roof, nearly sending them all over the side without breaking a sweat.

Did something like *that* sweat?

"Do you know what that was? Have you ever encountered anything like that before?"

"Like that? No," Plor said again. "I am aware of many who can command the weather and other elements, earth, fire, bend them to their wills…it is said the druids Ériu, Banba, and Fodla created a magical storm to drive the Milesians away when they first invaded our homes, but Amergin managed to calm the seas and guide the Milesian ships back into port."

"Yeah. Well, maybe we could use this Amergin guy's help."

Plor snapped angrily at the suggestion. "'Twas because of Amergin's treachery the Milesians were able to return to our shores, battle the Tuatha Dé Danann, and kill our kings; MacCuill, MacCecht and MacGréine, the last rulers of our world. The Tuatha Dé Danann were defeated in battle and tricked into living underground, forced to the *sidhe* mounds, to *Tir na nÓg.*"

"Whoa, easy. Down, girl. All I'm saying is we need somebody *like* him. Someone that can stand up to…whatever that was."

"Now that I know the extent of its powers, I will defeat the demon when next we meet, have no fear of that, Sean Regan." She turned, clearly intent on leaving. "We must return to the museum and safeguard *Lia Fáil.*"

"And how do you intend on doing that?"

"By taking it."

Regan blinked. "You want to steal that rock from the museum?

142

Are you crazy? We barely got out of there without being arrested the last time."

"Do you have a better suggestion, Sean Regan?"

*Good question,* Regan thought. And the short answer was no. But stealing a priceless artifact—even if it was a hunk of rock—was simply out of the question. While Plor was obsessed with Ciag and his obsession with some ancient *objet d'art,* he was more concerned with Kurt Kegler's and Brad Dumas's killer and the risk of more murders. "Unless they're connected."

Plor gave him a puzzled look. "Explain."

"This is twenty-first-century Boston. Weather-stirring druids and magical, lantern-carrying, conjuring leprecha—fear darrigs are not the norm here. What if the appearance of that…thing on the roof that's killing these people, and Ciag and his pursuit of your king maker's rock—"

"The *Lia Fáil.*"

"Right. *Lia Fáil.* In a conversation I had earlier with Dee—"

"Your betrothed, she is well?"

"Yes. She's fine. But what I was saying is there are no coincidences. What if this snow-controlling creature thing is here for the same reason Ciag is?"

"To take *Lia Fáil.*"

"Or to keep us busy while Ciag takes it."

Plor dropped her hand to the hilt of her sword. "Then they both must die."

"Okay. Easy there." Regan returned to the kitchen to fetch another beer. Drinking, he paced the living room, thinking. Still trying to wrap his head around all the weirdness, he was reminded of a famous, oft-quoted line of Sherlock Holmes: *When you have eliminated the impossible, whatever remains, however improbable, must be the truth.*

That fell neatly in line with what Plor had been saying all along. Trust what you saw, what you experienced, as real, no matter how unlikely or implausible your brain told you it was. What other explanation could there be?

Holmes was, of course, a fictional character. Still, Regan's military training supplied him with yet another axiom that might fit well, too: *the Kiss Principle—keep it simple, stupid.*

He had to keep this simple. Treat it like any other law-enforcement problem. Kegler and Dumas were murdered, so follow the clues to the murderer. Who or what that was, they could deal with later. The same went for Ciag. Stop the burglary, then deal with the perpetrator.

Suddenly, as if a heavy burden had been lifted, a weight taken from his shoulders, he could think clearly. "I know what we need to do next."

He told Plor about Saito Izumi, the new medical examiner who had suddenly started when the two strange deaths occurred. He told her that Saito was Asian and how he sensed, felt, from what little he saw of her face, that the entity they'd fought was Asian, too. He told Plor of Saito's bruised cheek, about the undisturbed snow around her car. The physical evidence didn't support her story, he said, and then there was her less than meticulously styled hair. As if she'd smoothed and placed her hair in the clip in a hurry.

Certainly all that wasn't enough to make a capital murder case against her, but it made her a legitimate person of interest. And now, unencumbered by all the mumbo-jumbo mystical malarkey, those were clues he intended to pursue, especially since other than the medical examiner, his suspect pool was zero.

Plor stood, silent and stoic as Regan continued to make his case against the beautiful, Asian medical examiner. When he was done, he said, "Well, what do you think?"

"I believe we must go see this woman."

*We?* Regan thought, panicked. That wasn't exactly what he'd had in mind.

# CHAPTER 17

IT WAS AFTER one o'clock when Plor and Regan arrived at the medical examiner's office. Plor had changed into yet another of Deidre's left-behind outfits, this one a sleeveless, cobalt-blue top, black cropped pants, and black suede wedges. She wore a headband, but still her thick mane of auburn hair tumbled over her shoulders and down her back in waves of shimmering brown and red highlights.

After arguing over whether she could bring her sword—he made her keep it in the trunk of the Camaro—Regan guided her through the lobby of the government building, where she turned heads, male and female alike.

The morgue was in the basement. Regan guided her to the stairwell and down the steps, marveling again at her statuesque beauty and wondering still if she was looney-tunes crazy or not.

If she was, he felt like he was slipping around the bend then, too.

"This way," he said, opening the metal fire door at the bottom of the stairwell.

Plor paused at the open door. "If this woman is indeed the being we faced last night, I believe it is a mistake to confront her without *Claiomh Solais.*"

He pushed the door closed again. The last thing he needed was to have someone eavesdrop on this argument. "Plor, for the last time, we're not here to engage this woman in some epic warrior woman battle royale. We're simply here to talk to her, to gather intelligence."

Clearly not in agreement, she ceded the argument. "As you wish. But should this woman have other intentions, I will be the one to say, I told you so."

Regan sighed. "If that happens, we'll deal with it."

He pulled the door open and led Plor down the brightly lit corridor. "This way."

At the door marked autopsy room, Regan again asked Plor to let him do the talking. "And," he added, "there may be things in here that you'll find disturbing."

"Such as what things?"

"Dead bodies."

That caused her to pause in surprise. "Why? That would certainly indicate this woman is—"

"No, no. That's her job," Regan explained. "She's a doctor. She dissects dead people to examine them, to determine how they died."

"What does it matter? They're dead."

"When doing police investigations, we don't always know why people died just by looking at them. If the ME can determine the cause of death, it can help us figure out who the killer is."

Regan pushed the door open. He found the autopsy room the same way he'd found it the day before, empty except for a single covered body on an autopsy table.

Plor followed him in, her expression bright with curiosity. Like a child let into a candy store, she looked around and reached out to touch things.

"Don't break anything," he whispered, then called out, "Dr. Izumi. It's me, Sean Regan."

When the woman didn't appear, Regan said, "Stay here. And stop touching things."

He left Plor near the door they'd come in and crossed the room to where another door led to the hallway and suite of offices beyond. His sneakers squeaked on the highly polished linoleum floor, wet from trudging through the snow outside.

At the doorway where he'd collided with Saito Izumi the day before—her office, he assumed—he knocked lightly on the open door and went in. It was an office all right, complete with a desk, chairs, bookcases, and a light box for looking at X-rays. Along one wall he noted another door, this one closed, but not all the way. Bright light shone across the carpet from where the door remained ajar. Regan eased into the empty office quietly and made his way over to the door.

From where he stood he saw movement from inside the room, a room that was a bathroom. Okay, that makes sense, he thought, until he noticed that over the sink, where a mirror would normally hang, the wall space was empty.

Regan furrowed his brow. Who doesn't have a mirror over their sink in a bathroom?

The figure inside moved past the door, and though her back was to him, he recognized it to be Saito Izumi. Her long, black hair, this time not braided, coursed down her bare back, combed in a long, corn-silk-like, shimmering wave. She busied herself at the sink, the one with no mirror, doing what Regan couldn't see, but it had to do with scissors and tubing and what looked like an intravenous bag of blood. She wore only a black, sleeveless shirt with a scoop neckline and a pair of slacks. Part of the pantsuit she wore earlier but without the jacket.

Regan was about to clear his throat to announce his presence when Saito Izumi whirled, suddenly aware he—or someone—was there. She yanked the bathroom door open. "What are you doing lurking about here?"

Taken aback himself, Regan stammered, about to utter an apology, but stopped short when he noticed Saito's shoulder. As she had rushed toward the door, her hair spun away, sweeping past her bare shoulder, revealing to him a black crudely inked tattoo of three symbols in a vertical row, in Japanese or Chinese kanji.

血
吸
鬼

Saito locked her eyes on Regan as she grabbed for her jacket from the back of the bathroom door. She quickly put the jacket on, then grabbed a lab coat, donning that too. She flipped her hair out from under it so it fell down her back outside the coat.

"Officer Regan, why are you here skulking around my office?" she demanded again, switching off the bathroom lights as she came out into the office, pulling the door shut behind her.

"Oh, I, um, I can see how you could interpret it that way, but it's not...I called out." He pointed toward the open office door behind him. "Out there. You weren't there and then the door...it was open. I didn't mean to interrupt."

The anger that had flared in her eyes vanished, as if suddenly everything was okay. Saito smiled. "It's all right. No harm done. I was just cleaning up. What can I do for you?"

Regan stared at her face. He opened his mouth to speak, then snapped it shut again, trying to take in all he'd just seen.

He had experienced so much over the last two days.

"Is everything all right, officer?" Saito asked.

"What? Oh, sure." He pointed toward her cheek. "I was just noticing...you must heal pretty quickly."

"Heal?"

"That black eye you had this morning, from slipping on the ice? You said you hit your head on the bumper of your car."

Saito touched the skin under her eye. "Oh that. I guess it looked worse than it really was. It still hurts to touch." She forced a smile. "You'd be surprised what a good concealer can cover up."

She brushed past him, going briskly into the autopsy room.

"I wouldn't be surprised at all," Regan muttered under his breath as he fell in step behind her.

Over her shoulder, Saito said, "You told me yesterday you weren't a detective any longer. That you weren't investigating—"

She stopped short, seeing Plor na mBan in the outer room.

Because of her abrupt stop, Regan practically bumped into her.

"I see you've brought a guest," she said.

"Yes. This is Plor. She's a...friend."

"Plor," Saito said. Smiling, she strolled over to Plor. "What an unusual name. Very pretty."

"It means 'flower of women'."

"I'm Dr. Izumi. It's a pleasure to meet you, Plor." Saito stuck her hand out to shake and Plor stared down at it. Behind Saito's back, Regan mimed people shaking hands in greeting. *The way I did with Dixon, the museum security director*, he thought. *You saw that.*

Plor saw him and grasped Saito's hand. She shook it, awkwardly, but she shook it. And to Regan's relief, she didn't crush it.

Once Plor finally released Saito's hand, the medical examiner glanced over her shoulder at Regan, an inquiring expression on her face, a look that said, "Is she all right, or just a little weird?"

Regan sprang forward, giving Saito his most endearing smile, and clapped his hands together in a way that said, *Okay, let's get started.* "So did you get a chance to take a look at our latest victim, Brad Dumas?"

"I haven't begun the actual autopsy yet, no, but I have completed my preliminary examination." Saito stepped over to the occupied autopsy table. She reached for the sheet covering the body but paused to glance over at Plor, who, like Regan, crowded around her to see. "It's pretty gruesome."

"She'll be okay," Regan said. *I hope.*

Plor nodded and Saito shrugged. She pulled the sheet down to the cadaver's chest. Like Kurt Kegler, the corpse appeared to be in the very late stages of decay. The skin was a darkish green color and had begun to slip, causing gaps to have opened up around the closed eyes where the flesh drooped, to gather in leathery folds over the ears, like on a pug's face, but this was anything but cute. The skin also had sloughed off the exposed torso and dangled from the arms in limp wrinkles, as if the body under the skin had evaporated, leaving the epidermis to sag like a wet paper bag.

"The degree of decomposition is not as advanced in comparison to the condition of Mr. Kegler's remains, but as you can see, Mr. Dumas's remains are well into the active decay stage."

*Because I interrupted the attack,* Regan thought.

"What does that mean?" Plor asked.

"When a person dies," Saito explained, "the body goes through several stages of decomposition."

Plor knotted her brow.

"The body rots," Regan explained.

"In a body left unattended, and depending on many factors, such as environment, body mass, digestive tract contents, post-mortem scavenger disturbances, submerging or burial of the body, even the amount or type of clothing worn, it can take several days to a few weeks for the remains to reach the skeletonized stage. By any known scientific standards this body has to have been dead for no less than ten to twenty days."

"Well, we know that's not right," Regan said. "This young man was alive when I arrived on the scene."

Saito nodded, agreeing but clearly no less perplexed. "And testimonial evidence proves Mr. Kegler was alive only a few hours before his remains were found, though his body was even further along in the decaying process, much closer to diagenesis than Mr. Dumas here."

"Diagenesis?" Regan asked.

"Sorry," Saito said with a smile. "Full skeletonization. The final stage where all moisture has left the corpse and the flesh is gone, leaving nothing behind but bone and some hair."

A bit excitedly, Plor said, "Is this where the conditions of the dead tells us what caused their death?"

"In theory," Saito said. "But nothing we know of can cause this type of death, this accelerated, rapid decomposition and body decay. It's unheard of. And there's something else."

She led them around to the other side of the table. There on the stainless steel bridge over the body, where she had the tools of her trade—sparkling, shiny scalpels, forceps, dissecting scissors, needles, and cavity mirrors—she had an iPad tablet.

Clicking open a page, she read from her notes, "In addition to the unnatural accelerated rate of decomposition, the corpse also displays a remarkable lack of discolored livor mortis, indicating a complete absence of blood pool patterns and no indication of autolysis occurring."

"What does that mean?"

"Autolysis occurs during decomposition, usually four or so days after death, after the bloating or putrefaction occurs, a breaking down of the body's tissues by autologous enzymes. In both of these cases, that stage didn't occur."

"And your explanation for that?"

"I don't have one. It can't occur."

"Except your own findings say it did," Regan said.

"Yes," Saito agreed. Hesitantly, she went on, looking nervously from Regan to Plor then back again. "I do have one idea, but I'm afraid you won't believe me. You'll think I'm crazy."

Regan stole a quick glance over at Plor. Saito had wanted to tell him something yesterday when he was here. Maybe this was it. "You'd be surprised what I've come to accept over the last two days, Doctor. If you've got something that can help, let's have it."

Saito nodded, clearly undecided about the path she'd chosen to go down, but also too far along to back up now. "How familiar are you with ancient mythology?"

Regan and Plor exchanged glances.

"Have either of you ever heard of the Yuki-Onna? It is a Japanese legend, a myth actually, of a snow spirit, a being called a succubus who appears around the time of October thirty-first."

"On Halloween," Regan said.

Plor said, "Samhain."

*Oh, Saito, you've gone and done it now.*

Her sudden concern came from the strange looks her two visitors were giving her.

Sean Regan stared wide-eyed at her, while the tall, odd woman with the enviable mane of auburn hair cocked her head, appearing more curious than incredulous. It was she who said, "Tell us of this Yuki-Onna."

Now, thinking she was really deep into it, Saito said, "I'm no expert in ancient Japanese mythology, but what I have found in examining these corpses fits with what the ancient stories tell of the Yuki-Onna." Saito tried to backpedal. "But it's silly. Old, foolish superstitions. Stories told to frighten young children."

"Doctor, you started this. You had to have a reason, so don't stop now. Tell us about this, this Yoko-Ono thing, then why you think it has something to do with these deaths."

"Yuki-Onna means snow woman, and she is a *yōkai,* a ghost or a spirit, from old Japanese folklore. It is said she comes at night and that she is tall and beautiful with long black hair and blue lips. Her skin is so pale as to be translucent. She commands the snowstorms that accompany her, and she floats over the snow, leaving no footprints. Some say she may actually have the ability to ride the winds and even transform into a cloud of mist or snow to escape from harm."

Regan felt weak in the knees. What she described was exactly what they had experienced, down to the finest detail. These were the details the police were holding back, stuff not even Saito as a medical examiner would know.

"Since examining the first victim," she went on, "the condition of the body brought back memories of stories told to me by my mother when I was a child. Stories I'd long ago relegated to fanciful myths and folktales, long forgotten. So I decided to research the Yuki-Onna further. I found many stories, many of them also in direct conflict with one another—I assume having been passed down from generation to generation stories get changed, embellished—but in the majority of the tellings, the Yuki-Onna appears, often for three nights, always during a snowstorm, and always to kill."

"For what purpose?" Plor asked.

Saito shook her head. "It is hard to say. Some say she kills simply for the pleasure of watching her victims die; other legends depict her as a succubus, a being that needs to survive by draining others of blood or their 'life forces.'"

"Sounds like a vampire to me," Regan said. "And that's just ridiculous."

"A vampire, yes, but certain aspects of the legends do strike eerily close to home."

"Such as?" Regan challenged.

"I believe what killed these two men was lyophilization."

"What is that?"

"Lyophilization is the process of freezing a material, then keeping it under pressure. The frozen water sublimates, turning it into a gaseous state, removing it—"

"Wait a second. Are you saying these men were...freeze-dried?"

"In a manner of speaking, yes. The human body is made up mostly of water, seventy percent. The rest is proteins, fats, carbohydrates, DNA, inorganic ions, and other free radicals. In both men, I found evidence of frostbite, around the lips mostly but also on the internal organs. Everything organic about these men, down to a cellular, molecular level, was ripped away, stolen from the inside out, by an impossible, inhuman means."

Plor stepped forward. "And what can do this to a man, Doctor?"

Saito shook her head. "Nothing natural. Nothing I've ever heard of...except a Yuki-Onna."

# CHAPTER 18

REGAN PUSHED THROUGH the revolving glass doors, exiting the building housing the headquarters of the Office of the Chief Medical Examiner and stood on Albany Street blinking in the harsh sunlight. Plor came up alongside him. Regan fished a pair of sunglasses out of his coat pocket, put them on, then took his notebook from another pocket, flipped it open to a clean page, and started to draw.

"You're upset?" Plor said.

"What did you make of all that?" he asked, drawing furiously, pausing only to lift his pen and wave it around. "All that talk about a Yoko-Ono thing?"

"I believe she called the creature a Yuki-Onna."

"Whatever." Without looking up he went back to drawing. "A succubus. Could she be a succubus?"

"I am unfamiliar with the word, so I cannot say. What are you drawing? Why is it occupying all your attention?"

"Something I saw. I want to get it down before I forget it."

When he finished, he turned the book around and showed her what he'd drawn. Though rather crude, he thought it was a fair representation of the kanji he'd seen on Saito's shoulder.

"Do these symbols mean anything to you?"

Plor shook her head. "They do not. What are it?"

"That, Ms. Na mBan," Regan said with some satisfaction, "is what we call in my business a clue."

Before Regan could explain further, they were interrupted by an unwelcome voice. "Well, what a surprise finding you here at the ME's office the day after another strange body turns up. What's the matter, Regan, couldn't sleep again?"

Regan turned away from Plor to see Mike Hall standing behind them, his hands in the pockets of his trench coat, his hat low over his eyes, a fat cigar stuck in the corner of his mouth. Smoke curled up into his face, making him squint so he could see through the blue haze encircling his head.

Regan shrugged. "We came in for a late breakfast this morning."

Hall's eyebrows lifted. "At the morgue?"

"What? Of course not. There's a breakfast place." He looked first one way down Albany Street then the other. "Down here."

"Name? Name of what?"

"The place you ate at, you know, for breakfast."

"Oh. Yeah, right. It's café something."

"Laz Café or Andre's?"

*Crap,* Regan thought. Of course Mike would know every single place in the city to eat. All cops do. "No. It's neither one of those."

"So you've got to mean Grille 705. It's the only other place that serves breakfast around here."

Excited, Regan snapped his fingers. "That's it. Great place."

Still dubious, Hall said, "That's all the way over on Massachusetts Avenue, Regan. What are you up to?"

"Nothing. Food. Then we went for a walk afterward. Nothing like a good, hearty stroll to work off a heavy breakfast." He patted his stomach.

Hall frowned and returned his cigar to his mouth. He puffed. "What are you really doing here?" He nodded toward Plor. "And who's this?"

"I am Plor na mBan. It means the flower of women." She stuck her hand out to shake.

"I'm sure it does." Hall took her hand. They shook. Suddenly Hall's expression darkened. His forehead furrowed under his hat and he looked down at his hand. Plor was squeezing it. He tried to pull it away.

"I sense you do not believe what Officer Regan is telling you."

"Plor," Regan cautioned.

Hall tried harder to disengage his hand. "I didn't say I didn't believe him. I just thought it was a…bit of a…coincidence."

"Plor," Regan said more forcefully.

Plor released Hall's hand. He stepped quickly back, rubbing his hand, one in the other. "That's, um, some grip your girlfriend's got, Regan."

Regan moved closer to her, putting his arm around her

waist. "Yes, well, it's sure great to run into you, Mike." Gently, he pulled Plor away. "We've gotta run though." He patted his stomach. "We're starving. It's good to see you. Good luck with, you know, the case."

"Regan, don't think you can worm your way into this case. Use it to somehow earn back your gold shield."

With a hand at the small of her back, Regan pushed Plor forward, moving them quickly down the street toward Massachusetts Avenue and away from any more scrutiny from Detective Mike Hall.

"Furthest thing from my mind, Mike," Regan said as they kept walking.

"It's not gonna happen, Regan!" Hall shouted to him.

"That man. Who is he?" Plor demanded to know.

"A friend." Regan continued to propel her along the sidewalk. "Now keep moving before he tries to ask us any more questions."

"He did not sound like a friend. I do not like him," she declared.

At the street corner, Regan guided her to hang a left. He glanced back to see Hall still glaring at them. "It's complicated."

"Explain it."

"It's...I did something I thought was right. It turned out others didn't agree. Mike Hall was one of those other people. So no, he's not very fond of me lately."

Regan walked Plor back to his car. He opened her door, she slid in, and he climbed into the driver's seat.

"What did you do?" she asked.

Regan sighed, not really in the mood to discuss it. He turned to tell Plor that, but she stared at him with such intensity, he doubted she'd let it go. "Fine. I used to be a detective, like Mike Hall."

"Are you not both protectors?"

"We are. But our jobs are different. I wear a uniform and work patrol. I try to make sure bad things don't happen before they do, if that makes sense. Hall, he's a detective. His job's to investigate crimes after they happen, try to figure out who did them and bring them to justice."

"Why can't you do both?"

"It's…that's just the way things work here. Anyway, a couple of years ago, when I was a detective, I began investigating a case where drugs and money were being stolen from dealers and junkies. Turns out the drugs were being resold out on the street by cops, bad cops. One of those bad cops was a friend of mine since we were kids, a guy named Dale Brandigan."

"This investigation you conducted, it revealed this?"

"It did."

"So these bad protectors were doing bad things and they were caught. You stopped them."

"Yes." Regan stared out through the car windshield. To hear Plor say it, it sounded so simple. So straightforward.

"What is the problem with that?" she asked.

And so naive. "They were cops, Plor. My coworkers. My friends."

"But they were doing wrong. I do not understand."

Regan thought about that for a minute. Then he twisted the key in the ignition and fired the Camaro up. "Sometimes neither do I, Plor."

A half hour later they arrived at the Museum of Antiquities and Early History. He pulled into a curbside spot, put the car in park, and shut off the engine. Plor squinted through the bright sunlight at the tinted glass front of the building. Pedestrians walked by, but no one paid them any attention.

When Regan made no move to get out of the car, Plor asked,

"Are we not going inside?"

"Not yet." Regan pulled out his cell phone and clicked on the Internet app. Then he pulled out his notebook and laid it faceup on the console between them so he could see the page he'd drawn the kanji on.

"I believe we should go inside," Plor insisted. "To secure *Lia Fáil* as we discussed."

"In a minute." Regan continued to scroll through the Google results on his screen. "This is bothering me. I need to check it out."

He left it at that, clicking through electronic page after page on a kanji translation site he'd found. He learned there were over fifty thousand kanji in existence, but only about two thousand were in common use. Though it took him over an hour and bleary eyes from squinting into the tiny cell phone screen, Regan found the middle character he'd written down first, and what it represented sent a shiver down his spine. According to the site—he checked two more to make sure he wasn't wrong—the first symbol was for blood. The next one he found meant ghost or devil, and finally the third translated into suck, inhale, sip.

But it wasn't until he put the three kanji together, in the proper order, and ran it through an English-Japanese translator that his blood ran cold. When used together literally meant blood-suck-demon, and most commonly translated into bloodsucker or vampire!

"Oh, no. Hell, no." Regan tossed the phone onto the seat, as if by throwing it away he could deny what it told him. "That can't be right. Christ, no."

With concern, Plor said, "What is it? What's wrong?"

Regan pointed at the phone, but he had trouble forming the words. Finally, after three tries he said, "Those symbols I showed you earlier. The ones I told you were tattooed on Saito Izumi's shoulder. I saw them when she was in the bathroom." Suddenly a thought struck him.

"Crap! The mirror. There was no mirror."

Plor's expression was a cross between worry and confusion. "What are you trying to say?"

"The tattoo. It means vampire. Saito Izumi is a vampire."

"Vampire? That word holds no meaning to me," Plor said.

Regan quickly filled Plor in on the conventional explanation of what a vampire was. When he was done, she said, "They sound like vile creatures."

"There's an understatement if I ever heard one."

"You believe this Saito Izumi to be one of these undead?"

"It fits. You saw her eye. She had one hell of a shiner last night, and now it's completely healed inside of what, twelve to fifteen hours? She had no mirror in the bathroom. Who doesn't have a mirror?"

"Her handshake was exceptionally strong for a mortal human," Plor said, concurring with Regan's assessment. "And cold. Her hands were cold."

"Sure, besides, what other reason would she have for having the kanji meaning vampire tattooed onto her shoulder?"

Plor stared out at the museum. "An excellent question. Do you suspect her to be this snow woman? If so, how does she connect to Ciag?"

"First things first." Regan picked up the cell phone and began to scroll through its Internet pages again. Reading, he said, "According to this, a succubus is different from a vampire. Vampires kill their victims by biting them, usually in the neck, using their fangs to pierce a vein, often the jugular, and draining them of blood. Life-sustaining blood."

"These victims were drained of more than blood."

"That's right," Regan agreed. "Fitting the description of a succubus: 'one who drains the life essence, the soul, of its victims either through a kiss or sexual intercourse.' Also, Saito told us the area around both victims' mouths and their throats showed evidence of frostbite. Indicative of a kiss."

"A kiss of death. But why would she reveal this information to us? It seems to serve only to trap herself."

"Or she's trying to throw us off the track. Slow the investigation. She must know we could never bring this information to Detective Hall or the police brass."

"Why not?"

"Because they'll think we're nuts. They'll throw us in the loony bin."

"That does not sound like a pleasant place to be." Plor remained silent for several minutes. "All of this is meaningless. It brings me no closer to Ciag than before."

"Not so fast, doubter-of-mine." Again Regan clicked on a few links on the phone and handed it over to Plor. "An article in the *Boston Globe*."

Plor read the story from the screen. It was a follow-up article to the burglary story. "Due in part to a recent vandalism incident, the famed Museum of Antiquities and Early History in Boston's South End has announced plans to move an exhibit of ancient Celtic artifacts on loan from the Natural Museum of Ireland in Dublin, part of their Irish archaeological collection, including historically significant items such as the Four Treasures of the Tuatha Dé Danann."

She looked up from the glowing screen. "Move it where?"

"I don't know, but I think we need to find out."

"Agreed."

# CHAPTER 19

MIDNIGHT. HALLOWEEN. The witching hour.

Sean Regan got called into work early. All Hallows' Eve tended to be an active night for police, and this Halloween would turn out to be no different. A bright, clear, crisp night and all manner of ghosts, ghouls and goblins swarmed the city streets. Their tiny hands clutched pillowcases and paper bags weighted down with assorted candies and gum and other treats; most of them were tripping over their too-large costumes.

Regan reported for roll call at 6:00 p.m. and had seven arrests under his belt (mostly incidents involving vandalism, public intoxication, and one street brawl that took three other cops to break up) before things began to slow down as the clock ticked closer to midnight.

To his relief, Regan encountered no ghouls more dangerous than a PCP-tripping addict with a knife and a painted scar down his left cheek. When he lunged at Regan, he stumbled, fell, and hit his face on a curb, breaking a front tooth. Regan landed on top of him and had his hands pulled behind his back and cuffed before the guy knew what hit him.

Still, through it all he couldn't shake an ominous feeling that haunted him. He worried the Yuki-Onna would return and that he would not be close by to help, that someone else would die.

And then there was Plor. She'd refused to leave St. Elias Church except to change into her "work clothes" as Regan called them and to get Enbarr. Twice through the night he'd called her on the cell phone he'd given her, and both times she assured him she was in hiding along the dark, tree-lined streets where he'd told her to remain atop Enbarr, watching the church they were told now housed the Four Treasures of the Tuatha Dé Danann collection.

From his car that afternoon Regan put in a call to Dr. Abigail Buckley and asked that she meet with him in the plaza in front of the museum. Better they meet outside than risk another encounter with Security Director Dixon. Regan didn't believe that could end without one or both of them landing in jail. At Buckley's hesitation, Regan assured her he had vital information concerning the security of some of her Celtic artifacts. Reluctantly, she agreed to meet him.

When they met, Regan asked Buckley, "I read a news article that said the exhibit has been moved. Is that correct?"

Buckley nodded. "It is a traveling exhibit after all. The items will be on display at various locations throughout the city before moving on to other locations: New York, Chicago, Philadelphia, Dallas, and finally Los Angeles. It will be returned to Ireland at the end of the year."

"Where is the exhibit now?" Regan feared she'd say New York or someplace equally inconvenient.

"The bulk of the exhibit remains here as we continue to assess the damage done." She glanced at Plor. "You're not really with the insurance company, are you?"

Regan tried to refocus the doctor's attention to the matter at hand. "What parts aren't still here at the museum?"

"None of the damaged pieces have been moved. There's no point in

166

that." Her tone was full of regret. "The Four Treasures have moved on."

"Where are they?" Plor demanded.

"They've been sent to St. Elias Church on Boylston Street in the Back Bay, all part of the original schedule. As I understand it, they requested the pieces as part of the one-hundred-and-fiftieth anniversary celebration the church is holding on All Saints Day, tomorrow, the day after Halloween."

November 1. The Samhain. The Gaelic holiday that marked the end of harvest season and the beginning of winter. What they called the dark half of the year. *Terrific.*

When they were finished speaking with Dr. Buckley, he and Plor drove over to St. Elias Church, a large stone building set on three acres of property surrounded by a stone wall topped with wrought-iron fencing. They found the parking lot empty, except for two large white party tents. Regan assumed they had been put in place as part of the prep for the next day's activities.

Next they climbed the massive front steps and entered the church proper through a set of two-story tall wooden doors. They passed through the narthex with its statutes of the Mother Mary and other significant figures from Catholic history whose identities Regan could not dredge up from his years of religious instruction as a boy. He did dip his fingers in the holy water and cross himself. Some things were so ingrained you never forgot.

They found the nave devoid of people, only row after row of hard, dark-wood pews, the smell of candles burning, flickering to the right of the altar, and colorful, diffused light shining down from the exquisite, stained-glass windows. Regan quickly checked all the doors within the chancel, then out in the hallway outside the nave. He found them all secured.

"Let's check the rectory out back." His intention was to find a caretaker or church official, but before Regan could complete that task, his cell phone rang, the call to report into work early.

Regan tried to wiggle his way out of it, but Patrol Captain Nichols was having no part of it. Report in immediately or face disciplinary charges.

There was little more they could do here anyway, he told Plor.

She set her fists on her hips and defiantly refused to leave. Regan sighed; she reminded him of Deidre. What was it with him and stubborn Irish women?

"If Ciag wished to take possession of *Lia Fáil,* he would do so this night," she told him.

"Why's that?" asked Regan.

"'Tis the last night of Samhain. The veil between these Otherworlds is weakest during the high holy times, especially Samhain and Beltane, the Gaelic May Day. After tonight, his ability to travel back will be made more difficult."

After much consternation, Regan got her to agree to simply keep an eye on the church for trouble and to take no action should the little lawn gnome appear except to call him. Regan then left to begin his regular patrol shift.

Parked at the curb under an overhanging elm on Gold Street, in a residential neighborhood of Southie, Regan had the window rolled down. Though he was a little chilly with only his uniform bomber jacket for warmth, he left the window down and the engine off so he could listen as he kept watch, scanning the dark street ahead of him and then behind him using the side and rearview mirrors.

"Lot of good that'll do me," he groused under his breath. "Looking for a vampire."

At least it wasn't snowing, which Regan took as a good indicator their serial succubus hadn't made an appearance yet. All over town the meteorologists were still grumbling about that, the unusual weather, not the succubus. Regan could only wonder what the news—and the public—would make of that, if they knew the truth.

Succubi, vampires. He shook his head. He was truly losing his mind. And let's not forget the people of the Tuatha Dé Danann, Ciag the fear darrig, and Plor na mBan and her miracle horse Enbarr. *Yep. My brain's definitely fried.*

A rustle of leaves caught Regan's attention. Behind him. He glanced at the side-view mirror. A gust of wind swooshed a colorful cornucopia of red, yellow, and golden leaves across the street. In the reflective glass he saw nothing but leaves and a few bits of paper, candy wrappers, and the like.

*Of course you wouldn't see anything, you idiot. Vampire reflections can't be seen in mirrors.*

Gingerly, Regan pulled the door handle, opening the door as quietly as he could. He kept his hand on the butt of his gun and searched his memory for everything he knew about vampire lore as he moved toward the rear of the patrol car. Same as everybody he guessed: they only come out at night, they hate garlic and crosses and can't be killed by bullets, except silver bullets—no, that's werewolves—wooden bullets, and stakes. And in real life they don't sparkle.

*In real life. Listen to me.*

In the next instant, several things happened almost at once.

Regan heard the fast, now familiar clop-clop-clop of hoofs across pavement. He whirled, instinctively drawing his service weapon, and saw Plor riding Enbarr. They bore down on him from the intersecting street—F Street—her cape billowing behind her, her mane of auburn hair, too. And her sword raised high, as if to strike.

Regan shouted, "Plor! What the hell are you doing?"

"Duck, Sean Regan! Duck!"

Regan dropped to one knee and crouched low behind the trunk

of his cruiser. As he did, he glanced overhead.

Plor swung *Claiomh Solais*. The blade swished over Regan's head, aglow from the reflective bluish moonlight, cleaving the air behind him. He spun in time to see a shadowy figure, what looked like a black cape, and a frenzy of movement too fast for Regan to tell what it was, but the gasp it let out told him Plor had struck her target.

Enbarr came to a stop. He thumped his front hoofs on the sidewalk before rearing up and thrashing his forelegs, snorting and whinnying with anger and excitement. Plor held the reins tightly in one hand, staying in the saddle, just barely it seemed, as she took another swipe with *Claiomh Solais* at the…whatever it was.

Regan saw only black swirling shadows and the vaguest of shapes because of the speed with which the thing moved. He rose up, bringing his weapon up, supporting his gun hand with his right hand, trying to track the thing. And failing. It was that damn fast. "Don't move!"

From atop Enbarr, Plor commanded, "Stay back, Sean Regan!"

His effort to intervene distracted Plor, and her adversary took full advantage of it. It leaped.

Regan shouted, "Plor! Look out!"

An expert shot, Regan fired twice. Both shots missed. The thing was too fast.

It crashed into Plor, getting under her swinging broadsword. When it did, Regan could at last see it was definitely human in shape. Two legs wearing black pants. It wore black boots, and what he thought was a long black cape turned out to be a black leather coat and flailing, long black hair.

Enbarr snorted angrily from the impact, which shoved both horse and rider to the right. The beast struggled to keep his legs under him. Plor had no such luck. With arms flung high, she was thrown from the back of the animal. Her attacker had succeeded in tackling her to the ground. They hit the ground hard and rolled, like two kids fighting in the schoolyard.

Regan scooted around the back end of the horse, protecting his face with one arm from Enbarr's wildly thrashing tail. Having cleared the animal's hind end without getting kicked in the head, Regan leveled his weapon and came around in time to see Plor kick her assailant off and into the air.

Black-shrouded arms and legs and hair and long coat flapped. The shadowy figure pinwheeled before it landed, almost catlike on all fours. It crouched low, its long hair hanging in stringy ropes over a paste-white face.

When the thing looked up, Regan gasped.

It *was* Saito Izumi, but her features were altered: inhuman, misshapen, her skin deathly gray. Her eyes glowed a bright, hellish red and her mouth was open in a wide, snarling hiss, her blood-red lips gleaming around white, glistening fangs.

It was true. She was a vampire!

She stared Regan for a beat, then sprang nearly straight into the air.

Plor raced forward, slower than the escaping vampire, but fast enough to grab Saito by the ankle and arrest her leap. "You shall not escape this night, evil spawn." Plor pulled Saito out of the air, slamming her back to the sidewalk, a blow that would've surely broken the back of anything mortal—or alive.

Saito gasped sharply. She hissed and rolled away.

Plor moved in closer and stood over Saito, her hands fisted.

Saito clawed her hands, hissed again. It was a god-awful sound, Regan thought. Regan saw her nails for what they were for the first time. They were not human nails, but long, black talons.

"Be careful," Regan cautioned as Plor reached down to fist

Saito's leather coat, to pull her up off the ground.

But Saito struck. She swiped her arm, raking Plor across the face, not unlike what the conjured vulture had done two nights earlier. Plor fell back, staggering from the blow.

Taking advantage of Plor's unstable stance, Saito kicked out, executing a martial-arts-style attack. Her booted foot struck Plor squarely in the gut. Plor exhaled with a forceful woof as her body sailed backward to slam into Enbarr's flank.

The horse leaped away and Plor landed on her butt.

Left in an awkward position, Saito twisted, trying to roll off her back and get up onto her hands and knees. She either had forgotten about Regan or considered him such a low threat she ignored him.

But that was her mistake. An arm's length away, he pressed his Glock firmly against the back of her head. "I don't know if a bullet to the brain can kill you or not, but I'm guessing it might slow you down and probably hurt like hell."

Saito froze, then hung her head, an act of submission. "I do not wish to fight you. Either of you."

"Why'd you attack us?" Regan asked, taking a second as Plor climbed back onto her feet to walk over to join them. He was relieved to see she appeared relatively unharmed.

"I did not attack," Saito said, staring ember-red daggers at Plor. "It was she who attacked me. I came here to talk to you. To explain."

"Are you the Yuki-Onna?" Even as Regan asked the question he knew in his gut she was not. There was no snow. Her coat was not white.

"No, I am not. But I have seen it, fought it. Last night on the rooftop near Fenway Park."

Regan was stunned. While he hung over the side of the building, hanging onto Plor for dear life, the black shroud that attacked, that had saved him... "That was you?"

"Yes. Now may I get up, please?"

Regan glanced quickly over at Plor. She nodded, holding her sword at the ready. "Okay," he said, "but no sudden moves. I mean it."

Regan took a cautious step back, keeping his gun trained on Saito as she climbed to her feet.

Her almond-shaped eyes continued to glow with red animal shine, and her fangs remained visible, indenting her shiny, lower lip like a macabre overbite.

Regan took a moment, trying to come to grips with what she was, what he was dealing with. "Now you have a lot of explaining to do. Start spilling."

"No!" Plor snapped. "There is no time."

Startled, Regan asked, "What are you talking about?"

"The reason I returned here," she said. "At the church. There is activity. I fear Ciag has arrived to complete his task."

"Maybe it is you two who need to explain," Saito said.

Plor ignored her. "We must go. Now!" She leaped onto Enbarr's back and turned the giant steed with a tug of the reins. "Follow me. Ciag might already have *Lia Fáil* and made off with it."

Before Regan could stop her, Plor spurred Enbarr about and they galloped off.

Saito watched the woman and horse gallop away. "What was that all about?"

"I'll fill you in on the way."

Saito looked quizzically at Regan. "You wish me to join you?"

"Do you want to kill me?"

"No. Of course not."

"Then get in. I want to know everything I can about this Yuki-

Onna we're chasing, and you seem to know a lot about it."

Regan pulled his patrol car door open and slipped inside the driver's seat. "Besides"—he thought back to their last encounter with the creature—"we might need your help in defeating the damn thing."

"Fair enough." Saito went around to the passenger side and climbed in.

Regan didn't activate the lights and sirens. The last thing he needed was unwanted attention.

When they were on their way, Saito said, "Where should I begin? Do you wish to know more about the Yuki-Onna that I have not already shared with you, or do you prefer to know about me?"

Regan kept both hands on the wheel, flooring the gas to keep up with Enbarr. "Why don't we start with you."

"My story? It begins in the seventeenth century."

Regan shot her a look. "Wait a minute. You're telling me you're four hundred years old?"

She gave him a sly smile. "Not yet. In about twenty more years. If you wish, I can bore you with the details when we have more time but for now simply accept I was born in feudal Japan, a samurai warrior from the Higo Province, which is where I died at the age of twenty-seven years. And where I was turned by another like I am now."

"My God."

Saito shook her head sadly. "I do not believe God had anything to do with it."

"It is true then. You drink blood to live. You feed on people."

"Humans. Animals. Yes. But I do not anymore."

Skeptical, Regan asked, "How do you survive then?"

"I take what I need from the dead that pass through the morgue." The revulsion showed on Regan's face; he couldn't help himself. Saito's own expression grew dark and angry. "Yes, it's disgusting, but better that than killing and mutilating innocent victims, do you not agree?"

"I..." Regan didn't know what to say.

Still angry, Saito said, "I've stalked and hunted and preyed on innocent victims during my existence, for more years than you have lived. I am not proud of that. The cravings cannot be ignored, cannot be denied. Like a drug addict or an alcoholic's need, only a million times worse. Overwhelming. Decades ago, centuries past, I had no choice. Nor did I know any better. Since then, I've learned to...adapt."

"What the hell does that mean?"

Saito made an attempt to harbor her anger but failed. "They do not give you a vampire handbook when you're turned. You are alive one minute, undead the next. You are all alone. There is no one to show you the ropes. At first, yes, I hunted. I slaughtered. I killed. It was the only way to survive."

"But," Regan interjected, "you found another way?"

"The killing disgusts me. But in time, I learned I did not need to hunt, to kill to live. I just needed blood. Now I go where dead people already are: hospitals, funeral homes, morgues. Wars are good for me," she added with a bitter grin. "I've been a doctor several times, a nurse more than a few times, a mortician twice, I think, and now a medical examiner. I take jobs that give me unquestioned access to freshly dead corpses."

"In the bathroom, when I saw you..."

"I guess you don't watch *The Vampire Diaries*, do you?" Saito looked away, ashamed. "Blood bag. Dinner. Unlike the Hollywood version of vampires, being turned doesn't make you suddenly evil; it doesn't radically alter who you are. You are the same person. You have the same personality you had before. But the cravings, the need, and what you must do to survive, what one must live with knowing, what they've done. It is that which changes you, corrupts you, what makes vampires become the things people so rightly fear."

"What? There's…more? How many?"

"Did you think I was the only one?"

Regan shrugged. "Hoping. How do you, they, stay hidden? That many vampires…they can't all be doctors. Wouldn't there be an epidemic of blood-drained bodies found?"

"Have you any idea how many people go missing in the United States each year?" She didn't wait for him to answer. "Annually, fifty thousand. In this country alone. A vampire learns to be very good at disposing bodies where they'll never be found. Vampires are not responsible for all of them of course."

*No, meaning there are other…things out there. Worse things.* Regan shivered. As he tried to cope with it all, he changed the subject. "Tell me about this Yuki-Onna. What exactly are we up against?"

"Are you sure you're prepared to know?"

Regan waved at Plor up ahead and then at Saito. "Seriously, how much worse can it be than you two?"

"You make a fair point," Saito conceded. "I have never encountered a Yuki-Onna before the other night. The Yuki-Onna is driven by only one thing, a thing I'm familiar with, her need to feed."

"Like a vampire. No offense," Regan quickly amended.

"Yes, like the vampire and blood, the succubus feeds on the soul of its victims to rejuvenate, to revitalize, to survive. According to legend they appear annually, for three nights to feed, then return to…wherever they're from, their youthfulness restored for the next year."

"So after tonight, it'll go away?"

"After it feeds one last time, yes."

"After one more death." Regan didn't accept that as good news. They turned onto Boylston Street having not aroused any suspicion along the way.

"Tell me about her," Saito said, referring to Plor.

"She tells me her name is Plor na mBan. Her mother was someone called Niamh and she's from a place called *Tir na nÓg*. It's some Otherworld that used to be Ireland, no, wait, she said it's under Ireland. Does any of that mean anything to you?"

"Strangely, it does."

"You're kidding."

"You are Irish, are you not, Officer Regan?"

"I am. Through and through."

"Then you've heard tales of how Ireland came to be. Of the people and gods who occupied that land. No?"

"If you mean the old Celtic legends and mythology, sure, from stories my mom and grandma told me when I was a kid. I haven't heard them in years."

"Officer Regan, Niamh is the queen of *Tir na nÓg*. The land of the forever young."

"Yeah, Plor mentioned something like that."

A bit incredulous of Regan's naïveté, Saito said, "What you were told as a boy, what Plor is telling you, they are not merely stories. They're myths, yes. Legends, sure. But they are—or were—real. Niamh is the daughter of the Manannán mac Lir, the Celtic god of the sea. That makes Niamh—"

"A goddess," Regan finished, his mouth falling open. Could this night get any stranger? "Making Plor a goddess, too."

"Well, a demi-goddess, actually," Saito corrected. "Her father was human. A poet by the name of Oisín."

Regan stared at her, open-mouthed. "You're putting me on. How do you know all this?"

"As a vampire I make it my business to be well versed with the things that go bump in the night. Mythical things. Supernatural things. It is best to be familiar with that which you might encounter." She smiled in an attempt to ease Regan's discomfort. Not an easy task with a mouthful of fangs and glowing, blood-red eyes. "I have been around awhile, and I cannot go out during daylight hours. That gives me a lot of time to read."

Regan shook his head, putting into words what he couldn't believe. "I've been running around town with an honest-to-goodness demi-god."

"Goddess, but yes, it would appear so."

# CHAPTER 20

REGAN PULLED THE cruiser to the curb in front of St. Elias Church. He put the vehicle into park and shut off the engine. Saito Izumi sat in the seat beside him. They hadn't spoken since she revealed to him Plor na mBan was a goddess. He had a thousand questions for her, about that, about her, and was afraid to ask any of them. *I'm riding around the streets of Boston with a vampire in my car, looking for a Celtic warrior goddess on horseback, all so we can stop something called a* fear darrig.

How insane was that?

Saito leaned forward to glance out the windshield up at the stone front of the one-hundred-and-fifty-year-old cathedral with a foreboding expression on her face. A face that was more or less back to normal, meaning no more red eyes, ghostly gray skin, or fangs.

In fact, he marveled at what a lovely face it was. At how such beauty could mask such…at first he was going to say evil, but that wasn't it. That wasn't her. He believed her when she said she was what she had always been. Not evil, just a person. A person who'd managed to not lose her humanity because of what she'd become, the things she'd been forced to do to feed her…addiction. He marveled at the strength that must have taken.

"Don't tell me. You need to be invited in to cross the threshold. That goes for churches, too?"

She shook her head. "Hollywood hype, I'm afraid." Still she looked uneasy. "But places of worship do give me the heebie-jeebies."

"A vampire with the heebie-jeebies." Regan grinned in spite of himself. "Shouldn't it be the other way around?"

"Let's just say, God and I are not exactly on speaking terms. I don't see Plor."

"She's here. Ciag came to this world to steal something called the Stone of Destiny, an ancient Celtic artifact that's supposed to have some magical juju that can bestow mystical power on whoever has it. Whomsoever possesses this stone can proclaim themselves to be the ruler of…whatever."

"Surely the fear darrig does not believe he can rule *Tir na nÓg*?"

"No, he's just the errand boy, sent here by some guy named Tethra."

"King Tethra. The ruler of Magh Meall."

"Yeah, Plor said something about that. You sure know a lot about Celtic mythology."

Saito climbed out of the cruiser. "Come on. We better find her."

Regan joined her near the front of the car. The headlights shone into the night, illuminating the sidewalk and the leaf-clogged storm drain in harsh, glaring light. "I don't know what it is she thought she saw. You check around that way." He pointed down the street. "Make your way around the perimeter of the church. I'll see if she's gone inside."

Saito set off, heading north. Regan gave the church a second look. The place was downright eerie at night, shrouded by trees and surrounded by a stone wall topped with wrought-iron fencing, each picket crowned in a carefully sculpted spiked tip. Thick, high hedges grew behind the fence, which made seeing into the churchyard impossible.

The gothic-style church, constructed of gray stone, consisted of two towers capped with soaring spires and a three-story portico with pointed arch entry doors and windows on either side made of cut stained glass and a round rose window. All of it was dark, gloomy, and cold. Trees stood like gigantic sentries on either side of the gated fence, still full of broad leaves rustling in the icy wind.

Regan curled the collar of his bomber jacket up around his neck and pulled the heavy three-cell Maglite from his belt loop, clicking it on. The halogen bulb flooded the granite steps and sidewalk leading up to the front of the church with bright white light. The massive front doors appeared closed and undisturbed.

What had he expected, for them to be blown off their hinges?

With a wry shake of his head, he reminded himself to not expect, or be surprised, by anything after what he'd experienced over the last three days. "Vampires and a demi-goddess," he muttered under his breath. "What's next?"

"Excuse me! Officer?"

Regan whirled at the voice behind him. The flashlight beam landed on a slight woman wearing a long white trench coat made of leather, her head bowed, causing her hair to obscure her face. She shied away from the light.

"Oh, sorry." Regan aimed the flashlight down and away. "I did not mean to startle you."

Aware of his racing heartbeat, Regan cataloged the woman's appearance. Long white coat. Long, straight, corn-silk-like black hair. Afraid to jump to conclusions or be accused of profiling, he said, "What can I do for you, ma'am?"

"I'm afraid I am lost." She withdrew her hands from the leather coat pockets. Clutched in her long, delicate fingers, a piece of paper snapped in the stirring breeze.

Regan stepped closer. He shone the light on the tear of notebook paper she held even as his instincts shouted at him to be careful. In the flashlight beam, Regan noticed the first snowflakes falling. Tiny white crystals, like dandruff. Amounting to nothing, he thought, except in this case, death. He snapped his head up.

The diminutive woman stared at him with a cruel smile on her face. Her eyes flared blue-white and icy cold.

Regan took a step away, reaching for his gun.

The woman's hand shot out so fast it was only a blur before it seized Regan by the throat and lifted him off the ground.

He grabbed her wrist with one hand but had zero chance of breaking her grip and he knew it.

She squeezed.

He gasped, unable to breathe as his feet dangled inches off the ground. In his mind, he saw the dehydrated, sucked-dry remains of Kurt Kegler and Brad Dumas, his imagination flashing a vivid image of his own similar demise.

Anger more than fear surged through him. Determined not to end up like that, Regan abandoned his futile attempt to break the creature's grip. He let go of her wrist, near the point of blacking out from the pressure her long, thin fingers exerted around his throat. Still he managed to stay conscious long enough to pull his gun. He cleared leather and pointed, pulling the trigger three times.

The air exploded with the crack of gunfire.

The creature's body jerked and she shrieked, releasing her grip on him.

Regan fell to the ground like a dropped sack of potatoes.

The Yuki-Onna vanished in a sudden swirl of snow and wind.

Coughing, Regan massaged his throat, trying to fill his lungs with air, taking slow, painful breaths. What seemed like minutes ticked by before his vision cleared and he could breathe without coughing.

A shiny black Lexus pulled to the curb. The side window was open. A woman sat behind the wheel. "Sean, is that you? Sean!"

Deidre jumped out of the car. She ran over to him, her heels hitting the pavement and sounding like rifle shots. She dropped to one knee and wrapped her arm around his shoulder, squeezing his upper arm with her other hand. "Are you all right?"

With her help, Regan climbed unsteadily to his feet. "I think so, yeah."

"What happened? Did you slip on ice or something?"

"You didn't see..." Fuzzy brained, Regan asked, "What are you doing here, Dee?"

"See what? Who? I heard what sounded like gunshots—" She saw the gun in his hand. "Who were you shooting at?"

"No one. It doesn't matter. What are you doing here?"

"I followed you."

Regan's head throbbed. "You what?"

"I've been following you ever since you and that woman left the morgue."

"Ever since..." Regan struggled to comprehend.

"And I've seen an eyeful, Sean, let me tell you. A real eyeful."

"Like what?"

"Like that woman, your girlfriend Plor, galloping around the city on a horse. For God's sake, Sean, tell me what's going on. And that other woman, the Asian one, what's her story? I saw the two of them fighting."

Regan rubbed at his forehead, which was slick with sweat despite the cold and snow. Oh Christ. It was snowing heavily now. "You're mistaken, Dee. Horses. Girls fighting. Really? I think you need to go home and get some sleep."

"I am not mistaken, Sean Regan. You were there. I saw you break up that fight."

"I'm not getting into this with you right now. There was no fight, no woman on horseback. In downtown Boston, Dee? That's insane. And Plor is not my girlfriend."

A sudden commotion erupted behind them, from the churchyard.

In unison, Regan and Deidre spun around. The hedges surrounding the churchyard rustled with an abrupt, violent flourish. A blur of wind-whipped white streaked toward them. Regan instinctively wrapped an arm around Deidre's shoulders and pulled her down to the sidewalk. Wildly waving black hair and the white hem of a leather trench coat spewed from the eye of a sudden snowstorm.

The Yuki-Onna was back, riding a vortex of wind and swirling snow.

A second later the night air filled with the angry snort of a charging horse. In pursuit, Enbarr leaped easily over the six-foot-tall hedges and fence, Plor on his back, swinging *Claiomh Solais* like a polo mallet at the Yuki-Onna.

The snow demon ducked and tumbled to the ground, the wind cut out from under her.

Deidre stared daggers at Regan. "Insane, huh?"

Enbarr landed cleanly and circled a safe distance around the snow witch, who had landed on the sidewalk on her hands and knees.

Plor steered the animal back toward her adversary and aimed the tip of her sword at the creature. "Rise, vile creature. Face your destiny."

Deidre started to say something, but Regan shushed her. As his mind cleared, he wondered what had become of Saito Izumi. "Plor?"

Too late, the Yuki-Onna began to rise, a grimace of fury on her face, creating a mini tornado of snow and wind and leaves and grit around her. The gathering storm pushed Regan and Deidre back. He pulled Dee from the vortex's grip, putting himself between her and the wind, squinting and shielding his face with his forearm.

Enbarr snorted, more angry than nervous it seemed, as he backed away, his tail flicking. Branches and leaves and debris were caught up in the cascading, swirling wind. The force of the wind grew stronger as the creature began to rise off the ground.

"She's getting away!" Regan called out. His pants cuffs snapped at his legs like hurricane flags.

"Sean!" Dee shouted. "What's happening?"

"Stay back," he yelled, feeling Dee try to come out from behind him. "Plor!"

Through the swirling grit-filled cyclone, Regan could no longer see Plor or Enbarr. He drew his weapon, tracking the center of the storm, but he couldn't shoot for fear of missing and hitting Plor or the animal she rode. For all he knew, the Yuki-Onna was impervious to bullets anyway. She'd certainly recovered from his three point-blank shots just moments earlier, with little adverse effect.

As the funnel grew wider and larger, and though he couldn't see her, he knew the Yuki-Onna was riding the storm up, escaping, and he was powerless to stop her.

Before he could shout out a command to Plor, thinking Enbarr could jump and still give them a chance, a black blur streaked up and over him and Deidre. He ducked and Dee screamed.

Saito!

Her arms were outstretched, hands clawed. Her leather coat and black hair splayed out behind her. Her porcelain face was frozen in a horrific expression of furrowed, wrinkled, ghoulish flesh, with blood-red lips and gleaming white fangs, long, deadly, and saturated with saliva.

Deidre's eyes went wide and her hand covered her mouth. "Dear God."

"I have it on good authority God had nothing to do with that," Regan said, no less awed.

Having reached the apex of her leap, Saito dropped into the maelstrom, the fading echo of her growling hiss the only evidence of her sudden appearance.

The trajectory of the twister lurched drunkenly, weaving in one direction then another, erratically, not unlike a drunk heading home after closing time. Yet still the disturbance continued to rise, the wind whipping faster, the debris field widening. Twigs and branches lashed at Regan's face. Both Plor and Saito were lost inside the storm.

He tucked Deidre into his chest, covering her face with his arms.

"It's not stopping," he shouted.

Suddenly the disturbance took another drunken turn, twisted, and Plor and Enbarr were ejected from the swirling whirlwind of snow and wind. The animal landed awkwardly and stumbled as he struggled to stay upright. A few more steps at a gallop and he was able to control his wobbling gait and come to a stop.

Regan and Deidre ran over to them.

Plor slid off the animal, her sword still in her gloved hand. Agitated, the animal danced and stomped. It was clear he was unwilling or unable to settle down. Maybe he was anxious for another chance to go after the Yuki-Onna.

"Plor, you need to do something. Saito's in there."

"I am aware. All we can do is watch and wait to see where they come down."

With his head tipped back and his hand shielding his eyes, he tracked what he guessed to be the center of the storm, adding, "And pray Saito's still alive when they do."

# CHAPTER 21

IT DIDN'T TAKE long to see where they ended up. The tornado swirled and spun, its center mass rising and moving in an erratic northwesterly direction, until it paused, hovered over the church, then dropped two figures like conjoined stone.

There was a horrendous crash followed by a spewing geyser of stone, timber, shingles, and other debris. The resultant silence after the roar of wind and lashing hail was unsettling. In the abrupt stillness, the spiraling leaves and twigs and branches dropped to the ground, as if the unseen force had suddenly released its hold over them.

Regan shouted the obvious. "They crashed through the roof and are inside the church!"

Plor mounted and spurred Enbarr, who reared up and thrashed his front legs, eager to give chase. Before Regan could call out instructions, or cautions, they were off, charging up the granite steps and across the walkway leading to the church portico.

"Plor…" he called out, watching the horse run headlong for the oversized and closed solid wood doors. "Plor! The doors…"

They were closed. He needn't have worried. At the last moment, Enbarr leaped. Both animal and rider leaped into the air and through the huge, round rose window over the portico, crashing through sparkling cut stained glass in what was nothing short of a spectacular manner.

Glass rained down, tinkling across the stone porch and steps. Then quiet once more settled over the night.

"That did not just happen," Deidre said once she snapped her mouth closed again. She tugged on Regan's arm. "You are going to tell me what is going on here. This minute."

Regan knotted his brow. "Are you serious, Dee?"

"Dead serious. Damn it! Did you see that?"

Regan walked away from her—he had to. What was he going to say? How could he explain…that?

But her clicking high heels followed him as he rounded the corner of the block with a purposeful stride, returning to his cruiser. There he opened the trunk.

"Damn it, Sean. Talk to me."

"People are in danger, Dee. I'm going in there to help them."

From the trunk Regan pulled the department-issued twelve-gauge pump shotgun and a pouch of shells. The pouch he cinched to his gun belt. He slammed the trunk shut, broke open the shotgun and jammed two shells into the breech.

When he had the weapon loaded, he rested it on the crook of his shoulder and turned toward Deidre. "Dee, there are things going on here you can't understand. Hell, I've been living with them for the past few days and I don't understand half of it."

"What are you trying to say, Sean?"

"I'm saying you need to go home. Go home and forget about everything you've seen here tonight."

Her reaction was exactly what Regan expected—indignant outrage. "Sean Regan, are you crazy? There's a story in there." She pointed at the church. "A whopper of a story and I intend to get it."

"There are people in there fighting for their lives, Dee. It's too dangerous. I won't allow it."

"Won't allow it?" She stomped her feet like the stubborn, unreasonable child he knew she could be sometimes. "Who are you to not allow it?"

"The police," he said.

He grabbed her arm, quickly and forcefully, before she had time to dig in her heels. He dragged her to the back of the cruiser, yanked the back door open, and shoved her roughly inside before slamming the door shut, locking her in.

Through the closed window, he said, "I'm sorry, Dee. But you didn't give me a choice, and I don't have time to argue."

Without a second glance, Regan trotted back to the church and up the walkway. He had to be careful. The stones were already slick with a coating of snow and ice, slowing him down. "Damn snow. I hate winter. I bet crap like this doesn't happen in Miami."

He reached the bottom of the stone steps leading up to the church entrance. Regan hoisted the shotgun to his shoulder, set it firmly into the hollow of his shoulder, and fired two deafening rounds. The muzzle flash blazed yellow and illuminated the puffs of gun smoke escaping from the breech.

The heavy oak around the wrought-iron decorative door handles and lock mechanism splintered. Regan jogged up the steps and pulled the hanging, twisted door pull. It came off in his hand. He tossed the handle aside, relieved to see the door was ajar. He kicked it the rest of the way open.

Regan stepped through into the narthex, holding the shotgun, ready to fire. The interior was dark. He ducked in around the ruined center door. With his back to the other closed door he kept to the shadows.

Breathing hard, he paused, giving his eyes time to adjust to the darkness inside.

Facing him were oversized, heavy wood doors that separated the narthex from the nave. There, beyond those doors, he heard what sounded like Armageddon raging. Light pulsed and ebbed from the gaps of space between the doors, the frames, and the floor. The doors vibrated, as if trying to contain whatever was happening inside the church.

Regan sucked in a deep breath and pushed at the door in front of him. It resisted his attempt to open, as if something inside were pushing back. Regan put his back against the door, planted his feet, and shoved with all his might, his teeth grinding with the effort. Finally, he'd made an opening wide enough to slip through. As he did, the door snapped shut again with enough force to sever his arm if he hadn't pulled it through in time.

Relieved to still be in one piece, he gasped at what greeted him inside. This was so far beyond Armageddon it wasn't funny.

A howling wind swirled around, trapped inside the nave except where it whistled through the gaping hole in the ceiling. Books, pamphlets, candles, coins, and bills from the smashed collection boxes, scraps of cloth, and things like challises and small crosses and pictures ripped from the walls whipped around the room like missiles.

Regan would have been swept up in it, too, if not for the windbreaks created by the thick, ornate columns and arch supports, one of which he clung to for dear life.

Through squinted tearing eyes and his arm shielding his face from the brutal wind, Regan saw Saito, Plor, and Enbarr rushing at the Yuki-Onna, who stood in the apse, her arms raised, as the vortex raged around her.

Repeatedly, the three of them rushed at the snow witch, only to be repelled by hurled concentrated bursts of swirling snow, hailstones, and wind.

Regan moved forward, crouched low, staying below the level of the pews where the wind was less fierce, pulling himself from one pew to the next. The wind tore at his hair. His skin stung, being pelted by ice and sleet. He held one arm across his eyes, only able to look down at his feet to keep from being blinded.

The snow inside the church was already ankle deep, and his shoes, socks, and the hem of his trousers were soaked through, chilling him. He gritted his teeth and trudged ahead. When he'd reached the transept, the area separating the nave from the chancel, Regan dropped to one knee, shielded by the front pew.

There he replaced the two shells he'd used to blast through the front door and set the shotgun to his shoulder once more. Unable to see more than vague shadowy forms at the storm's center, Regan forced himself to wait, his nerves grating on him, but he waited.

Plor had leaped onto Enbarr and charged, coordinating her attack with a savage assault by Saito, who rushed at the Yuki-Onna's left side. But the Yuki-Onna rose above them, riding a funnel of wind above where Saito had leaped, too low. Plor fared no better, making a last-ditch attempt to swipe at the rising Yuki-Onna with her sword.

And finally, Regan had the opening he needed.

He tracked the snow witch's rise with the barrel of the shotgun...and fired.

The blast was earsplitting in the enclosed space. Its boom echoed through the chamber only to ultimately get lost over the howl of churning wind. Regan cared nothing about the noise. He grinned. The round had struck its mark.

The Yuki-Onna lurched.

Regan knew she couldn't be killed by being shot. He'd seen that when she'd survived three point-blank shots to the gut earlier. But she could be hurt. And that was enough for him at the moment. He pushed through the wind to his feet, aimed, and fired again.

This time the Yuki-Onna's wobbling became even more erratic, like a top reaching the end of its run. Regan pressed his advantage. He loaded and fired two more times.

His ears rang, but with each shot the Yuki-Onna reeled, pitched, flipped, then finally dropped. It crashed to the carpeted apse floor, further cushioned by the two inches of accumulating snow.

"Well done, Sean Regan," Plor shouted as she dismounted and rushed with Saito toward the downed creature.

The whipping wind and twisting, howling storm suddenly ceased as well.

Regan breathed a sigh of relief, lowering the shotgun to his side and trudging slowly through the snow toward the altar. There was no way in the world what had just happened had really happened, he told himself. His brain refused to process it.

Then without warning, both Saito and Plor flew away from the altar, propelled into the air as if they were marionettes suddenly yanked back by their strings.

Saito hit the ground first. Her arms and legs splayed in the air, like someone trying to do the backstroke through a tsunami. She crashed into the pews somewhere in the rear of the nave, near the cathedral doors.

Enbarr reacted with a speed that was remarkable. He leaped, timing it so Plor's flung body slammed into his hind end. She slid, twisted, and scrambled on board. It wasn't a pretty mount by any means, but it was the most magnificent thing Regan had ever seen. It also kept Plor uninjured and in the game, something Regan could only pray was the case for Saito.

"No way that just happened," Regan said. But despite his

disbelief, he rushed the altar.

The Yuki-Onna stood with her head hung low, her hair curtaining her face. A silvery-gray goo bubbled down her chest. Was it blood?

Regan didn't know, but clearly the thing could be hurt. And if it could be hurt, then it could damn well be killed.

Regan dug two more shells out of the pouch tied to his belt. He loaded and leveled the shotgun so the barrel lined up directly with the Yuki-Onna's body. The second shot would be the head shot, he decided.

About to pull the trigger, Regan aborted the shot at the last second. The entrance doors banged open. He twisted to see. In silhouette, Deidre stood with the lunar midnight sky framing her. She looked disheveled and had a stunned expression on her face. She shivered in the cold.

*How'd she get out of the damn police car?* Regan wondered. He got his answer when the doorway behind her filled with an eerie green-yellow glow.

Deidre rubbed her hands up and down her arms, as if trying to get warm. *Good luck.*

Ciag, the demented little lawn gnome with his long, crooked nose and twisted, jaundiced face of evil and his ridiculous red top hat, came up beside her.

"Deidre! Run! Get out of here!" Regan had no idea whether she could even hear him over the howl of the wind. In the end, it didn't matter. She appeared to be in shock, her unblinking, vacant eyes not registering anything that was going on around her.

The Yuki-Onna snapped her attention toward Deidre, a fresh soul and little more than helpless prey. The wounded snow witch rose slowly but with gathering speed, rising as if on a cushion of snowy wind. She soared a dozen feet in the air, gliding forward, her sights clearly on Deidre.

Enbarr and Plor made a run for her but were forced back by a conjured mini-blizzard.

Regan tracked the demon like one would anticipate the firing of a clay pigeon while skeet shooting. *Pull.* He fired. The shotgun slammed into his shoulder where he hadn't properly seated it. His shoulder exploded with pain. Regan ignored it and fired again.

Neither shot hit their target. Or if they did, this time they had no effect.

The Yuki-Onna swooped down and seized a startled Deidre by the throat, lifting her up off the ground even as the succubus's feet touched down.

Ciag danced a jig, holding the pale-yellow glowing lantern as high as his four-foot frame would allow. He swung it back and forth, casting an eerie, jaundiced glow over the broken pews and snow-covered nave.

Regan pushed through the wind, trying to rush forward. His rushing amounted to the same slow progress one made on Storrow Drive during rush-hour traffic. Namely, none.

The Yuki-Onna brought a struggling Deidre's mouth to hers and covered it with a kiss.

A kiss of death.

Deidre fought hard, but quickly it became obvious her strength was waning. Her kicking and thrashing arms lost their vigor as her very soul was being sucked from her, sapping everything from her, leaving her ultimately with nothing. Not even her life. All while strengthening the Yuki-Onna, a creature already proven to be more powerful than they could defeat, even with the addition of Saito Izumi's incredible power and speed.

Ciag cackled and danced, his snaggletooth grin wide on his misshapen face.

Plor and Enbarr were too far away to intercede; the hurricane-force winds kept them at bay.

Regan shouted, leaning against the unyielding wind, helpless to do anything to stop the demon but determined to try. Then he blinked.

Through the howling, blizzard-strong winds, a dark figure rose from the rumble of pews.

Saito Izumi. She was alive.

In a blur of movement she rushed forward and grabbed the Yuki-Onna from behind. She spun her around and violently tore Deidre away, breaking the soul-sucking death grip. Thus released, Deidre fell to the debris-covered floor.

The demon howled in anger and frustration.

Saito slammed her forehead into the Yuki-Onna's face. It was a head butt any WWE wrestler would have be proud of. The Yuki-Onna staggered back, disoriented from the blow and having been ripped from her final meal, leaving her thirst unslaked.

Ciag, the coward, seeing his team's advantage slipping away, tapped his hat three times and vanished. *Good riddance,* Regan thought. *One less thing for us to worry about.*

The winds abated some as the Yuki-Onna's attention was diverted to fighting for her life against a very pissed-off vampire. Regan and Plor continued to press forward, making slow but better progress, advancing, but their efforts were too slow, too late.

As the demon struggled against Saito's frontal assault, the vampire bared her fangs. Her eyes glowed the color of hot burning coals. Saito threw her head forward again, this time with the intention of sinking her fangs into the Yuki-Onna's pale-white throat. She slipped, losing her balance on the piled-up debris underfoot. The Yuki-Onna grabbed her by the lapel of her black leather coat, yanked Saito to her feet, and mashed her desperate, soul-stealing mouth down over the vampire's lips. A muted scream erupted from the union.

To Regan, it was the scream of every lost soul in hell.

The two unholy creatures thrashed about, embraced in mortal combat, but then something changed. Suddenly, it wasn't Saito who fought to break away. It was the Yuki-Onna who tried to pull back, to sever the death kiss between them.

Saito seized the soul-sucking demon's face with both hands, her long clawed fingernails digging into the white flesh of the Yuki-Onna's skin, the demon's flesh growing paler as she continued to try yet failed to pull away. The snow witch's eyes went wide, full of surprise and panic.

With a final, desperate surge of strength the Yuki-Onna managed to rip herself free. She staggered away from Saito, drunken and bewildered. Still she stared at the vampire with confused, icy-blue eyes, twin portals of shocked anger and disbelief. Staggering, unable to stand on her own, she dropped to one knee, suddenly looking older, not younger than before. "No. How?"

The billowing wind around them died down to a soft breeze.

Plor charged the disoriented demon as she remained down on one knee.

Plor raised *Claiomh Solais* over her head, holding the hilt in a two-handed grip. She plunged the broadsword through the demon's chest, pinning her to an angled pew behind her. The Yuki-Onna let out a final, blood-curdling scream.

Her eyes wide and with silvery-gray syrup-like blood leaking from the corner of her darkening purple lips and from around the embedded blade, still the creature thrashed, unwilling or unable to die.

Regan rushed to Saito. The vampire had also been weakened by the encounter. She had trouble remaining on her feet, reaching a splintered pew and one of the church's columns to arrest her fall.

Regan reached her in time to catch her before she collapsed. He lowered her to the floor, cradling her in his arms.

"Saito. My God. Are you all right? What happened?"

Exhausted, she leaned heavily in his arms. Blood caked at the corners of her mouth. Her eyes had lost their demonic glow and returned to their natural dark brown. "I don't have a soul. Whatever she sucked out of me, I guess it didn't agree with her." She forced a smile. "I think I poisoned the bitch."

"I'd say you're right."

"Your wife, Regan, go to her. I'll be fine."

"You're sure?"

"Yes. I'm just…I need to rest." Saito closed her eyes and went limp in his arms.

He lowered her to the ground, afraid she was more gravely injured that she was letting on. He felt for a pulse and then a heartbeat. He found neither. Of course, he wouldn't. Frantic, he didn't know what to do. Mouth-to-mouth? CPR? How do you revive a vampire?

He looked up. Plor stood over him. She held Enbarr's reins in one hand.

Regan swallowed hard. "I don't know what to do."

"Is she dead?"

"She was already dead." He climbed to his feet, never feeling as helpless as he did at that moment. The only idea that came to him was to feed her blood. He looked around, saw Plor's sword hanging by her side, and held out his arm. "I have an idea. Slice my wrist."

Plor gave him a concerned, dubious look. "For what purpose?"

"Vampires feed on blood. It's what gives them strength. Maybe if—"

Before he could finish, the floor shifted under their feet.

Regan wondered, *What the hell now…an earthquake?*

The floor shook worse, then heaved up like a geyser, tossing pews and debris in every direction. Chunks of floorboards and timber joists buckled. Large chunks of wood, metal, sheetrock, and plumbing pipes spewed into the air from below along with plumes of smoke and steam, all belching upward as if a volcano had suddenly erupted underneath the church.

Then like a giant sinkhole, everything collapsed, falling into a chasm below.

# CHAPTER 22

REGAN FOUND HIMSELF riding a chunk of floor as he—
and everything else around him—dropped to the level below. It
seemed as if the entire nave floor had caved in. Through the plumes
of gray dust, smoke, tumbling pews, and heavy, wet snow he heard
Plor gasp with surprise and Enbarr whinnying, a sound full of both
anger and fear.

Helpless to stop his fall, Regan scrambled up the slab of flooring,
trying to get to the top of it, but to no avail. The section of wood he
rode hit below with a flat, jarring impact. He bounced, struck his
head, and grunted. The blow to his forehead made him see stars.

Thankfully the drop was only down to the next lower level—and
not all the way into the depths of Hell—to a basement floor below.

He covered his head to protect himself from the nonstop debris
raining down around him. Regan tried to take in a dust-filled breath
and winced. The pain felt like a tight band around his waist. A busted
rib maybe. Through it all he managed to hold onto his shotgun.

*Go, me.*

When the bulk of what was coming down had settled, Regan

turned his head to look around. He coughed, winced again. When he looked up, he caught sight of a large section of floor—now the ceiling—dangling directly over him, swaying as it hung from a stretched silver conduit and brass pipes. The metal creaked with the strain. Some of the wires encased in the conduit sparked. Just as his mind caught up with the realization that the whole thing was about to come crashing down on him—it did.

The last conduit brass pipe snapped under the weight. The chunk of wood joists and floorboards and plywood broke loose. It was too late to get out of the way. He wasn't going to make it.

*But I'll die trying.* He scrambled on all fours, still clutching the shotgun in his left hand.

From somewhere out of the billowing dust a gloved hand grabbed the back of his collar and pulled. It was a slender hand with long fingers. The wrist was encased in a decorative armband, bronze, with intricate but crude reliefs hammered into the metal. Vaguely, Regan's brain recognized the armband and realized who had seized his collar and pulled him to safety: Plor na mBan.

Regan's body seemed to fly. He tumbled into her. The two of them twisted away from the falling wreckage. The section hit with a thunderous clap of noise. Dust and chunks of plaster and wood and other debris pelted them, painfully jabbing them. They huddled into each other, covering their faces with their bodies, their heads with their arms.

When it was over, Regan rolled away and the two of them sat up. Scraped, bruised, bloodied, and covered in dust, but they were alive.

"Thanks," Regan managed after a coughing jag.

"You are welcome."

Regan, still more than a little dazed, asked, "What the hell caused that?"

"I am not sure," Plor said, the first one to climb to her feet. She extended a hand down to Regan. He took it and let her pull him up.

"Whatever it was, you can bet it's not good." He fished more slugs from his ammo pouch and pressed them into the chamber, reloading the shotgun. "Come on. We've got to find Saito and Deidre."

Regan and Plor split up to urgently traverse the damage. A sick feeling stirred in the pit of Regan's stomach as he began to realize just how much debris had fallen through.

They were in a large square room with a tile floor, rows of cafeteria-style tables, most of them smashed to smithereens, and Regan noticed a service window into a kitchen area off to their left. The room must have served as a meeting area, a place where they had refreshments after services and probably a cafeteria for the religious instruction classes and a daycare center.

"Deidre! Saito! Call out!" Regan tugged some wood studs out of the pile and tossed them aside. He squatted to look under a pile of concrete and thick cast-iron drainage pipes.

He shouted to Plor. "See anything?"

"Not yet," she called back.

"You think that the Yuki-Onna thing is finally dead?"

Before Plor could answer, the pile of rubble before him burst upward, a sudden geyser of debris. Regan staggered back, grimacing at the pain in his side. When the remains fell back to the ground and the dust settled, a figure stood before them. A giant figure.

"Oh, come on. I can't take anymore," Regan complained, but it was clear the new arrival wasn't going away because of Regan's grousing. "Plor, what in the hell is that?"

"Cernunnos." Plor spat out the name in disgust. "The Stag Lord."

"Let me guess. He's not one of the good guys."

"No," Plor confirmed. "He most certainly is not."

"Crap."

Cernunnos stood twice as large as any man, fifteen feet tall at least, and as wide as the side of a barn. Regan remembered Plor talking about the Fomorians. Giants, she said they were. He hadn't believed her. Now he did.

And damn if they didn't live up to that description.

Concrete dust fouled the air. Regan waved clouds of it away, coughing, trying to get a better look at what they faced and giving himself time to come to grips with it. What Plor called the Stag Lord was bare-chested with a human-like torso, male, by the looks of him, with shaggy brown hair, except for the large palmate antlers sprouting from his forehead, a rack that would do any moose proud. A ring of metal hung from one antler branch and Cernunnos clutched a second one in his hand.

As the Stag Lord climbed to the top of the ruins, a chill iced Regan's spine. Cernunnos wasn't humanoid at all, but more akin to the Minotaur of ancient Greek mythology. Its entire lower half was covered in thick, brown fur. Its legs were that of the Cervidae, right down to its shiny clove hoofs.

"You should not have interfered, little princess," Cernunnos said to Plor, his deep voice booming in the hollowed space. He took a step out of the rubble. Boards snapped under his hoofs like toothpicks. Chunks of concrete crumbled to dust.

Plor took a step closer to him. "You are unwelcome here. Leave this world, Cernunnos, and never return."

Cernunnos laughed heartily. "Who would spend a second more than they needed to in this forsaken Otherworld? Are you daft, woman? I am here for one thing and once I have it, I am off."

The bandage around Plor's arm, from when Ciag's conjured vulture attacked her, was dark with blood. Her exposed arms, upper chest, and face were covered with scrapes. How serious they were was impossible to say, and who the hell knew about any internal injuries she might have sustained. The woman had taken several bad beatings already over the last few days.

Regan worried about her, and he had no misgivings about this new threat. It was clear to him Cernunnos would not be an easy enemy to defeat, not even for Plor.

"Plor, be careful."

"Find the vampire and your wife, Sean Regan, and get yourself to safety. This fight is mine and mine alone." To Cernunnos, she said, "Be off, jackal, and be seen nevermore."

"Soon, my pretty one, but not without that for which I have come."

"*Lia Fáil.* It shall never be yours. Not so long as I live to prevent it."

Again the giant laughed. "Do you think me afraid to fight you, little girl? Your death shall be a sweet extra. One I will cherish."

"Then why don't you stop talking, or 'tis your aim to bore me until I surrender?"

Cernunnos raised the metal ring he carried over his head. As his hand arced downward, swiping the ring at Plor, the neck ring expanded in size, becoming something more, a *chakram* with a honed, razor-sharp edge.

Plor leaped free of the weapon but came down on the uneven debris awkwardly. She slipped and went down on one knee, using the splayed fingers of her opposite hand to maintain her crouched balance.

Cernunnos switched the *chakram* to his other hand and took another swipe at Plor.

Regan leveled the shotgun and squeezed the trigger. The recoil slammed him back, but he hit his target. Cernunnos stumbled to the side and snarled with anger and pain, his upper chest, shoulder, and arm bleeding profusely. *Take that!*

Cernunnos fixed his attention on Regan. Another snarl erupted from the giant's throat.

Regan's *take that* became an *uh-oh* as he found the shotgun empty. So too was the pouch hanging from his gun belt.

"Leave Cernunnos to me!" Plor shouted, moving between him and the advancing giant.

"Fine by me," Regan said. "But I'm thinking he's got other ideas."

Plor leaped between Regan and the advancing giant. She threw a punch across the giant's jaw. "Find the others and go!"

Cernunnos staggered back from Plor's assault, but he did not lose his footing. He shook his head to clear it. Then he looked back at Plor, his sinister features twisted into an amused grin. His way of saying, this he was looking forward to.

Regan pulled his service Glock and fired twice. The round tore into the giant's shoulder but barely seemed to register more than a bee sting. "Tiny man, your annoyance will no longer be tolerated."

Cernunnos waved a hand, like he was swatting away a flea.

Regan knew not to laugh, but the giant was thirty feet away from him. What had Cernunnos hoped to accomplish with that? Knock him down with the wind of swing and miss. But what little smugness Regan enjoyed was short-lived.

From somewhere in the back of the room, hidden from sight by the piles of rubble, something stirred. Rocks and wreckage shifted and fell. From behind Cernunnos debris bubbled up then dropped down, displaced by something moving through, burrowing through the building wreckage.

"Now what?" Regan's imagination was too fried to even contemplate what new threat this might be. And when it erupted through the concrete and timber and steel his mind screamed at the impossibility of it.

Like a whale breeching the water, a snake of incredible size, unearthly size, burst forth, arcing into the air. Beyond the creature's bulk, the dimension of a tree trunk, what made it even more incredible—if more was needed—was the beast's head. It wasn't serpent-like at all. It was a horned ram's head!

Yet it hissed with a flickering forked tongue and bared sharp fangs Saito Izumi would envy and a mouth large enough to swallow Regan whole.

"Holy mother of God."

Regan dove away from the serpentine attack.

The ram-snake slammed face-first into the ground where Regan had stood seconds before. It hissed and slithered away, made a serpentine turn, and returned, moving as fast as a freight train.

Regan planted his feet, trying to determine which way to go as the ram-snake spun in a circle, hissed, and coiled for a second attack. Left. Right. Could he jump out of the way fast enough and for how long?

"Plor, do something!"

Plor heard Sean Regan's cry for help, but she was powerless to do anything to assist. Cernunnos had her in his grip. His hand wrapped around her upper arm. His fingers completely encircled her bicep, like one would hold a walking stick.

He held her up by that arm, pulling her completely off the ground. His grip was like a vise.

Plor didn't care. She could endure that. She glanced over her shoulder at Regan. It was he she worried about. Though he had scrambled back, the ram-serpent was nearly upon him.

Plor stuck two fingers into her mouth and whistled.

"What is that, weak woman? You wish to defeat me by injuring my ears?"

*No,* Plor thought. *God or not, Cernunnos was a simpleton.*

She unclasped her cloak from around her throat and twirled it into the air, twisting it, spinning it. She heard the charging of Enbarr's hoofs even as Cernunnos did. The Stag Lord turned his head, distracted by the sound of the advancing horse.

Plor noted through the gray dust that had settled on the sweaty flank of the horse a deep, bleeding gash. Enbarr was hurt, which explained his delay in aiding her. Poor, loyal horse. *I will make it up to you, my friend. Once I am free of this swamp-smelling monstrosity.*

"Not me, Enbarr," she shouted. "Assist the man. Sean Regan."

Cernunnos's expression clouded with dull-witted confusion. He'd expected, and prepared for, the horse to attack him, but instead the steed galloped past them.

Cernunnos shrugged off his confusion and shifted his attention back to Plor.

As he did, Plor snapped her cape like a whip. The metal fasteners that clasped the cowl around her throat struck Cernunnos in the eye.

The giant released his grip and howled, covering his damaged eye with both hands. He staggered away, bent over, whimpering. "Wretched girl. I will kill you for that."

Plor dropped to the ground, landing hard on her knees and her hands. Something sharp and jagged sliced through one palm. She cried out in pain.

No time for that now, she mused, coming to her feet. She started at the sound of Regan's projectile firing weapon going off. Twisting, she was pleased to see her concerns were misplaced. Enbarr and Sean Regan had managed to deal with the ram-serpent on their own.

Enbarr had reared up and pinned the giant serpent to the rubble on the floor with his forehoofs long enough for Regan to take a

shot—she believed that was the correct term. His projectile pierced the beast's eye, causing the creature to thrash and rear its head up. With fangs gleaming, half blind and disoriented, the ram-serpent shot forward, on the attack. It opened its great maw and struck.

But Regan was prepared. He'd pulled loose a long straight metal pole from the wreckage. As the ram-serpent drove its open-mouthed head downward, Regan jammed the metal pole upward, using it like a spear and sending it through the roof of the creature's mouth and out its skull. The beast shrieked and writhed, skewed on the pole, until it died.

Plor smiled. She was pleased. Sean Regan had turned out to be a rather capable warrior, a most valuable ally. But her smile faded as Cernunnos roared behind her.

Plor turned around. The giant stood, removing his hand from his left eye. The orb was milky with fluids and blood coursed down the Stag Lord's cheek. Like the ram-serpent he controlled, he was half blind. Unlike the serpent, he was not yet dead.

"Plor! Look out!" Regan warned needlessly.

How she wished she had *Claiomh Solais,* but her sword was buried somewhere under the rubble, still pinning the thrashing snow witch Yuki-Onna to a slab of wood.

Plor turned to face her enemy. Somehow she would prevail. All of *Tir na nÓg* counted on her. As did this world. Regan's world. She would not let them down.

"Come, you foul-smelling leech of a god. Come and do your worst, if you can. But be forewarned, wretched Stag Lord. I will not be easily defeated."

Cernunnos charged.

Regan raised his Glock, fired, and...click.

The gun was empty.

Cernunnos swung his torc in a savage arc.

Plor ducked, her speed the only thing saving her from being guillotined. What she couldn't do was recover her stance in time to avoid Cernunnos's follow-up attack, a sledgehammer-like fist that came down across Plor's jaw. Her head snapped down and away from the advancing giant.

Bright lights of pain flashed before her eyes. She took several staggering steps away from Cernunnos, but she was too slow, too off-balance.

Regan shouted out a warning.

Cernunnos swung the torc ring again, taking an uppercut swing at Plor.

The razor-edge torc sliced through her upper arm. Blood fanned out from the deep wound. Plor winced and grabbed her arm, blood leaking from between her fingers. She sidestepped, staying out of the giant's reach. But for how long?

Regan grabbed a chunk of rock the size of a football and threw it at Cernunnos. The rock hit the side of his head, skimmed off, and left a gaping wound, but Cernunnos simply laughed.

Regan searched for another, heavier rock but froze. Enbarr snorted a warning behind him. Regan turned. Slithering around the smashed and upturned pews, chunks of concrete and flooring, coiled and sparking electrical wires, all covered in a melting layer of snow, were not one, but two more giant, ram-headed serpents.

Regan called out, "Plor! We're screwed."

"I need *Claiomh Solais!* You must find my sword." Together they would face and defeat the ram-serpents or they would die trying.

"No." Regan backed up against Enbarr's side. "For all we know it's the only thing keeping the Yuki-Onna out of this fight. Besides, I have no idea where it is."

"Find it, Sean Regan. It is our only hope."

Cernunnos charged, and Plor, even without her sword, welcomed the chance to fight. No longer distracted, she planted her feet and balled her fists. When Cernunnos was within striking distance, racing toward her, overconfident and with his guard down because of a few luckily landed blows, Plor leaped into the air and drove her fist down into Cernunnos's jaw.

The giant spit teeth and blood, staggered forward, and crashed to the floor.

He twisted to face Plor, setting up her next strike perfectly.

She swung a right punch up and across his face. The power behind the blow lifted and spun Cernunnos across the great chamber like a whirling dervish.

Plor chased after him, determined to press her advantage.

Cernunnos slammed into the far wall. The foundation of the entire structure shook, dropping loose rocks and dust down on the shaken giant.

Plor grabbed him by the chest plate and groin and lifted the giant over her head. She spun and threw the Stag Lord across the room and through the far wall. Large cinder blocks exploded into dust from the impact; the wall shattered behind the giant, and Cernunnos disappeared in the large gaping hole that had seconds before been a solid block wall.

With his mouth agape, Regan said, "How strong are you?"

From the black maw behind the ruined wall a guttural roar shook the building. Two giant hands grabbed at the edge of the opening. Cernunnos pulled himself back into the room with a frightening bellow.

Plor said, "Not strong enough."

"We need to do something," Regan said, not being very helpful.

"My sword, Sean Regan. Without it, all is lost."

In his expression, she saw resignation and acceptance. He knew she was right. There was no other choice. "All right. Hold him at bay. I'll try and find it. And deal with them, too."

The ram-serpents were slithering inward toward them in ever-tightening circles. Animals playing with their food.

"Normally, I'm a fairly upbeat guy, Plor," he said as he frantically tore through debris, desperate to find *Claiomh Solais*. "But right now, I'm thinking we're not going to make it."

# CHAPTER 23

PLOR DIDN'T REPLY to Regan's dire prediction.

Sure they might be his final words as he scrambled to find the sword while avoiding being eaten by giant, ram-headed serpents the size of giant redwoods. Do it so they might take out a god—a god, mind you that had already proven more powerful than they were.

A rock and a hard place, Regan thought while looking around for where the skewered snow queen and Plor's sword might be, and if luck would have it, a weapon he could use in his and Enbarr's battle against the twin snakes from hell.

*Hopeless,* he thought, but he refused to give in. They'd find a way.

And though Regan didn't recognize it immediately as such, it came from the most unexpected source: Ciag, the demented, deformed lawn gnome.

He appeared like an apparition in the gaping hole Plor had created by throwing Cernunnos through the wall. Poof. He bounded up and down and held his swinging jaundiced lantern high—as high as a four-foot being could—and chanted.

"I have it! I have it," the gnome sang.

Everything seemed to stop at once, except for the sparking live

213

electrical wires. Even the ram-serpents coiled, settled down, and watched, still ready to strike.

Ciag danced into the room, followed by a lumbering, horned brown and white ox. The beast of burden moved slowly, its gait halting, as it was harnessed and struggling to pull a wooden cart behind it. The sight was like something out of a Paul Bunyan and Babe the Blue Ox story.

Damn the creepy little red man and his conjured up creatures.

"Have what?" Regan called out, but his sinking heart knew the answer.

"*Lia Fáil!*" Cernunnos shouted triumphantly. "The Stone of Destiny is mine."

"No, that cannot be." Plor looked stricken.

But it was.

Regan saw the granite-colored, rough-hewed stone sticking out of the back of the cart. It was too large to fit completely, tilting the cart back at an angle. No wonder the poor ox was struggling. Not that Regan could believe he was seeing that, either.

"We have it. We have it," Ciag sang, still dancing his jig. "We can go now. Leave this vile Otherworld."

Regan rolled his eyes. *Oh Christ.*

Plor whirled back on the giant. "I will not allow you to take *Lia Fáil*. It is forbidden."

Cernunnos let out a deep, loud belly laugh. "Weak girl, the battle was fought for as long as it needed to be fought. You are, and never were, worthy of my interest."

"A distraction," Regan said. "To keep us busy so Ciag could load the stone into the cart."

"And damn hard work it was, too," Ciag chortled.

"I shall not let you go."

Cernunnos grinned. "Accept defeat like a warrior, not a sniveling baby child."

"I will not accept defeat at all."

"Plor…"

She ignored Regan. "Come and fight me, sham god that you are, to the death."

"Plor, let it go."

She whirled on Regan. "I shall not. You know not what you ask."

"I think I do."

"Listen to the human, girl," Cernunnos said. "The time for fighting is over. Now is the time for the righteous king of *Tir na nÓg* to be crowned."

"And who's that? You, big guy?" Regan began to move in a wide circle, moving toward Plor.

Cernunnos glanced contemptuously at Regan. "Your attempts at humor are anything but, human. Mock me again, and it will prove deadly."

"Big words coming from a guy who hangs around with a leprechaun too stupid to wear green. Go on, take your stupid rock and get the hell out of here. Good riddance to you."

"Sean Regan. Stop."

Regan stole a glance at Plor. "He's right, Plor. We're defeated. We need to help those we can help. Deidre and Saito are hurt. They need us." He was close to her now. He grabbed her arm. Under his breath, he whispered, "Trust me."

"Listen to the pitiful, human, Plor na mBan of *Tir na nÓg*. 'Tis sense he speaks."

She shook her arm away. "No."

"Alas, it is already too late," Cernunnos pronounced. "Behold!"

He ceremoniously waved a hand toward Ciag and the ox, like the ringmaster in the circus, directing the audience to a new feat of derring-do.

And this one was a doozy.

The archway where the fear darrig stood swirled in a blue-gray mist with white, sparkling, firefly-like lights. The area behind him darkened from magenta to purple to midnight blue to black. Like a violent storm, the swirling mist churned and a widening vortex took shape.

"The druids have seen. They are calling us home," Cernunnos shouted over the sudden roar of wind.

"Tell me that's not a portal to some Otherworld."

"'Tis a portal, human. A portal to Magh Meall."

"No!" Plor shouted as she ran for the vortex. Her intentions were clear; she would stop Ciag and *Lia Fáil* from entering the vortex or she'd jump right in after them.

But Cernunnos was faster. He reached the portal first and blocked it with his massive form. As Plor came up short, Cernunnos swatted at her, striking her backhanded across the face. It wasn't Cernunnos's strongest shot of the day, but it was enough to send the exhausted Plor reeling.

Cernunnos advanced on her, fully prepared to finish her off.

Regan darted forward, skidding and skirting over the piled rubble. He dropped into a crouch between Plor and the giant. "Enough!"

Cernunnos came up short.

"You've got what you came for." Regan signaled at the vortex. Ciag, the ox, and *Lia Fáil* were already gone. Quickly following the fear darrig, the two ram-headed serpents slithered their way to the opening and plunged in, disappearing as if the vortex were devouring them.

*One could hope,* Regan thought, but he knew in his heart they were simply transporting from one realm into another.

"Coward." Cernunnos waved a dismissive hand as he backed

toward the portal. "What Tethra wishes with this world I do not understand."

Plor tried to get to her feet.

Regan pushed her back down. "Let him go."

Regan stared hard at her, trying to get her to understand, to trust him. With his expression, he tried to tell her it was going to be okay.

Cernunnos stepped into the portal, his loud laughter fading as he disappeared. The portal went black, then snapped shut with a reverberating pop.

Plor went limp against Regan's pushback. All resistance, all will to fight, was gone. "That 'tis it, then. Cernunnos has the *Lia Fáil*. All is lost."

"No, Plor, it's not. That's what I'm trying to tell you."

She stared at him with narrowing eyes. "Sean Regan. You are a fool who has condemned not only my world to destruction, but your own as well."

"I haven't. That's what I'm trying to—"

His words were drowned out by a loud explosion from overhead. They both cast their eyes about. The vortex hocus-pocus had destabilized the cohesion between the two worlds, Regan thought. Or maybe having the floor drop out from under the one-hundred-and-fifty-year-old church left the walls and roof without any means of support, so now they were about to collapse on top of them.

Yeah, maybe that.

"We've got to get out of here," Regan said, scrambling to his feet. "This whole place is about to come down on our heads."

He reached down to help Plor up. She stared at his hand, pushed it away, and got to her feet on her own. It was clear. She would accept no assistance from him.

Regan returned her steel-hard gaze. "Whatever. Be an ass, but help me find Saito and Deidre."

"Of course we will not leave without what *you* are concerned about."

"Plor, it's not like that. Look out!" The south wall buckled and the roof timbers splintered. A joist broke away and tumbled down toward them. Regan pushed Plor out of the way. The joist swung like a pendulum and struck a pile of rubble within a foot of where they stood. "We'll talk about this later."

She nodded, firmly. "We will indeed. There."

Regan followed where she pointed. "Deidre." He rushed toward his ex-wife.

"I will find the vampire...and my sword."

The sword. He was convinced it needed to stay where it was, pinning the Yuki-Onna, the only thing keeping her at bay. But there wasn't time to argue. "Just hurry."

Regan dropped down beside the legs he saw. Across Deidre's body lay a broken section of pew. Several prayer books were scattered around. He pulled at the pew and luckily it dislodged easily. He shoved it off to the side with a crash. Ominous creaking from the ceiling above continued to fill the chamber. He checked Deidre for a pulse. He found one and breathed a sigh of relief.

"Come on, kiddo."

He tucked his arms under the crook of her legs and behind her shoulders, cradling her head against his chest, and he lifted her. Smoke and concrete and drywall dust fouled the air. He coughed, juggling his wife to get a better grip and wincing as pain knifed through his side. Yep, definitely a broken rib.

She stirred in his arms. She looked up at him, her skin coated with a fine layer of dust. "Sean?"

He smiled, trying to be reassuring. "Hey."

Then her head lolled. She slipped back into unconsciousness.

Over his shoulder, Regan heard more debris, some of it rather large, being tossed about, hitting walls and the floor, debris cascading down piles. He twisted around to see Plor digging through the rubble. Angry. Getting her frustration out by pitching debris in every direction as she searched for Saito and her sword. Good, he thought, better than wanting to shish-kebab him with that sword of hers.

A minute passed. "I've found the vampire," Plor called out.

Not a moment too soon. "Grab her and let's vamoose."

Carefully, but with urgency, Regan climbed up the sloped piles of wood and rebar and concrete and stone. It was like climbing a constantly shifting Mt. Everest, but he got close enough to the higher floor to lift Deidre up to chest level and slide her onto the upper floor.

Winded and with his arms feeling like they might fall off, he climbed up and sat down next to her inert body. He gave himself a minute to gather his strength before going back down to help Plor. But his help was not needed. Plor emerged from the hole carrying Saito slung unmoving over her shoulder.

"Here," he said, "let me give you a hand."

Plor rolled her shoulder and transferred Saito's dead weight into Regan's waiting arms. When he had her fully, he set her down next to Deidre. He reached out a hand to Plor, but the Celtic demigoddess turned around and retreated back down to the lower floor.

"Where are you going? We need to get out of here."

As if to emphasize Regan's urgent plea, another section of the roof split off and came crashing down to the ground. Regan hunched over Deidre's and Saito's prone bodies.

"Not without *Claiomh Solais*. I would sooner leave without one of my arms." Once more Plor dug through the rumble, flinging stones and chunks of wood in every direction.

Regan got down on his hands and knees. Looking down into the crater below, he said, "For the last time, Plor. We've got to go."

The expression on Plor's face was nothing short of fury. "You have doomed my world, and yours, to years of destruction and war. You have conscripted untold thousands of lives to death because of your cowardice, Sean Regan. I will not have *Claiomh Solais* lost for eons as well because you lack the bravery to fight your enemies. I was wrong about the sort of man I thought you were."

"Plor…"

She waved him away. "Say not another word."

"It's…okay." The voice was barely heard over the shifting and thumping of thrown debris. "It's okay," Saito said again.

Regan crawled back to her side. "Saito, you're alive."

"No, I'm not. But I understand the sentiment."

"Thank God."

She smiled weakly. "You keep giving credit to the wrong deity." She gave him a thumbs-down signal, indicating her so-called continued existence was more the doing of the dark lord below than the Almighty above.

"Whatever, I'm sure glad you're a…here. What did you mean by 'it's okay'?"

Saito shifted, struggling to get into a sitting position. "Plor. Let her retrieve her sword."

"But the Yuki-Onna?"

"It's not the sword trapping the Yuki-Onna. There is but one way to kill a Yuki-Onna. She must be buried under a cairn of holy stones." She waved a weak hand around her.

Regan quickly followed her gaze. Sections of the roof dropped down around them like rainfall. It was only a matter of time before the whole damn thing came down.

"You're saying this will fit the bill."

She nodded and coughed.

He turned to the hole and called down to Plor. "Okay, find your damn sword and be quick about it, and just make sure you bury that snow bitch under a ton of rock, will ya?"

"Thy task will be done. Aye. There she be."

Plor climbed across some boulders and found the Yuki-Onna still pinned to the pew she'd been skewered to. The lower half of her body was additionally pinned to the floor by a slab of rock easily twelve feet long and as thick as an altar top. Plor looked around and found another stone of nearly the same size and dropped it on the witch's chest, just below where her sword protruded.

Plor clasped *Claiomh Solais* by the grip and quickly withdrew the sword. Once she'd pulled the sword free, Plor held it triumphantly over her head and announced, "Now we can leave."

But Regan shouted, "Look out!"

The Yuki-Onna opened her glacier-blue eyes and seized Plor around the ankle.

# CHAPTER 24

PLOR STARED DOWN at the wretched monster holding her. The thing's claw-like grasp was weak. The succubus had not fully recovered from her ill-conceived attempt to steal the vampire's soul that which the creature of the night did not possess, or which was so poisoned the succubus could not stomach it.

"Die now and forever more," Plor commanded and stabbed *Claiomh Solais* upward, aimed at the crumbling roof two stories above her head. "Die in the name of Núadu and the divine people of *Tir na nÓg.* Die."

A flaming light streaked from the blade of the broadsword. The light struck the dark, crackled and splintered timbers. The wood burst into flames. Fire whooshed and raced in both directions along the exposed joists.

"Holy crap!" Regan shouted. "I didn't know it could do that!"

"You thought the name Sword of Light was without meaning?"

"I didn't really give it much thought at all, to tell you the truth," Regan called down into the pit. "You better get out of there now."

Burning embers fell from the ceiling, dropping down into the massive hole in the nave floor like fire rain. Burning chunks of shingle and plywood and lathing splattered the Yuki-Onna still trapped beneath the pile of rubble. The creature screamed as the hailstorm of fire pelted her and burned into her flesh. Holy fire.

Still, the Asian demon held tightly to Plor's leg.

"Enough!" Plor adjusted her grip on *Claiomh Solais*, holding it overhead once more. She stabbed down at the trapped snow witch. Her blade severed the demon's arm at the wrist. Plor shook her leg and the detached hand fell away.

Plor whistled. "Enbarr!"

The great white steed trotted over to her, slowing only enough as he circled around her so Plor could leap onto his back, now with one arm over her head to protect herself from the destruction she'd unleashed overhead.

"Come on," Regan urged.

The amazing animal galloped around the mound of debris before finding a path to navigate their escape from the lower level. But once a course was chosen he quickly charged up to the second floor, slipping only minimally until he could make the final leap up to the church's main floor.

Enbarr skidded to a stop where Regan waited with Saito and Deidre; both women were lying on the floor beside him. Saito was only marginally conscious and Deidre not at all. Enbarr bucked urgently as more of the ceiling came down on them.

"Agreed, Enbarr," Plor said. "We must go."

"Can you walk?" Regan asked Saito.

"I'm not sure yet." Her voice was weak.

Overhead, there was a tremendous crack of timber. Regan glanced up and said, "Well, we don't have time to find out. Plor?"

"Yes, put her on Enbarr. I will take the vampire from here."

Regan helped get Saito to her feet and with Plor's help hoisted her on to the back of the horse. "Neither one of you can be here when the police and other first responders arrive. Take her away from here. Get her somewhere inside before the sun comes up."

"Where?"

"My apartment isn't far from here."

"I will take charge of her, Sean Regan," Plor said, her voice formal, icy. "The woman has proven her bravery and deserves no less."

"Good. Afterwards we'll talk, Plor. I didn't do what you think I did."

"Since we first met, you have been forced to believe the strange things, the unbelievable things you have witnessed. Yet now you ask me to not trust what I watch with my own eyes. I know what cowardice thing you have done, Sean Regan. And what the consequences will be."

Sirens could be heard over the crackle of burning wood.

"And I'm telling you, Plor, you're wrong. Just hear me out, but later. Now, go."

Regan slapped the horse on its bloody rump, avoiding the nasty cut on his hind end. Plor pulled on his reins and moved Enbarr to the left and away. They trotted toward the front doors, one of which now lay on the floor.

Regan returned his attention to Deidre. He squatted and, after getting an arm under her shoulders and the crook of her legs, he lifted her and carried her toward the doors.

She began to stir and then woke up. "Sean, what's going on?"

Carrying her, Regan picked his way carefully through the rubble, relieved now that Dee was awake that Plor, Enbarr, and Saito Izumi were gone. "We've got to get out of here."

"Okay," Deidre said, licking her dry and gray soiled lips. An explosion ripped through the basement, shaking the church to its foundation. Broken pipes were flooding the place with gas. "Did I just see a woman on a horse?"

Regan gave her an *"are you crazy"* look. "What? No. Of course not."

With her in his arms, he weaved his way through the rumble and climbed over the inclined wood doors of the destroyed sanctuary. As they went outside, the first responders were rolling up, screeching vehicles to angled stops at the fencing around the church. Red and blue lights pulsated, reflecting off the surrounding trees, buildings, and the facing stone wall of the church.

The approaching dawn stretched a ribbon of maroon and orange light low across the eastern horizon.

He carried Deidre down to the sidewalk below, careful not to trip on the chunks of concrete and other building materials strewn over the stone steps. Inside, more explosions rocked the church foundation. In response to a torturous creaking sound, Regan snapped his head around.

He watched as the south wall of the church faltered, the top of it crumbling, and then gave way, falling in on itself. And thankfully, thought Regan, burying the Yuki-Onna under tons of rock and rumble. He could only pray it was holy enough to entomb the foul creature for all eternity as Saito had promised.

Cops and a fireman ran to them and took Deidre from his arms.

"Wait." To Sean she said, "What happened in there?"

"We'll talk later, Dee. For now, just let these people help you."

Then she was gone, but one of the uniformed cops remained. "Christ, Regan, what the heck happened?"

Regan glanced up at the church. Flames from as deep as below ground level clawed their way into the sky, chasing thick black columns of billowing smoke.

He thought he could hear the faraway sound of a woman's scream. Or, maybe it was simply his imagination.

"Gas leak, I guess."

"And what were the two of you doing in there?" the cop asked.

An unmarked dark blue sedan pulled up to where the police and fire engines were parked. Mike Hall climbed out of the car and with his overcoat flapping around his legs and a cigar firmly seated in the corner of his mouth, the tip glowing red, he mashed his rumpled hat down on his oversized head and stomped over to the ambulance where Deidre was being tended to.

"You okay, Dee?" Regan heard Hall ask.

"Yes, I am. Thanks, Mike."

"Good." He looked at Regan and his face was beet red with anger. "I'll check in on you once I've had a word with your hubby here."

He stomped over to where the cop and Regan stood.

To the uniformed officer, he said, "Ain't you got anything to do? Set up a perimeter or something?"

"Yes, sir."

When the cop was gone, Hall drilled down on Regan. "Start talking and don't stop until I know everything."

"There's nothing to say, Mike. I responded to an emergency call of a gas leak, got here a few minutes ago. The place exploded. I went in to look for survivors."

"And your wife?"

"You know her. She followed me in. Guess she hoped to get a story out of it."

It was a story so full of holes it was more vapor than substance.

But Regan was operating on the fly, and he was exhausted, overwhelmed, and too worn-out to even think straight. He just hoped to buy himself a little time to come up with a better lie.

"Hockey puck who-ha," Mike said. "There was no 911 call. And dispatch doesn't have a record of a call. I also checked with the gas company. No calls reporting any gas leaks. You were in there with that crazy woman I saw you with earlier. Your new girlfriend."

"Girlfriend? What are you talking about, Mike?" He waved

around. "There's no one around here like that."

A few early morning lookie-loos had shuffled up to the hastily placed police line strung up by two of the cops. A man stood with a cup of coffee and holding a dog on a leash. The little rat-thing growled and barked, straining at the leash. His focus was not on the cops and other people but squarely on the church. Regan wondered if the dog with its heightened senses could detect, maybe smell, the evil that was now buried under the rubble of the church.

Meanwhile, firemen were pulling hoses and positioning rigs.

"Ever since that dead body turned up the other night, you've been acting really weird, Regan. Weirder than usual."

Regan brought his attention back to Mike Hall. "I don't know what you're talking about. Now unless there's something else, I'm going over to check on my wife. Excuse me."

"Soon to be ex-wife," Hall called out, fuming, puffing on his cigar and snorting like a steam engine.

Regan felt the man's eyes boring into his back. He didn't turn around.

At the back door of the ambulance, Regan clasped Deidre's hand. It was ice cold. She clutched a blanket tightly to her throat.

"How is she?" Regan asked the paramedic.

He looked up from the abrasions he was applying antibiotic ointment to. "Oh, outside of some cuts and bruises, she's fine. A few days' rest and she'll be good as new."

"Great to hear. Thanks. Can we have a minute?"

"Sure." The paramedic snapped his case shut and walked back to the front of the ambulance, where he grabbed a clipboard and began writing, documenting the aid he'd administered and accounting for the medical supplies he'd used. Regan knew from procedure.

"Are you really okay?" Regan asked.

Deidre swiped a lock of dust-encrusted red hair off her face and tucked it behind her ear. "I will be once you tell me what the hell is going on."

"How much do you remember?"

"I remember you locking me in the back of your police car."

"Um, yeah. Sorry about that."

"We'll table that one for now and deal with it later."

Regan bet they would.

"I remember banging on the back window, trying to figure out a way to smash out the side window—"

"Never would have happened. They're shatter resistant."

"I remember being inside the church. That's where it gets a little fuzzy."

"Do you remember how you got out of the police car?"

She looked away, searching her memories. "No. I..."

"It's okay." *Thank the heavens for that*, Regan thought. "What else?"

"Snow, mostly. And wind. And being very, very cold." Deidre shivered. Then she tilted her head to the side, as if at that angle it might bring the memory into focus. "The rest is all a jumble. Something about a woman in black clothes. And a horse."

"A horse?"

"It sounds crazy, I know, but I'm serious. And there's something else. A woman in white. She was really scary looking. And someone you called Plor."

"Deidre. You met Plor. Yesterday afternoon. At my apartment."

"That's right. The girl you're shacking up with."

"I'm not shacking up—"

"Is she here? Plor?"

"No, she isn't. You sustained a nasty cut on the head. You were knocked out cold. I'm sure this is all just jumbled memories and thoughts."

"I know it sounds insane, but I know…an Asian woman came at me. She kissed me."

"Kissed you? I didn't see that…and believe me, that I would have remembered."

"Don't be a child, Sean. It happened."

"It didn't. You did bump your head pretty hard."

She instinctively reached up and touched the tender spot on her forehead. "How?"

"There was an explosion, Dee. The ceiling caved in. What you think you saw…" He waved his hand in circles in the air. "…it's your mind filling in blanks with crazy images. It's all in your imagination."

"I…don't…think…so."

Regan placed his hands on her shoulders. "Trust me, Dee. It's all in your head."

Stubbornly, she said, "I saw a horse in that church. I did."

Regan simply gave her a look, a patient, "*it's okay, dear*" look.

Deidre nodded and hugged the blanket the paramedic had given her tighter around her throat. "Maybe you're right. Maybe I just need a good night's sleep."

"Now you're talking." Regan flagged down a passing cop. He told him who Deidre was and where she lived. He instructed him to take her home and get her settled.

Regan kissed Deidre on the cheek.

"I'll check in on you in a few hours."

"Good," she said, then whispered in his ear, "and I hope you're really ready to talk then. Because I will get the real story from you, Sean Cassidy Regan, not that gas-leak line of BS you're trying to run past everyone." She kissed Regan on the cheek. "Bye, Sean, honey. See you soon."

Stunned, Regan stood back and watched her go.

What else could he say except, *Aw crap*.

# CHAPTER 25

BY NOON REGAN had extricated himself from the crime scene, having explained his involvement in the destruction of the church repeatedly to Mike Hall, the fire chief, the arson investigators, the deputy chief of police, and even an IA dick named Holmes. Holmes, could you believe it?

Finally, the preliminary report from the arson investigators came in, and while the fire and explosion were still classified as suspicious, they told Hall, Holmes, and the other police brass they couldn't find anything to contradict Regan's version of what happened.

*Pure fantasy,* Regan thought, driving away. They should hear what really happened and get a gander at what's really buried beneath that mess. It would turn their hair white. He frowned. There was one more thing he needed to do before he could drag his exhausted butt to bed. He needed to set things straight with Plor. He just hoped she wouldn't impale him before he got a chance to explain.

He called her on the cell phone, asked her to meet him, and gave her directions to Boston Commons. She told him she'd treated Enbarr's wounds and he was once again returned to Regan's garage, where he was happily munching hay and grain and had a belly full of apples. That thing could eat like…well, like a horse.

"Plor," he said, seeing her standing on the banks of the lake watching the swan boats. She was dressed in more of Deidre's clothes. This time she'd selected blue jeans and a gold shimmering blouse. Her hair was tied in a thick ponytail and draped over her shoulder.

"Sean Regan." Cold. She turned. She clearly hadn't forgiven him for betraying her, for betraying her people. He couldn't blame her for that because she didn't know.

"Let's walk." As they started out, Regan asked, "How's Saito?"

"Resting. She needed to eat. She gave me directions to her dwelling and at her instruction I found bags of blood in her ice box."

"Refrigerator."

"Yes, that is what she called it, too. When I returned to your living space, she drank." Plor shook her head. "Ate."

"Whichever."

"She stated that she felt better. I left her to rest. I told her one of us would return to check on her later."

"Good."

They continued to walk, following the red line of the Freedom Trail. As they walked, Regan talked to her about America's fight for independence, about how his small, newly formed country had chosen to fight against an overwhelming, powerful force, a nation that up until that time had never been defeated in war.

"You know how they did that?" he asked.

"They had to have been strong warriors. Very brave."

"That's true, and they were, but they also had to be clever. Their enemy was the most superior fighting force on the planet. The most well-armed, experienced, well-funded army in the world. My countrymen couldn't fight them in a straight-up battle and expect to win. They had to outsmart them, sometimes trick them. They had to fight in ways that were new and unexpected and different."

"You are making a point, are you not, Sean Regan?"

"My point is this. If what you say is true, that Cernunnos works for this powerful Tethra god and Tethra wants to invade this world, I say let him try. Others have tried to dominate us, and others have tried to destroy us. It hasn't happened yet, and I say it never will. He won't win, especially if we have people like you and Saito on our side."

"You may be correct, Sean Regan. Your world may prevail against Tethra and his Fomorian forces when they arrive. But it will have been a preventable war, a war that will cost your planet hundreds of thousands of lives, millions of lives. It will be a war that is fought because of your cowardly actions this day. You might—"

"No, Plor," Regan said sharply, "you're the one who's wrong. If this Tethra is hell-bent on invading this world, he'll do it, with or without the Stone of Destiny. Men like him, creatures like him, are nothing if not determined. If he didn't get *Lia Fáil* today, he'd have simply found another way to gain the power he craves, to convince the small-minded who would follow him that they should." Regan turned and began walking again. "I guess we'll just have to see what that something is."

Plor took a moment, not following his meaning. "Wait. What are you saying?" She caught up to him and grasped his arm. "You did something."

"No, Plor, I knew something. Something Cernunnos didn't know. Something you didn't know."

"What? What was it?"

"Like the brave men and women who fought victoriously against the British right here where we're standing now, if we're to prevail against a far superior fighting force, we can't fight them the same old way. We'll need to be smarter, fight in a way they don't expect, in a way they can't anticipate."

"What is it you knew?"

"The Stone of Destiny. *Lia Fáil*. Plor, it was a fake. It was just a stone, a stone like any other. It wasn't real."

Stunned, Plor stared at him. "What? How did you know?"

"You told me."

"I? How did I—"

"Your sword."

"*Claiomh Solais*. I do not understand."

"At the museum. Remember you and Dr. Bradley were going on about the four treasures, the cauldron, the spear, *Lia Fáil* and—"

"And *Claiomh Solais*. They had Núadu's Sword of Light on display."

"That's right," Regan said. "But how could that be when we had *Claiomh Solais* in my car?"

"If I possess the real sword…"

"The other one had to be a replica. That made me realize, if it wasn't real, then all of the four treasures were fakes." He smiled as Plor began to smile too.

*Good, maybe now she won't run me through with the damned sword.* "I didn't get it until that moment. But it made perfect sense. Cernunnos and Ciag left this world with a useless hunk of rock. Nothing more."

What he didn't tell Plor was that he gambled, that he didn't know for sure at the time but suspected, guessed. It was only while he waited for her to come meet him he'd had the time to check the Internet on his phone and verified that what is believed to be the real Stone of Destiny, *Lia Fáil,* remains in its place on the Hill of Tara, in County Meath, Ireland.

He had gambled, and won. Thankfully.

At that point, Plor did something she'd never seen her do. She laughed. And it was a deep, hearty laugh, full of mirth and relief.

"You tricked them, Sean Regan."

"I did."

"Then I have a new regret."

"What's that?"

"That I will not be present to see the expression on Tethra's face when *Lia Fáil* fails to sing for him, when a worthless piece of stone refuses to bestow on him the magical gifts he expects."

"Yeah, I bet that's gonna be a downer of a day."

They walked on in silence. Then Plor stopped. "Sean Regan, I must apologize. I did not trust you and I should have. And for the terrible things I said."

"No worries, Plor. It took me awhile to come around and believe in you, too."

"Yes." She nodded in total agreement. "You are a stubborn man."

He shrugged. "A trait of the Irish, I'm afraid."

They walked on down to the harbor. There Regan told her the story of the Boston Tea Party. She smiled at the telling and when he concluded, she said, "I believe I will enjoy remaining here among these people. An intriguing lot, you appear to be."

"Hey, hold on. What do you mean? You're staying? But your mission, it's over, isn't it?"

"No, Sean Regan. My mission 'tis far from done. And even if it were not, though Cernunnos made it appear simple, and 'tis true the barrier veils between Otherworlds diminish with each passing day, 'tis still a difficult accomplishment to breach the mists at will. It takes the most experienced of druids to achieve the feat, at the most exact time and place."

"So what you're saying is you're stuck here? At least for now."

Plor nodded. "Unless you are aware of a powerful druid who might—"

Wishing he had concealed his glee a bit more, but unable too, he spurted out, "You'll be sticking around for a while. That's great. I mean, I'm sorry for you, but—"

"If by sticking around you mean I must remain in your world, then the answer is yes. I believe that to be what I said."

"Yeah, I guess you did." Regan smiled. "That's great. I mean cool." An idea struck him. "In that case we should celebrate. And I'm hungry. Have you ever had pizza before?" Excited and with a wide grin he answered for her. "No, of course you haven't."

Blinking, and somewhat surprised by Regan's burst of enthusiasm, she said, "No, I've never had nor even heard of—"

"Pizza!" He led her toward a pizzeria shop he knew down the street. "You're gonna love it. Trust me."

"Tell me, Sean Regan, can this pizza be consumed with that most excellent ale you slaked my thirst with before?"

Regan grinned. "Oh, my dear Plor, that is absolutely the best way to consume pizza." He took her by the arm and said, "Come on."

Read on for an exciting short story featuring
Saito Izumi

NIGHT.

Two dark-clad figures faced each other in a courtyard, just beyond the long, ominous shadow of the *tenshukaku,* the castle keep, of Kumamoto Castle. Pastel moonlight cast the grounds in an ethereal blue glow. Dressed in samurai armor, *tosei dō gusoku,* each warrior was armed with a long sword called a katana.

They bowed, respectfully, then positioned their feet, prepared to fight.

Their blades—forged by fire from three kinds of steel—were curved, folded, shaped, and burnished to a mirror's shine and a razor's edge by skilled craftsmen, each engraved by gifted artisans with *kanji* symbols and a dragon motif. The grips were handcrafted and wrapped in *samegawa* to custom specifications.

Samurai Saito Izumi made the first move.

She swung her sword horizontally, right to left, leveling the blade of her katana with her left hand, cutting the air with a *whoosh.* The polished steel reflected the blue hue of the glowing full moon overhead. She'd put everything she had into the swing.

Her opponent, Katō Ichirō, a second earlier standing on point, his katana aimed at Saito's nose, swiftly dropped his hand down and to his left, blocking her swing.

Steel blades clanged crisply in the night air.

Pain reverberated up Saito's arm. She grunted.

She withdrew her katana quickly and advanced toward Ichirō, who pulled back and raised his own katana over his head.

He stepped forward, slicing his blade down and to the left, his attack aimed at Saito's shoulder. If successful, the blow would have cut through flesh, muscle, and bone, and severed her arm from her body.

But Saito had already crouched and moved beyond the swinging blade. She now stood behind her opponent. Saito spun, holding her katana in a two-handed grip, level with Ichirō's waist.

Surprised and off-balance, Ichirō ducked.

Saito's swing missed all but the outer layer of Ichirō's *tosei dō gusoku*, chinking the small iron scales and sending several metal links flying.

Ichirō spun on his heels, sliced his katana low, mirroring Saito's attack, but aiming for her knees.

Saito easily jumped over the swipe of his blade.

"Why not?" Saito asked. It was a question she'd asked many times before. One they'd argued over often. And one she returned to again. Her booted feet hit the ground, raising puffs of dry, brown dust.

"Because I told you…there's more to it than—"

Saito thrust her katana forward. Ichirō dodged, avoiding the blade.

They continued their duel, part dance, part fight, in a flurry of swings—blocks—strikes—counter-strikes—and parries. The intensity of their battle intensified.

Saito wiped a bead of sweat from her brow.

She jabbed.

Ichirō darted out of range, his speed inhumanly quick. One instant there—

Saito blinked when he disappeared.

The next he was several meters to her right.

She spun.

He smiled, pleased with himself.

"Not fair, Ichirō-sama," she admonished.

Ichirō tilted his head ruefully, then bowed. "My apologies, Saito-san. But being impaled is not high on my list of things to do this night."

"See?" Saito dropped her defensive posture, lowering her katana. "You prove my point even as you argue against me."

"And you ignore the whole, seeing only that which appeals to you. Imagine never being in the sun again, to never feel its warmth on your face, to be trapped in the night. Darkness. Cold. Your constant and only companion, beyond forever."

"I do not care about such things," she insisted.

Her feign succeeded.

Ichirō had grown wistful and let his own guard down. Saito struck.

A savage diagonal cut from left to right left a deep gash across Ichirō's belly, under his *mōgami dō,* cutting cloth and into flesh.

Ichirō winced.

He glanced down at the bloody wound under his heavy plate iron vest, pulling back the bloody material to examine the cut. Then he laughed. "Ha. I see you've listened when I told you to hold nothing back." He covered the wound with his hand. "You say you care not now, but when it is denied you," Ichirō said, returning to their prior conversation, "when you miss it and can never have it back, that then is a different tale. Besides, Saito-san, you need no supernatural advantage. Your skills are already quite formidable, perhaps greater even than mine."

"But I possess none of your speed," Saito complained. "None of your strength or your superior healing powers." Already Ichirō's stomach wound had healed, leaving no scar. "Your father's enemies are powerful, and many. He deserves the best possible protection he can have."

Saito and Ichirō came together, stood, facing each other, swords raised. Their katana tips touched in unison as they circled.

Ichirō withdrew his katana and feigned a diagonal cut.

Saito parried, counter-blocked. Clashing steel rang loudly in the crisp, night air.

A thrust came from Ichirō. "And father has it in you. The best samurai on all of Nippon."

Saito side-stepped. She brought her katana down, brushed Ichirō's blade aside, and spun.

"Do not patronize me, Katō Ichirō." Like wary cats they stalked about the courtyard in pacing circles. "You can avoid my speediest attack, overpower my most skilled assault. You can defeat me without expelling a single labored breath. A truth we both know."

"I do not breathe, Saito-san, a truth you know well, also."

Ichirō lunged and made a downward diagonal cut, then reversed it and swung his katana back from the right to the left, catching Saito in her heavily armored shoulder.

"You are samurai, Saito Izumi. Hand-picked for your skill and your bravery by the *daimyō* to be his personal protector. Katō Tadahiro does not make mistakes in such matters."

Saito rushed forward, feigned a thrust, then struck at Ichirō's unprotected thigh. Her blade cut a bloody line through his silk robe and his skin.

Ichirō leaped into the air. He swiped his katana downward, blocking

Saito's follow-up attack.

With her offensive abated, Saito was left off-balance, the ringing of their blades loud in her ears. Her breath grew heavier

Ichirō landed, twisted, then swept the ground with his feet, knocking Saito's legs out from under her.

She landed heavily on her *ketsu*—ass—knocking the wind from her lungs. A puff of dust plumed off the dry earth ground around her.

She gasped as Ichirō moved in, his katana raised over his head. "Only the very best get to be samurai for the daimyō. If you are not the best, Saito-san…"

Ichirō swung his katana downward, to deliver the killing blow—

But Saito rolled away.

Ichirō's blade cleaved the dirt where seconds before Saito had sat, stunned and sore. Now on her hands and knees, Saito spun and kicked out her legs like a mule. She drove her booted feet into Ichirō's knee, shattering it.

Ichirō collapsed with a cry of pain. Down on his one good knee, his injured leg stretched out, keeping his balance with one hand clutching the dry, caked dirt, Ichirō massaged the splintered bones back into place, wincing at the ache of bone and muscle as they knitted back together.

Saito didn't give him time to heal; with a two-fisted swing, she sliced her katana through the air.

Ichirō ducked, using all of his supernatural speed; otherwise, he'd have lost his head. He flung a fistful of dirt into Saito's face.

She cried out and staggered backward, her eyes burning. She dropped her katana and covered her face with both hands.

Ichirō jumped to his feet. He shook out his injured leg, not yet completely healed, but when he put his full weight on it, the knee held without buckling.

Saito remained bent over, rubbing at her eyes with her hands. She made whimpering sounds.

Ichirō rushed to her side, inhumanly fast, only a blur to anyone who had seen him move. He seized Saito's arms and straightened her up. Concern was plain on his face.

"Saito-san. My beloved. Are you hurt?"

Saito wiped dirt from her face, her breathing still labored. But when she lowered her hands, her dirt smudged face revealed tear-streaked cheeks. "I am unhurt, Ichirō-sama, physically. But damaged..." she tapped her chest over her heart, "...here."

He held her in his arms, pulled her close. "What is this obsession of yours, Saito-san?"

"It is not obsession. It is love, Ichirō-sama. Love for you, and frustration. You have these abilities. You have been cut. Your bones shattered. But you heal almost instantly. You have these wondrous gifts, yet you deny them to me. The woman you profess to love."

Ichirō pushed her away, clearly angry now, too. He turned his back to her. "You call these abilities gifts. And perhaps they are, but Saito-san, make no mistake. They come with a price, a very steep price."

Saito wrapped her arms around him, hugging him hard and strong. Her love for him was so deep, so all-consuming. She pressed her face to his armored back. "You do not age. You are immortal, Ichirō. You will live forever, while I..."

Ichirō looked down at her, brushing away her tears with his thumbs. "No one lives forever, Saito-san. Not even I."

"You will not grow old. You will not become wrinkled and haggard and crippled with age." Her voice was hard-edged, her eyes tear-filled again, but defiant.

Ichirō spread his hands, helpless.

"This is no blessing, Saito-san. This is a curse. There are dark and...horrible things about what I am. What I must do. Things you do not know about. Things so terrible as to be beyond your imagination. Things that...because I love you...you must never know. Never see, much less experience."

"If I experience them with you, Ichirō-sama, then it matters not. So long as we are together. Forever."

"It does matter, Saito-san. It is vile and disgusting. To be forced to roam the nights, skulk about in basements and shadows like a rodent during the days. Afraid of even the slightest touch of sunlight on my skin." He pushed her away. "What I do to survive is something you will never witness. I could never live with myself if you saw what it means for me to be...*kyuuketsuki*."

Saito looked longingly into his face. She reached out for him. "Please, Ichirō-sama, do not keep me out." Her fingertips stroked his cheek. "I wish to be with you forever. Whatever I must do, or be. That matters not." She repeated, "So long as we're together."

She pulled his face down to hers. She kissed his cold lips.

He pulled her into an embrace, returning her kiss, his body hard and strong against hers. Their love for each other was deep, neither doubted that. But could it endure? Could it survive this divide between them?

Saito was determined that it would. No matter the consequences. As they kissed, long and hard and with passion, Saito bit down on her cheek and tongue. She gasped as her mouth filled with blood. Warm, salty blood.

Ichirō pulled back, his eyes wide with surprise, his lips smeared with Saito's blood. "Saito-san, what are you doing?"

"Whatever I must to be with you, Ichirō-sama. Turn me. Please!"

Saito pushed herself at him, trying to get past his arms now holding her at bay.

He pulled away. "Stop it."

But it was Ichirō who could not stop. Who could not prevent

the longing, the craving, the bloodlust. His face lost color. His pale ocher skin became ashen; gray tinged the flesh around his mouth, his ears, the smooth line of his jaw. His almond-shaped eyes, usually an intense brown, brightened to glowing red orbs.

He snarled menacingly, baring white, gleaming fangs.

He pushed her away.

Saito stumbled back, her hand covering her mouth in horror at the sight. She tripped over one of the dropped katana and fell. She hit the ground hard but continued to stare.

Ichirō crouched and held his hands out with his fingers splayed, claw-like, his fingernails extended into actual claws and turned black as onyx. He lunged at Saito, snarling when he reached her.

He dropped down on top of her, their faces mere centimeters apart.

"To be *kyuuketsuki* is a curse," he snarled. "Is this what you wish to be? To kill so that you may live. To kill and drink the blood from living humans and animals alike to survive. To be feared and shunned because you are a vile... creature of the night."

Saito recoiled. She had known this but never seen it. She knew what a *kyuuketsuki* was, that her lover Katō Ichirō was a blood-suck-demon, one of the un-dead.

But to see him transform, to witness what it meant to change...

"This! This is what you covet?" Ichirō shrilled, blood-tinged spittle drooling from his mouth. "This? You foolish, foolish, girl!"

Ichirō squeezed his eyes closed and his body trembled. He made fists of his hands, his long, black claws digging into the flesh of his palms. He licked at his lips, then wiped Saito's blood away in disgust.

Finally...

Slowly...

And with great effort, his *kyuuketsuki* features faded; the nails receded and returned to their normal color. When he opened his eyes again, the fire in his eyes had dulled; his beautiful brown irises were returning. Ichirō closed his mouth and climbed off Saito, leaving her breathless on the ground.

When he opened his mouth again, his fangs were gone.

"Forget this, Saito-san," he said, his voice as cold as his flesh.

Ichirō whirled away from her and stormed across the courtyard, returning to the castle keep.

Saito Izumi remained in the courtyard for some time. Alone. Afraid. Shivering.

For how long she remained, she could not say except for the distance the moon had passed overhead. Which was a great distance.

When she finally gathered the strength—or was it the will—to go, she did so by studiously gathering up the weapons left discarded from their practice drill. First, she retrieved her katana, wiped it down, and slipped it into her scabbard on her left hip, opposite the *tantō*, her shorter, ornate, double-edged knife, which hung from her right side.

Lastly, she retrieved Ichirō's dropped katana and her own *yumi*, the longbow she had been practicing with when Katō Ichirō came out seeking to train with her. With the weapons and her quiver of arrows, Saito left the courtyard behind the *tenshukaku*, a structure eight stories tall with an ancillary five-story-tall keep attached to it. The most important, most fortified place within Kumamoto Castle, the stronghold and home to the daimyō.

Swollen black clouds rolled overhead. They obscured the bright full moon and threw a patchwork of shadows over the ground. The increasing darkness matched Saito's mood as she reflected over what she'd seen this night—Ichirō's transformation, his wild, unrestrained hostility—and worried about where it left her relationship with Ichirō and her place as samurai for Ichirō's father,

Katō Tadahiro, the daimyō of Higo Province.

**BUILT IN 1467,** Kumamoto Castle underwent an extensive expansion from 1601 to 1607 overseen by the great warrior Lord Katō Kiyomasa, a recognized master of castle construction. Considered to be one of the most fortified, impenetrable castles in all of Nippon, Kumamoto was built on the *teikaku-shiki* design, meaning that the *hon maru*, or main court, and within its walls the *tenshukaku*, was in the northeast section of the castle, at the highest and most defensible portion of the hilltop castle.

To the south and west—separated by high, sloped block walls called *kuruwa*—lay the secondary court, the *nino maru*, protected behind yet another series of walls and moats, and a third defensive court called the *san no maru*, beyond which were still more walls and moats.

Access from one area to the next was controlled by a series of gates, strategically built and guarded throughout the castle interior, separating the various *maru* tiers. Each tier could be sealed off in the event of an attack.

Saito now passed through one such gate, moving from the *hon maru* to the secondary *nino maru*. She carried her yumi and Ichirō's abandoned katana. Her katana and tantō were sheathed in their scabbards and bounced at her hip as she walked. She made her way to *Uto Yagura*, the turret tower built on the defensive wall in the northwest corner of the *nino maru* courtyard. It overlooked the lower *san no maru*.

Uto Yagura was the largest guard tower in Kumamoto; at four stories tall it had been the *tenshukaku,* the castle tower, of Uto Castle when it was under the Konishi clan and before the reign of Ichirō's grandfather, Katō Kiyomasa, before Lord Kiyomasa's expansion and fortification of the castle completed in 1607.

Entering Uto Yagura, Saito carried a lighted torch by which to see and set it in a wall-mounted iron sconce. The flame sent a curling ribbon of black, acrid smoke upward to where she heard palace guards pacing the upper floors.

At least a few appeared to have remained awake while on guard duty.

In a room set off from the main hallway, Saito placed her yumi on a weapons rack built into the wall. On the next higher rung, she placed Ichirō's katana, the curved blade up. Methodically, she crossed the small space and slid back a wall panel in the far-left corner to reveal a shelved closet. There she took off her *kubuto* and placed the heavy iron helmet on the upper shelf before beginning to unfasten her *mōgami dō*, the heavy plate-metal armored vest and back shield she wore, setting the cumbersome components of her *tosei dō gusoku* on the table beside her.

In the darkness, she had only the flickering torchlight to see by. The pungent smell of the burning, pitch-soaked wood and cloth irritated her nose and made her want to sneeze.

The firelight sputtered in a sudden, cold breeze that blew through the drafty bottom floor of Uto Yagura. Saito shivered, feeling the hair at the nape of her neck stand up.

From the darkness behind her a hand reached out and scooped her long black hair from her face, tugging it lovingly behind her ear.

Saito turned. "Ichirō?"

But she realized quickly, it was not.

Saito drew her tantō and ducked out from under the hand. She held the short blade at the ready.

The figure in the shadows stepped into the flickering glow of torchlight and raised his hands, palms out. "Easy, Saito-san. I am not an enemy."

"Kampaku Koken!" she said, her voice harsh. "What is the matter with you? I almost stabbed you."

Yagyū Koken grinned.

A handsome man, Koken had lived his whole life in Higo Province. He'd spent his childhood years growing up with Katō Ichirō and Saito Izumi. That Ichirō was the daimyō's son and Saito Izumi the only daughter of the most powerful samurai family in the province, while he was merely the son of a rice farmer, meant nothing. They had stuck together and remained as close as family. Yagyū Koken was now a great Regent, a chief advisor to the shōgun, Tokugawa Iemitsu, the most powerful leader in all of Nippon.

"And had you stuck me, it would have been well-deserved." Koken smiled. "What was I thinking, sneaking up on the greatest samurai warrior in all of Higo Province in the middle of the night?"

"Yes," Saito said, agreeing. "And if you mean to flatter me with your praise, making my heart go all aflutter, you will be disappointed. Better you put your efforts toward wooing the *yūjo* in the *Yūkaku* of Edo."

"Oh," Koken said, ignoring her insults about prostitutes and the pleasure district in Edo. "You're just angry because you and Ichi had a fight."

Saito spun around.

Koken leaned causally against the wall, his legs crossed at the ankles, his arms folded over his chest.

"What do you know of it?"

He shrugged. "I saw you. Heard you argue."

"So that is why you are here. You've returned to Kumamoto Castle to spy?"

"No," Koken said, defensively, straightening up. He let his arms drop to his side. "I came to the courtyard to speak with Ichi about…a matter of Regent business. I saw the two of you sparring. Rather than intrude, I watched. You fight quite well, Saito-san. Your skill has improved greatly since I left for Edo two years ago."

Saito stepped closer to Koken. "And what did you hear of our fight?"

"I heard you ask Ichirō to turn you. And I heard him refuse."

His words cut like a tantō. She loved Ichirō and wanted to be with him, forever, no matter what. Why could her lover not see that?

Saito lowered her head in shame. When she looked up again, she said, "Please, just go."

Koken grabbed Saito by the arms. "I am sorry Ichi treats you this way, Saito-san. You deserve better." He paused a beat. "I would treat you better."

"What are you saying?"

Visibly flustered, Koken looked away. "I mean you no disrespect, Saito-san. Only that Ichi should..." Koken closed his eyes then opened them again, steeling himself to get the words right, to get them out. "...respect your wishes."

Her silence spurred him on. "He should not dictate his will onto you. Who is Katō Ichirō to choose for you what you are...what you wish to be?"

Saito brushed Koken's hands away. He let his arms fall to his side. "He only wants what is best for me," she said.

"No, Saito-san. You are wrong. Ichirō is only interested in himself. He will not turn you because he does not love you."

"That is not true," Saito insisted. "Ichirō does love me."

Koken shook his head.

"He only pretends to love you, Saito-san. So he can control you. So he can treat you like his own personal *yūjo*."

"No! Koken, I am not his play woman. You do not know what you are saying."

Koken took a step toward her. "But I do, Saito-san. I am his best friend. He has confided in me."

Saito turned away, shying away from his words, his lies. What he said, she did not believe.

Koken took hold of her arm again. "He is afraid of you, Saito-san. Afraid of how strong you are. Should he turn you…should you become *kyuuketsuki*, combined with your skill as samurai, he fears he would be able to control you no more."

"He does not control me. He loves me."

"Then why does he deny you the one thing you wish above all else" Koken countered. "I do not fear you, Saito-san. I will turn you. I will make you my equal. Together we can have everything, do anything. Forever."

"Together? What are you saying, Koken?"

"I am saying…" Koken took hold of her other arm and pulled her into him. "I am professing my love to you, Saito-san. I have always loved you. Ever since…growing up together, playing…"

"No." Saito squirmed to break free of his grasp.

Koken held her tighter. His fingers dug into her arms, hurting her. His strength equaled that of Katō Ichirō. Koken and Ichirō were more than childhood best friends; they were also both *kyuuketsuki*—vampires.

"It is true." He pulled her into a tight embrace. "Forget, Ichirō. He is through. His father is done. Be with me. I will give you what you want, Saito-san. The strength. The power. Everlasting life. Everything you wish for—"

"No!" Saito pulled away. "I do not love you, Koken. I love only Ichirō!"

Anger and shame colored Koken's face as he stared at Saito. With a speed that was blinding, Koken lashed out and seized a fistful of Saito's hair. He jerked her back into his arms, encircling his arm around her waist. "You shall feel differently…once you've changed."

Saito struggled in his arms. "No!"

Koken yanked her hair, pulling her head to one side, exposing the side of her neck. Her carotid artery pulsed thick, hard, and fast. Koken's skin paled, becoming a ghoulish shade of gray. His eyes suddenly glowed red like the embers in a swordsmith's forge. Koken opened his mouth—wide—revealing long, gleaming white fangs. He growled from deep in his throat. Yagyū Koken threw his head forward, his sharp fangs aimed for Saito's pulsing carotid artery.

Saito Izumi did not scream. She did not cry. She withdrew her tantō from its scabbard and drove it upward under the hem of Koken's *mōgami dō* and into his gut. She rammed it as hard and as far as she could shove it, then twisted the blade, inflicting as much internal damage as she could.

Koken cried out and let Saito go as he staggered back, his hands grasping at the bloody wound to his side. Blood leaked through his fingers and dotted the tatami floor. Koken crashed into the wall, upsetting the weapons rack upon which rested Saito's yumi and Ichirō's katana.

Doubled over, Koken looked up at her, his eyes glowing red, his fangs pressed into his thin lower lip.

Saito set herself in a defensive position. She held her tantō—his blood dripping from the tip—to her side in her left hand, her katana drawn and held horizontally over her head.

Koken pushed off the wall, his face twisted into a grotesque mask of gray anger, pain and embarrassment. The hurt he felt at Saito's rejection was clear in his expression and in his fury.

Saito swallowed hard. Aware of her inferior strength, her lack of stamina and speed against the supernatural abilities of a *kyuuketsuki*, she knew in a prolonged battle against Koken she would not prevail, despite her superior swordsmanship skills.

If he attacked her, if his rage was that all-consuming, then

Saito Izumi had only one hope, one chance to survive. She had to strike first. She had to decapitate Yagyū Koken!

That was the only sure way to kill a *kyuuketsuki*, other than driving a wooden stake through its heart.

At the moment, she had none at hand.

Koken hissed a horrible, beastly snarl and rushed forward, but stopped when from outside came a thunderous explosion.

The sudden boom was quickly followed by a terrible scream. Then more booms.

Saito's blood iced. They were the sounds one only heard from a battlefield. "The castle is under attack," Saito shouted.

Saito sheathed her weapons and hurried back into her *mōgami dō*, strapping the chest plate and back vest in place before rushing over to the weapons rack. There she grabbed her yumi and a full quiver of arrows and strapped them to her back. She grabbed two more katana; Ichirō's and one other. The second one she tossed to Koken, who was up until then unarmed. She wondered at the wisdom of doing that.

He caught the sword by the grip and weighted it, expertly gauging its balance. He grunted his satisfaction, then looked over at Saito.

Before he could say anything, Saito said, "We shall settle this later, Yagyū Koken. For now, we must defend Kumamoto Castle."

He nodded. "To the death if need be."

-----

SAITO IZUMI AND Yagyū Koken rushed from Uto Yagura into the *nino maru*. What they saw stopped them in their tracks. Saito's mouth fell open at the sight.

Beside her, she saw Koken have the same reaction.

It was like nothing she had ever seen—or even heard of—before.

Thick, black clouds had rolled in and filled the night skies. An evil darkness had rolled in and blacked out everything except the torches that hung from the sloping interlocking walls of the castle.

But what awed them both was not the impossible black night sky or the flickering torch light in the suddenly strong wind. No, it was the streaks of fire raining down from the heavens. Dozens of fireballs the size of small boulders arched downward, a torrent fire and trailing smoke.

The fireballs smacked into the ground, trees, ancillary buildings, and off the sloped castle walls. The cherry blossom trees, just now coming into bloom, and the structures that were hit, constructed mostly of black lacquer wood, burst into crackling, bright, orange and red flames.

Geysers of dirt exploded into the air where the fireballs slammed into the courtyard ground.

Saito and Koken stood agape, as did the dozens of palace guards, emerging sleepy samurai, and other residents of the castle who'd come out to investigate the disturbance.

Fireballs burst up from where they hit to suddenly zip around the *nino maru*—not inanimate objects, weapons tossed down at them— but cat-sized creatures with short, blazing arms and legs, blackened claws, and flaming manes running down their backs all the way to their tails.

Their flaming bodies sizzled as they slingshot haphazardly throughout the courtyard, their mouths gaped open, screaming thunderous howls.

"*Raijū*," Koken said.

"Yes," Saito breathed. She had heard of this type of *yōkai* before, but she had never seen nor believed they could actually exist. "And so many of them."

From the gates nearest the *hon maru*, Katō Ichirō emerged.

Seeing him made Saito's heart sing. Not only because of the

love she felt for him, which was immense, but because that meant the *tenshukaku* was safe—at least for the time being—for Ichirō would never abandon the main court, or the daimyō and his family, to defend the secondary *nino maru* if the *hon maru* was not fully secure.

Ichirō saw Saito and Koken and waved, running toward them, dodging the *raijū* whizzing around the grounds, and the many samurai and palace guards now engaged in fighting them.

When Ichirō reached them, he put an arm around Saito and kissed her cheek. "I am relieved you are well, Saito Izumi. I feared the worst when the commotion began."

"I am well, thank you, Ichirō-sama." Saito handed him his katana.

"And you, Yagyū Koken," Ichirō added, accepting the sword from Saito.

"You as well, my brother-in-arms," Koken replied.

Saito heard his icy jealous tone. Or was that simply her imagination?

For a moment the three of them stood, watching as still more *raijū* pelted down around them, bounced, then careened in seemingly a hundred directions at once.

"These *raijū*. What are they?" Saito asked. "Why are they attacking?"

"I do not have answers to your questions, Saito-san," Ichirō said.

"Nor is it the time to ask them," Koken offered, raising his katana.

"Agreed," Ichirō said. "Now is the time to engage our enemy and destroy them." Ichirō hoisted his katana over his head. "Attack!"

Without hesitation, Ichirō rushed into the melee.

Saito and Koken followed closely behind him before veering off in opposite directions. Saito worried about Koken and what had happened between them, but that was a concern for afterward, once the current battle was won.

A flying *raijū* noticed Saito and altered course by bouncing off the trunk of a nearby cherry blossom tree, leaving behind its mark: several long, ragged, and black singed scars in the bark.

Saito planted her feet and drew her katana back over her shoulder.

She swiped at the speeding thunder-beast but missed.

It cackled as it passed, a booming noise ringing in Saito's ears. The creature hit into the back of a nearby samurai, singed his *mōgami dō* and knocked him to the ground. The thunder-beast recoiled and shot back again toward Saito.

Again Saito readied her stance, She raised her katana over her head, but rather than swing the long bladed weapon at the attacking creature…as it came near, Saito thrust her tantō upward and pierced the *raijū's* belly.

The cat-size beast screamed, a booming crack of thunder-like noise, and exploded into a flaming, multicolored ball of sparks. Saito twisted away and shielded her eyes as the creature disintegrated into an umbrella of hot flaming, falling embers that sprinkled harmlessly to the ground.

Similar battles were taking place all over the courtyard. The *raijū* were deadly of course, but they also died easily, and the samurai they attacked were skilled warriors, up to the task, if not for the sheer number of *raijū*. For every one killed, dozens more showered down from the sky, filling the *nino maru*, and exhausting the hard-fighting samurai and palace guards.

*There are simply too many of them,* Saito realized. *Eventually we will fall.*

A scream roused Saito from her morose thoughts.

She spun—katana in one hand, tantō in the other, backlit by a burning building. The flames behind her climbed several meters into the air, filling the dark night with thick, oily, black smoke.

The scream had come from a samurai attacked by two *raijū*. The man's *kubuto* had been knocked off his head and the side of his face was on fire. He dropped his katana and frantically patted at his skin with his hands, unable to put the flames out while the buzzing *raijū* continued to streak past him, slicing at his face with their claws and leaving deep, flame-filled gouges in his cheeks and across his forehead. One of his eyes had been scratched out. Bright yellow and red flame burned in the blackened void left where his eye had been.

Saito charged and sliced the head off one *raijū* while she gutted the other with her tantō.

The creatures burst into sparkling flames and died.

Saito knocked the injured samurai to the ground. There she pressed the fiery side of his face into the dirt, smothering the flames.

As more *raijū* attacked her, Saito was forced to leave the man's side, leaving him to roll around on the ground, moaning. He would not survive to see the sun rise, she thought, and considering his injuries she decided that was for the merciful best.

Saito ran, continuing to slash and slice her way toward the western wall, where the attacking *raijū* seemed to be concentrating their attack. It was as if their assault were orchestrated and not random fate.

Could the creatures be under someone or something's command?

That thought iced her blood. A coordinated attack by supernatural beings?

Such an occurrence was unheard of, unthinkable. Yet, could it be possible?

Again her musing was interrupted by a shout, but this time it was one of warning, and from a familiar source: Ichirō.

"Saito-san! Look out! Behind you!"

Saito spun around.

A giant figure loomed over her—a hideous ogre-like creature twice her height and as wide as a doorway. A tigerskin loincloth draped over its one shoulder and covered its hairy torso. It had two large horns protruding from a shock of wild, black hair. It carried a *kanabō* in hands that more resembled bear claws than human hands.

Saito knew the ogre-like beast to be an *oni*.

The giant grunted and brought the massive iron club down in an overhead swing.

Saito dived to the right.

The *kanabō* came swooping down, narrowly missing her but so close she could feel a breeze as the club passed. The head of the club hit the ground and shook the land with the intensity of an earthquake, sending large, jagged cracks through the surface of the earth.

Many of the samurai fighting the *raijū* around her were knocked to the ground, with devastating results. The *raijū* went into a sudden frenzy, viciously attacking the fallen samurai.

Saito herself was on the ground, her katana knocked from her grip as she fell. She crawled toward it.

The *oni* lumbered toward her, the ground trembling with each pounding step it took.

Its shadow crossed over her. Saito glimpsed over her shoulder.

The giant was nearly on top of her.

Saito desperately glanced around, looking for help.

She saw Ichirō across the courtyard, near the base wall of the *tenshukaku*. But he was too far away to help her and was engaged in his own battles at the moment. He and Koken stood back to back, their katana slashing, their blades dark—coated with the blood of their enemies.

Saito noticed two *oni* lying dead on the ground nearby; black blood poured from their slit throats. Clearly they'd been slain by Koken and Ichirō, but now the two *kyuuketsuki* faced another three *oni* and were surrounded by them.

Spurred on by fear and desperation, crawling, Saito redoubled her efforts to get to her katana.

A hand seized her ankle and yanked her back.

Dragged across the ground, Saito ended up with a mouth full of dirt and her weapon farther away than ever. She twisted so she was on her back.

The *oni* continued to pull her.

When she was close enough, Saito kicked her heel into the creature's mouth. She heard something snap, a tooth or bone.

The creature roared but did not let go of Saito's ankle.

Saito drew her tantō.

The creature lifted her up into the air.

Dangling by one foot, Saito swiped her knife at her captor's massive thigh. The blade cut cleanly through skin and muscle and cleaved bone, spurting a fan of warm blood, splashing Saito's face, chest and arm.

The creature dropped Saito.

She spit blood and dirt out of her mouth as she hit the ground and crawled once more, hard and fast, toward her katana. She reached it. Her fingers encircled the grip, the *samegawa* comforting in her hand.

The ground under her trembled as the *oni* lumbered toward her again. Injured and angry, it loomed over her and swept its hand downward.

Saito swung her katana, cutting the blade cleanly through the *oni's* wrist.

More blood sprayed out.

The *oni* dropped its *kanabō* to grasp its injured arm, a futile attempt to stop the bleeding.

Its roar rumbled in Saito's ears.

She winced, then thrust her katana hard and deep into the giant's gut.

"Die, monster!"

Again the creature bellowed.

Saito had to clasp her hands to her ears, the howl was so deafening. She scrambled back on all fours, crab-walking to get beyond the *oni's* reach.

The ogre doubled over, clutching its gut. Its arm and leg were covered in blood. More blood poured from its stomach, like a crimson waterfall. The creature glared at her with hate-filled eyes. Then the ugly, bloodshot orbs rolled back in its head and the *oni* fell like a cut-down tree.

Saito scrambled back, then rolled clear of where the monster would hit the ground. She made it, but just barely. The giant smashed into the dirt, sending more jagged cracks rippling through the ground away from under where it hit.

With the *oni* dead, Saito climbed to her feet, wiping blood from her face. She circled the downed monster to see how Koken and Ichirō were managing, fighting their own three hideous *oni*.

A *raijū* flew in to attack her.

With barely a glance up at the thing, she swiped at it with her katana, using a figure-eight swish and cut. The blade sliced through the creature, not once, but twice, and the thunder-beast exploded.

Saito spotted Koken and Ichirō.

They were still cornered by the *oni* on the far side of the *nino maru* from her, but neither appeared to be injured. For that Saito was grateful, but the *oni* were closing in on them, tightening their circle.

And there were three of them.

Saito rushed toward them, swinging her katana and her tantō, exploding a *raijū* to her left and another to her right. But a sudden, strange hiss caught her attention. It was a new sound, associated with neither the *raijū* nor the *oni*.

Saito stopped short, barely in time to avoid getting her face burned off by a stream of fire.

Breathless, Saito searched for its source and spotted yet another type of *yōkai*. This sort of creature she knew. It was an *itsumade*, a bird-like monster the size of a sparrow, with black, oily feathers, and glowing red eyes, a *yōkai* that could spit fire.

Saito speared it with her katana.

It cawed and flapped its wings before the ember red light of its eyes went black.

Saito flicked the dead carcass away as if it were a littered parchment stuck to the tip of her blade.

The dead *itsumade* tumbled through the air and into a zigzagging *raijū*.

The latter burst into crackling sparks and died too.

Will they never get ahead of the multiplying fire-*yōkai*? Saito wondered as she resumed her charge toward Koken and Ichirō, wary of the wave of *itsumade* that had now joined the attacking *raijū*.

Saito reached where the *oni* had Ichirō and Koken backed against a wall. When she was in striking distance, she leapt into the air and came down on top of the nearest *oni*, jamming her tantō into the giant's side.

It bellowed and staggered back, at first knocking Saito off its back, then swiping its mighty tree-trunk-size *kanabō* at her, missing by only a hair's breadth.

Saito remained crouched and sliced her katana across the *oni's* shin.

Again the creature roared.

With murderous intent, the *oni* searched for and found Saito. It narrowed its eyes at the sight of its own blood on her blade.

Saito had a split second to react, and it wasn't enough.

The *oni* flicked its club at her, sort of a weak forearm swat, but getting hit by the head of the forged iron club still sent Saito flying. She fell to the ground and skidded several meters across the hard-packed dirt.

Ichirō cried out. "Saito-san!"

He darted, *kyuuketsuki* quick, through the opening left by the *oni* now pursuing Saito and leapt onto the creature's back, leaving Koken to deal with two of the misshapen giants by himself. Alone.

Koken shouted, "Ichirō! Hey—"

Ichirō ignored his brother-in-arms and scrambled up the *oni's* back. He grabbed one of its horns and, using the horn as leverage, pulled its massive head to the side, exposing its throat. The *oni's* jugular vein was thick as a tree branch. Ichirō's expression and skin color paled, growing ghostly and cold. His eyes glowed ember red. He snarled and bared his fangs.

Ichirō slammed his face down into the creature's neck. His fangs pierced flesh and muscle and sank deep into pulsing veins. The *oni* roared and arched backward, dropping its *kanabō*.

The ground shuddered.

The *oni* twisted and shook and stomped in haphazard directions trying to reach Ichirō and get a hand on him, but Ichirō remained out of his grasp. While the creature flailed, Ichirō bit deep into the creature's throat, ripping and savaging through the tough skin and meat, tearing at the veins buried inside. Rivers of blood spewed from the ragged wound and coursed down the creature's torso and loincloth, coating Ichirō's mouth, his jaw, and even his *tosei dō gusoku*.

The *oni* staggered to his knees, weak from blood loss. Still it thrashed frantically to dislodge Ichirō, who hung on tighter and savaged its neck more viciously until the creature finally fell face-forward and died.

Ichirō leapt off the creature and landed a meter away in a three-point stance, his legs crouched and locked, his one hand on the ground ahead of him, his fingers splayed. His hair was a tangled mess, and his lower face coated with dripping blood. No one and no thing dared go near him...except Saito.

She ran toward him. "Ichirō."

But Ichirō straightened and turned away, thrusting a hand out toward her, stopping her. "Saito-san, no! Stay away."

He did not add *when I'm like this,* but it was unnecessary.

Saito knew he would never turn away from her, reject her, otherwise. And she ignored his demand now. She reached a hand out to him, stroked his blood-stained chin and forced him to turn toward her, to look at her.

"Saito-san. Don't," he said. "Please."

Undeterred, she stepped around to face him. "Do not turn away from me. Nothing you do, nothing you become, can change my feelings for you. Ichirō, I love you."

Saito stretched up on tiptoes and kissed his blood-smeared mouth. She would do anything to prove her love to him. Anything. When she stepped back, her own mouth covered with the warm, tangy *oni* blood, she wiped it away with the back of her hand.

"I love you," she said, reminding him again.

From across the nino-maru, Koken shouted, "That's sweet and all, but...a little help. Please."

Koken had managed to hold off the two remaining *oni,* but now they had him cornered against the sloping wall.

Saito and Ichirō exchanged glances, drew their katana, and

charged across the *nino maru*.

As one of the *oni* began to swing its club, clearly intent on bashing in Koken's skull, Ichirō leaped and grabbed the head of the *kanabō* with one hand and rode the arching weapon up into the air, then dropped down to sit on the *oni's* broad shoulders. He crisscrossed his arms—one around the *oni's* forehead, the other across its massive chest and shoulders—and twisted in opposite directions.

The neck of the colossus snapped like so much kindling. Its knees buckled and the giant fell. Two down.

Saito leapt past the tumbling *oni* and landed on the ground between Koken and the last *oni*.

She dropped to one knee and thrust her katana up, gutting the giant ogre, driving her katana nearly all the way to its hilt.

The beast doubled over and Koken leaped over it, using the wall to springboard his jump until he was high enough to drive his own katana straight down through the back of the ogre's neck, severing its spine from the base of its skull.

The blow caused instant paralysis, and the creature fell flat to the ground.

Three down and done.

Koken dropped to the ground beside Saito where she'd scooted to safety. He turned to face her. The look on his face said he wanted to say something, but Ichirō came over to join them. Together, they stood, reunited, three old friends against a common enemy.

Saito gazed over at Koken. They would need to deal with what had been started in the weapons room in Uto Yagura. But what would that mean? Would he attack her, kill her, for her rejection of him? Or should she kill him first? Or had his anger and embarrassment been doused by this new threat? Had this diversion caused Yagyū Koken to come to his senses?

Koken smiled at her and the coldness of it sent a chill down Saito's spine.

His message to her was clear. Before this night was over, Saito Izumi would be dead.

"The *raijū* and *itsumade* are concentrating their attacks on the gates," Ichirō was saying, "separating the *nino maru* from the lower *san no maru*. That is how the *oni* got in. The lower gates have been breached."

"Then the *san no maru* has fallen," Saito said. The outermost protection was gone.

Even now *oni* could be seen pounding their way through the gates, where the massive wooden doors lay on the ground, twisted off their iron hinges. And still more were climbing over the walls, wet from their swim across the moats, bloodied from injuries endured in the climb, from encountering the rows of spikes along the underside of the *yagura*—and from where samurai fired arrows and shot at the invaders with their *tanegashima*. The Japanese matchlocks banged out bullets, adding to the acrid smoke and echoing booms on the battlefield.

Yet still the *oni* came.

Saito worried their defense of the castle would ultimately fall.

Koken grabbed Ichirō's shoulder and turned him away from the west wall. "Um, Ichi…"

He pointed toward the inner gates, the one that led to the *hon maru*, and ultimately to the *tenshukaku*. A dozen or more samurai were rushing out from the *hon maru* to battle the many and various *yōkai*. Leading them in their charge was an older man, in full *tosei-gusoku*. "Is that not your father?"

Katō Tadahiro, the daimyō, was the last person in all of Nippon who should be on the battlefield. But, tell that to an old warrior and expect him to listen, Saito mused.

Ichirō shouted and broke into a run. "Father!"

Saito shouted, too. "Ichirō! No!"

Something had caught her attention. At least she thought it had.

Ichirō turned, his run abated. "What is it, Saito-san? What is wrong?"

Saito pointed to a column of smoke billowing upward from a burning *yagura* in the southeast corner of the *nino maru*. Totally consumed by blazing, crackling flames, what remained of the structure was little more than the charred and blackened frame. The horizontal beams gave way and fell into the fire, pulling their attached vertical studs down with them and sending sparks and whooshing fire shooting skyward along with a thick, swelling, serpentine pillar of roiling, black smoke.

Ichirō followed where she pointed with his eyes, confusion plain in his expression. "What?"

"Are you blind? Can you not see?"

To Saito the column of smoke was more than that. It weaved and coiled in a manner inconsistent with the blowing night wind. In defiance of it, she thought.

Ichirō turned his attention to the small knot of samurai fighting around and beside Katō Tadahiro. "I have neither the time nor the patience for nonsense, Saito-san."

Before Saito could reply, Ichirō rushed off to be by his father's side, to defend and protect him. The way a good son should.

*Where I should be,* Saito thought. Not looking for *yōkai* where they did not exist.

Did she not have enough of the real variety to worry about?

Saito twirled around, cut the head off a passing *raijū* and gutted another fire-spitting *itsumade* with her tantō. But even as she continued to fight, slicing and jabbing her way toward Ichirō and the daimyō, the curling smoke kept calling for her attention.

Again she glanced over at it. The smoke had climbed high in the sky and grown thicker and blacker. Earlier she'd thought she'd seen the smoke coalescing, coming together. Now it appeared to be spreading apart, away from the main column to form limbs akin to arms and legs.

But that...thought bordered on madness. Didn't it?

Saito stopped and stared, unable to tear her eyes from the smoke. Behind her, Koken said, "What is it you think you see, Saito-san?"

So lost in her thoughts, Saito jumped at his closeness.

"The smoke," she said, after finding her voice. "It appears... no, it is becoming a shape, taking form. Tell me you see it, Koken."

*Tell me I am not insane.*

"I am sorry, Saito-san, but I do not."

"Then I am going crazy."

"I do not believe that," Koken said with a shake of his head. "Describe to me what you see."

"Arms and legs." She pointed, trying to outline the formation of features with her finger, features which were becoming clearer and clearer to her. "A head, but not human. Animal."

"What sort of animal?"

Saito squinted.

The smoke was so dark against the black-clouded night sky it was difficult to tell where smoke stopped and the cloud-covered sky began. Around her the thunderous booming of exploding *raijū* continued, as did the constant vibration of the ground, the shaking from every stomp of an *oni* or every time one fell in battle.

It wasn't her imagination. Saito knew that now, watching, mesmerized.

The smoke bent, swelled, twisted, and narrowed even as it grew larger. Saito could see it clearly now, but what she saw confused her. The limbs appeared to be human—sort of—taking on the muscular contour of biceps and triceps, thighs and calves, but the extremities were all wrong. Instead of hands and feet, the smoke-beast had tiger paws with long, extended claws, and its body was that of some kind of canine animal, perhaps a *tanuki*, a Japanese raccoon dog, and its head was oval with protruding ears and a muzzle-like mouth.

"Not an animal," Saito said in response to Koken's question. "Many animals. A hybrid beast."

"Describe it."

"Tiger paws and human arms and legs…a *tanuki's* body…with a monkey's head…and a tail…but not a tail."

"What do you mean 'not a tail'?"

"It's long and thrashes and snaps like a whip but there's something…unusual about it." A moment passed and the looming smoke-beast became clearer to see, more solid, black and gray and purple in color. "Wait. I can see it now. It's a tail that's a snake. It has an open mouth, fang-toothed, and a slithering, forked tongue."

Koken nodded.

"What you are seeing, Saito-san, is called a *nue*."

"And you do not see it?"

"No."

"Why not?" Saito demanded, still concerned her mind was playing tricks on her eyes.

"According to legend a *nue* can only be seen by one who is pure of heart." Koken waved his katana across the entirety of the castle. "I suspect in all of Kumamoto you may be the only one who can see it."

"Pure of heart. Me?"

Koken shrugged. "So legends say." His tone suggested they couldn't be believed.

"Myths," Saito added, no longer sure what she did—and

didn't—believe. All the while she kept an eye on the *nue*, now in solid form but with tendrils of fluttery smoke wafting off its body, like molting skin, obscuring the clarity of its form.

"I need to warn Ichirō." Saito took off running toward her lover, and her daimyō. If they could not see this new danger, they could not defend themselves against it. She had to be their eyes to tell them where it was, what it was doing. And defeat it if necessary.

As Saito ran she felt the *nue's* gaze following her. She glanced up at it, shuddering at its size as it hovered over the charred, crackling, burning remains of the *yagura*. The *nue* began to drift, floating down. It alighted on the ground near Saito.

She stopped. Would the nightmare never end?

The *nue* sat on all four paws and crouched low, like a lion, its claws extended and digging into the puffy, dry dirt. It brought its monkey-shaped head lower and closer to Saito, cocking it slightly to the side, as if the *nue* found what it saw intriguing. Its eyes were gray with diamond-shaped black pupils of simmering smoke. Saito could see her reflection in the dinner plate-sized eyes.

Saito shuddered. She held her katana and tantō akimbo, low and away from her body, but at the ready. "Proceed no further!" she commanded the *nue*.

From behind it, the *nue's* tail whipped lazily, its snake-like mouth open and fangs drawn. It hissed menacingly. The *nue* cocked its monkey-head back the other way and smiled, revealing a row of sharp, gray teeth.

"You can see me, child."

Saito's mouth dropped open. It could speak. The *nue's* voice twittered pleasantly, almost birdsong in its cadence, a sound paradoxical to the smoke-beast's ferocious appearance.

"I can," Saito managed to answer over her shock. "Move away or die by my blade."

She raised her katana to emphasize her resolve.

"Try, child, but ask yourself, how does one kill smoke?"

Its monkey mouth twisted into a sardonic grin. To demonstrate its incorporeal form, its head, body, and legs began to break apart, drift, become inchoate, the way smoke would waft away in a gentle but persistent breeze.

Saito didn't have an answer for it, but neither did the *nue* wait for one.

The smoke-beast crouched even lower, nearly lying on its front forepaws, arching its back. The tendril snake-tail whipped around, more agitated than before, snapping and hissing, its tongue flicking menacingly at Saito.

Saito settled into her battle stance, katana in her right hand held high, her tantō held in the left, lower, and closer to her body.

The *nue* sprang off the ground, a high, short leap, pouncing like a cat attacking a mouse.

Saito crouched to the right, windmilled her katana, and rolled under and away.

Her blade nicked the *nue's* forepaw. A tendril of smoke followed the blade, much like a stream of blood would trail a cut in a corporeal being if it were submerged underwater.

Only a flesh wound. But Saito smiled.

The cut had elicited a high-pitched yelp of pain.

Saito regained her footing and twisted around to face her enemy once more.

The *nue* twisted its body and turned. As it padded towards Saito, it favored its left, front paw; a coil of smoke drifted gray-black from the wound. The *nue* winced each time it put weight on that paw.

Saito's smile grew wider. "A *yōkai* that can be hurt is a *yōkai* that can be killed."

The *nue* was through talking.

It circled, stalking its prey. Then it attacked, rushing in. It took a swipe at Saito with its uninjured paw, a paw that was easily the size of her head.

Saito bent forward.

The paw sailed so close over her head that her hair became entangled in its claws. Saito staggered forward, the pain of her hair being pulled out of her head bringing tears to her eyes.

Saito stabbed the *nue's* paw with her *tantō*.

Once.

Twice.

Three times.

Smoke drifted up from the wounds and the *yōkai* howled, hopping on its hind legs.

Saito sliced her katana through the tangled lock of her long, black hair, cutting it off close to her scalp to free herself. Hair will grow back, she thought, as she adjusted her grip on her sword and brought it down, savagely slicing the *nue's* paw off its front leg.

The *nue* jumped back with a sharp yelp, withdrawing its paw up to its chest. The detached limb lying on the ground disintegrated into a thick, black puff of smoke. The *nue* sat back, a stunned look on its face. From behind it, the snake tail swished and spit angrily.

With her focus solely on the *nue*, Saito swatted at a flitting *raijū*, barely noticing it.

Her blade cut it in half and the little thunder-beast exploded.

"Saito-san!" Ichirō cried out from the far end of the *nino maru*, where he and his father and others battled several *oni* and dozens of zigzagging *raijū* and diving *itsumade*. "What are you doing? Come! Assist us!"

Saito ignored Ichirō's plea, aware he could not see the *nue*. Thus, he could not know what she faced or what danger he and the daimyō were in for from this enemy. An enemy unseen by all except her because she was pure of heart, if Koken were to be believed.

*Bah.*

She dismissed such foolishness. There had to be another explanation.

To the *nue*, she said, "You are behind this attack. Admit it."

The *nue* looked hard at her. Its eyes were smoldering swirls of purple and gray smoke. Its broad brow hooded and its monkey face grinned.

"So what if I am? What are you to do about it, child?" he taunted.

Saito saw its paw had begun to reform. She needed to attack it now. Saito charged, her blades held high.

The *nue* at first didn't seem to react; it simply remained seated, its injured leg cradled in its other forelimb, the end of it swirling smoke knitting into a nebulous proximity of a tiger's paw.

It wasn't until Saito got close enough to thrust her katana into the side of the *nue* that she realized the mistake she'd made.

Suddenly and without warning, the snake-tail snapped up from where it had been lazily coiled around the hind end of the *nue*. Now it struck. Opened-mouthed, it lashed toward Saito, nipping her arm before she could spin away.

She cried out and grabbed at the two long, jagged gashes in her upper arm.

The *nue* followed up with a swipe of its fully-formed paw.

Extended claws gashed Saito's cheek.

The blow knocked her off her feet.

Saito lay on her back, too dazed to move.

The *nue* slinked toward her. Its snake-tail swished and snapped.

It bared its fangs, flicking its purple, forked tongue.

The snake-tail struck, aiming for Saito's face.

She rolled.

The snake-tail's head slammed into the ground.

It whipped back up, shaking its head and spitting dirt, angrily searching for Saito.

But Saito struck first.

She slashed her katana upward, nearly lopping the snake-head from its thick, scaly tail-body.

The *nue* screamed in agony.

About to attack the smoke-beast again, Saito stopped short.

Beyond the *nue* she saw something that froze the blood in her veins, hardening it to ice.

Rising out of the dirt amid the battling samurai, palace guards, Ichirō, and the daimyō, a creature rose, shaking off clumps of dirt.

A *gashadokuro*!

A giant skeleton formed of the old, brittle bones of the dead.

It rose up, fifteen times larger than the average man.

Saito watched as the *gashadokuro* assembled itself before her very eyes, amid a horrific clattering of bones, clicking and rattling.

"Ichirō!" Saito shouted in warning.

She pointed at the giant skeleton.

What she saw...it could not be!

The ghastly thing had its orange glowing eye sockets locked on the daimyō, who at that moment was unaware, valiantly fighting an *oni* with the aid of two samurai.

"It's after your father!" Saito shouted to Ichirō, frantically waving at the *gashadokuro*. "Protect the daimyō!"

Saito moved to dart around the *nue*.

But the smoke-beast was too quick. It spun and pounced. Its powerful paws pounded the ground, kicking up puffs of brown dust and wafts of smoke, blocking her path.

"Get out of my way," Saito demanded. "Or you will die."

Saito hoped her bravado would hide how empty the threat sounded to her.

The *nue* grinned. "Really?"

Its snake-tail had its nearly severed head reattached. Once again it slithered and hissed but kept a respectable distance from Saito and her poised blades.

"The daimyō. He will be killed," Saito said with panic in her voice.

"That is the plan," it said.

"To kill the daimyō. Why?"

What possible reason could an army of *yōkai* have for wanting the daimyō dead? It made no sense. None of it.

Saito sidestepped to the left, but the *nue* reared up and reversed direction, continuing to block her. It paced, keeping her at bay. Desperate, Saito looked around behind her.

Koken. He could help.

But Koken had his hands full battling two more *oni*, his katana slashing in fancy figure-eights, keeping them both at bay at once, locked in a stalemate with the two giant ogres and in no position to assist either her or the daimyō.

Saito darted close to the *nue*, then quickly ran to the left.

It turned as swiftly as she did. It swatted a giant paw.

Saito dodged it, backing up. The *nue* missed but was close enough to thrash her hair across her face.

If she were *kyuuketsuki,* possessing the speed Koken and Ichirō had, then she could get past the *nue*. She cursed. Instead, she was trapped, powerless to protect the daimyō, powerless to carry out her sworn duty.

Over the broad back of the *nue* and its slithering, hissing snake-tail, Saito saw her worst fear become a reality. The *gashadokuro* stomped toward the daimyō, swiping aside warriors and *yōkai* alike with its massive skeletal hands. Unimpeded by the finest samurai in all of Nippon, the *gashadokuro* scooped the daimyō up like a child would carry off a stuffed doll. Its stiff, bone fingers completely encircled Katō Tadahiro's torso as it squeezed its hand into a fist, the *gashadokuro's* bones creaking and popping.

The *gashadokuro* lifted the daimyō up into the air, high over its head. It dropped its lower jaw open. Gray, decayed teeth spread wide.

Saito's breath caught in her throat. The *gashadokuro* was about to eat the daimyō.

"Father! No!" Ichirō shouted.

Still with an *oni* between him and the *gashadokuro*, Ichirō bared his fangs. He swung his katana with renewed effort, cutting the blade deeply through the *oni's* thigh. He tried to dart to the side, past the *oni,* but Ichirō was yanked to a standstill. The two struggled. Ichirō seized the *oni's* arm with both hands and wrenched it down as he slammed his foot into the giant's knee.

Surprised by the sudden strength of Ichirō's attack and the crippling damage to its knee, the giant fell onto all fours. Ichirō reached up and exposed the giant's neck and threw his face into it, savaging through skin, muscle, veins, and bone. A gush of arterial blood fanned out. The *oni* howled and gnashed its ragged, sawtooth teeth as it struggled to escape, then quivered in its death throe, and finally, went still and died.

But Ichirō was too far away, too late to help his father.

Still, there might be a chance. Saito slipped her yumi off her back and notched an arrow. She pointed it at the *nue's* face.

"A puny arrow won't harm me," the *nue* warned.

"Good to know, but I'm not firing at you," Saito replied, shifting her aim from the *nue*—too late for it to jump in the way— to the *gashadokuro*.

She let her arrow fly.

Earlier she had watched as foot soldiers shot at the

*gashadokuro*. Their bullets and arrows had passed unimpeded through the creature's exposed rib cage or nicked off bone, harmlessly deflected away.

But Saito aimed higher.

Her arrow arched upward.

Saito prayed her aim was true.

The arrow shot into the *gashadokuro's* glowing eye socket.

The *gashadokuro* snapped its head back and slapped its free hand over the damaged eye socket with a clattering slap.

It was hurt.

Saito quickly notched another arrow. She lined the tip up with the undamaged eye, if she could just blind it...

She let her arrow fly.

But not before the *nue's* snake-tail lashed out and bit the back of her hand.

Saito yelped, even as she knew her shot was ruined. Yet, she remained unmoved, only lowering her yumi to watch.

But she'd been right.

The second arrow missed the *gashadokuro's* eye socket and glanced off the hollow bone of its cheek.

Saito lowered her yumi. There was no time left for a third try.

All she could do was watch in horror as the *gashadokuro* shook its skull. With the struggling Katō Tadahiro still held in both skeletal hands, it closed its mouth, snapping its teeth closed like a guillotine's blade. Its teeth sliced through the daimyō's neck and severed his head from his body.

The *gashadokuro* yanked the thrashing body away from its mouth and chewed on the daimyō's head, crunching it, pulverizing it, gnawing it to a pulpy mash.

Ichirō screamed. "NO!"

Saito cupped her mouth, her lips quivering as incredulous

anguish erupted inside her like lava spewing from a volcano.

The *gashadokuro* dropped the daimyō's body. It hit the ground with a dull, final thud. The *gashadokuro* then turned and strolled away, indifferent to the stunned silence its actions had caused to the crumbled dead and headless body of the great man it left behind.

Ichirō ran to his father's body and collapsed beside it. He cradled the headless corpse as blood poured from the open neck, soaking his father's body and his own armor. Ichirō pressed his face to his father's chest, rocking him and sobbing.

Off in the distance, Koken knelt on one knee on the chest of a fallen *oni*. His katana was at the giant's throat, but Koken's gaze was on Ichirō and the daimyō's inert, headless form. Koken exchanged a glance with Saito, then viciously swiped the blade across the *oni's* throat, sending a fountain of blood into the air.

Still stunned by the brutal death of the daimyō, Saito was slow to react, but then the *nue* snickered.

She returned her attention to it.

The *nue* paced, slinking back and forth in front of her. It wore a self-satisfied grin on its dark, monkey-like face.

"You," Saito said. "You are responsible for this."

"I am. But what does it matter now? Your daimyō is dead. You have no reason left to fight."

"Monster!" Saito charged.

She aimed her katana high, and as she'd anticipated, the *nue* dodged to the left.

Saito was ready.

She lunged, suddenly changing direction, and drove her tantō into the smoke-beast's flank.

The *nue* howled and reared.

Saito leapt up onto its back, riding it like a horse, her arm around its thick neck.

The *nue* shook its head and the snake-tail lashed, striking at Saito with its open mouth, biting harmlessly into the thick plates of the *mōgami dō* covering her back.

She ignored the snake-tail's assault, holding on, and jabbing her tantō repeatedly into the side of the *nue*.

The *nue* thrashed and yelped with each stab of the tantō blade.

Its attention on Saito, its head twisted around, the *nue* tripped over the outstretched arm of a fallen *oni*.

Saito dug her blade into the *nue's* shoulder as the creature started to fall.

Its front leg jerked with a spasm, unable to hold the *nue's* weight. The smoke-beast crashed to the ground, chin first, and slid, spewing up a coughing cloud of dust and spraying dirt and rocks in a hundred different directions.

Jarred by the impact, Saito lost her grip on the creature's neck and tumbled over its head to the ground. She rolled away but quickly came to her feet. With katana and tantō raised, she faced the fallen creature, prepared to fight on, to battle to the death.

It would be her final sacrifice for her fallen daimyō.

The *nue* tried to get up by putting weight on its injured foreleg, but sprawled onto its face.

Wasting no time, Saito rushed the *nue* and leaped as high into the air as she could. She seemed to hover over the creature for a moment before she dropped back down, two hands wrapped tightly around the grip of her katana. She drove the blade down between the bunched shoulder blades of the smoke-beast, its black-purple-gray skin quivering.

Razor-edged steel passed through the creature as if passing through air, with no resistance at all until the blade was driven a meter into the dirt underneath it.

The creature let loose a blood-curdling scream.

Saito released her grip on the katana and fell away to the side, off-balance but once more drawing her tantō.

The *nue* slammed its paws into the ground, trying to push itself off the ground. The snake-tail slashed around, hissing and frantic as it snapped at the air in search of a target. When it came within striking distance of Saito, she hacked at it with her tantō. The blade cut through the slithery appendage—

Once.

Twice.

Thrice.

The *nue* shrieked.

Three pieces of the snake-tail dropped to the ground, including the still hissing head with its wide jaw, tendrils of smoke drifting off where Saito's blade had sliced through. Soon the detached pieces dissolved, wafted into pure smoke, and drifted away.

But the *nue* remained pinned to the ground by Saito's katana.

Ribbons of smoke curled skyward from the various stab wounds in its upper foreleg and from around where the katana pierced the beast's torso.

Saito didn't know, but she surmised that so long as the creature was in contact with the steel of her katana, and the blade remained embedded in the ground, it was trapped in its corporeal form, tethered to the solid world by the contact and unable to morph into smoke and escape.

"Why have you done this?" Saito demanded, facing the smoke-beast. "Why have you attacked Kumamoto Castle?"

The *nue* winced as it continued to struggle. "What does it matter now, child? Your daimyō is dead. It cannot be undone."

Saito drew her yumi, notched an arrow, and shot it at an angle through the side of the *nue*'s chest. The arrow dug into the dirt, reinforcing the *nue*'s tether to the ground, keeping it in solid form.

The *nue* bared its teeth and snarled, more angry than hurt.

"Tell me or you will die."

A hand grabbed Saito from behind. She spun and raised her arms in defense.

It was Koken. His face was deathly gray and his eyes burned red like hot coals, but only the barest sight of his fangs could be seen in his closed mouth, their tips only slightly indenting his lower lip.

"Saito, what are you doing? You're shooting arrows into the dirt and shouting at air."

Was she losing her mind? Maybe all along the smoke-beast was made up, brought to life not by some supernatural magic, but by her imagination.

"No." She pointed with her yumi. "It's there. A *nue*."

"He cannot see me," the *nue* said. "He is a filthy, undead *kyuuketsuki*!"

"I see it," Saito insisted, ignoring the *nue* and determined to convince Koken and herself it was there. "It is the *nue* that is behind the attack."

"It told you that?"

"Yes."

"But why?" Koken asked.

"I do not know. It hasn't said." She turned her attention back to the *nue*. "Yet. Tell me why?"

"Withdraw your blade and your arrow and I will tell you."

"Is it talking?" Koken asked. "What does it say?"

Saito notched an arrow, drew the string back, and aimed the tip at the *nue's* feline-like eye. "You will tell me or you will die."

Smug, the *nue* shrugged its shoulder. Its decapitated tail swished in the air, still headless, still spewing tendrils of smoke. "Then my secret dies with me, Saito Izumi."

"How do you know my name?"

"I know all about you," the *nue* said. "About everyone here. You. The Daimyō Kotō Tadahiro. His *kyuuketsuki* son, Ichirō."

"Tell me what it is saying," Koken demanded. "Now!"

"How?" Saito asked, ignoring Koken. "How do you know of me, of the others?"

"I was told by the one who hired me."

"Hired you?" Saito repeated. "To attack the castle? Tell me who! I demand it!"

"Saito," Koken said. He grabbed her by the shoulders and shook her.

"Unhand me." She pushed him away and came once more face-to-face with the *nue*. Its smoky presence was cloying, scratching at her throat and tickling her nose. "If I promise to release you, will you give up your secrets?"

"For a promise? I think not." The *nue* gave a little shake of its head. "How naive do you think I am?"

"If I possess the pureness you yourself say is required to see you, and I must since I *do* see you, then surely as such, I cannot lie. Add to that, I am samurai."

The *nue* tilted his head, considering her words. "Your logic is not flawed, child." It nodded. "I agree."

Saito glanced over the *nue*.

Ichirō sat with his father's body draped over his legs, his headless form still cradled in his lap. Around him palace guards and others continued to battle the fire-*yōkai* and the lumbering *oni*. They fought valiantly, keeping all manner of *yōkai* from attacking the grieving Ichirō, knowing he was now the new daimyō.

"Tell me true," Saito said, refocusing her attention on the *nue*. "And I will let you live."

The *nue* looked past her. "Him."

Saito twisted around, following the creature's gaze. It landed on…Koken.

Unsettled by her stare, he said, "What?"

"No," Saito gasped.

She turned back, but the *nue* nodded.

"No," she insisted again. "You lie."

The *nue* shook his head sadly. "Though I possess the capacity to maim, to kill, to destroy, I am incapable of uttering even the simplest deceit, Saito Izumi. Ironic, I know." The *nue* shrugged. "I do not understand it. Now, I told you true. The one who orchestrated this raid, who paid me in gold, is your long-time friend, Yagyū Koken. That one. Believe me or not, that's up to you."

The *nue* made a show of looking around, of observing the destruction: the burning buildings and trees, the dead and wounded samurai, and those still fighting the frenzied whiplashing *raijū*, the flittering, fire-spitting *itsumade*, and the earth-stomping *oni*. Its gaze settled on Ichirō, seated, rocking his father's corpse.

"Amazing the extraordinary lengths, the destructive lengths, some will go to achieve their ambitions." The *nue* shrugged. "For what? To rule a castle? Impress a girl? Humans."

The *nue*'s grin turned menacing. "Now, child, all is known. All is revealed. My work is done and I wish to leave. Release me."

Saito moved toward the smoke-beast.

It watched her with a careful eye.

When she got close, she reached up for her katana, stretching to get her hand around the grip. She had to lean in close to the smoke-beast, and when she was practically on top of him, she quickly drove her tantō into the side of its neck and sliced it downward, splitting its throat open. A hot waft of smoke drifted skyward. The *nue* screamed, then lost its shape, dispersing into ribbons of harmless black smoke that spread thin and drifted away on the gentle night breeze.

She'd killed it rather than release it like she'd promised. She'd lied all along. A violation of the long-held honor code of the samurai. Yet, worse than that, Saito could not help but wonder: had the *nue* truly drifted into harmless smoke because she'd killed it, or had her deceit caused her to simply lose the ability to see it any longer?

Had she, with that one vengeful act, now become as dark as the enemy she fought?

She shook her head. Unimportant.

She had other matters to attend to.

To Koken, she said, "Is it true?"

"Is what true?" Koken asked.

"Are you responsible for this attack?" She waved her arms about the battlefield. "For all this?" Even as she asked the question, she knew the answer.

"No," he said defiantly, but without his usual bravado. "Why would I?"

Saito knew it was a lie. She rushed at him and slammed the heels of her hands hard into his chest.

Koken staggered back, not hurt but stunned, rubbing at where she'd struck his chest. His complexion paled, became gray, and his eyes burned red hot once more. Koken snarled and bared his fangs.

"Fine. Yes, Saito-san. I did it. Satisfied? I schemed with the *nue* to gather an unholy army. I paid it in gold, untold riches, to attack the castle, to burn it to the ground."

"And...the daimyō?"

"To kill the daimyō, too. That was the whole point."

To hear Koken say it, and with such glee, shocked Saito more than she cared to admit. "Why, Koken? Why?"

The light in his ember red eyes faded a notch and his voice

softened. He took a step toward her, but Saito backed up. "I did it for us, Saito-san. For you."

"Me?" She shook her head. "That...makes no sense."

"It makes perfect sense, Saito-san." Koken held out a hand, reaching for her. "I did it because I love you."

Saito took a moment to absorb that. She stood in her samurai armor, the yumi crossbow strung across her back, both of her blade weapons back in her hands where they belonged. Her arms hung down by her sides but she held them away from her body. Her hastily cut hair covered her face at scraggily and differing lengths. Several buildings burned brightly behind her.

"No. You did it to become daimyō," she accused, staring at him through a scraggily curtain of black hair. She paused, taking in his cold, hard expression, realizing the full extent of his plan. "But so long as Ichirō lives you will not be daimyō. You intended for Ichirō to die, as well."

"You're a smart girl, Saito. You figured it out."

Saito nodded. The *nue* had given her the answer, but she hadn't heard it. *To rule a castle? Impress a girl?* If both the daimyō and Ichirō were killed, there would be no living heirs. "The Katō clan would end and Tokugawa Iemitsu would appoint a close, political and personal ally as the new Higo Province daimyō. You."

"Me. And why not." Koken stepped toward her. "And there is still time for you, too, Saito-san. Do not simply be samurai. Stand with me. Be the wife of daimyō Yagyū Koken."

"Never. Ichirō still lives. Ichirō will be the next daimyō. Not you. Never you."

Koken pounded a fist against his chest plate. "Why not me? I am every bit as good as Ichirō. As smart as he, as good a fighter. Better, even."

Saito snorted. "Ha. You are none of those things, Yagyū Koken.

You are pathetic and you are a fool."

"How dare you speak to me with that tongue? I will be the next daimyō and you will serve me...or you will die."

"Then I die."

Saito rushed at Koken, her two blades raised high.

Koken rushed at her, his own katana poised high over his head.

At almost the same instant they leaped at each other. Like two giant rams about to butt horns...they collided in midair.

Saito stabbed viciously with her tantō. The blade cut into Koken's belly. She drove it hard up and under his *mōgami dō*.

Koken winced and grabbed at the wound with his free hand. The two of them twisted in the air. Koken tried to ensnare her with his arm, circling it around her waist, but Saito kicked out and shoved him away with her forearm across his chest.

Their embrace broken, Saito fell to the ground even as, seemingly from nowhere, Ichirō sailed through the night air and slammed into Koken. "Murderer! You killed my father!"

The two *kyuuketsuki* hit the ground hard and rolled, locked in a deadly embrace, fists striking crushing blows.

"Ichirō, be careful," Saito shouted.

Saito ran toward them, but the area between her and the dueling *kyuuketsuki* became increasingly filled with *raijū* and *itsumade* as if the fire-*yōkai* were purposefully keeping her from Ichirō and protecting Koken. She swatted at the frenzied beasts, ducking as her blade struck and ignited the flying *yōkai* into exploding fireballs. Still, they kept flying at her, cawing and spewing caustic flames. There were many of them, too many.

Ichirō struck a solid blow to Koken's jaw, sending him reeling.

Saito sliced the head off a passing *itsumade* and gutted another *raijū*.

Koken recovered and charged Ichirō. A swipe of his katana

cut a gash through Ichirō's thigh. It was a deep cut but ultimately harmless against the healing power of a *kyuuketsuki.*

Ichirō knocked Koken to the dirt. He dropped down on him, straddling his torso with his legs, his knees pinning Koken's shoulders to the ground. Ichirō had a hand around Koken's throat, the tip of his katana blade poised at Koken's neck, indenting the flesh, drawing steady droplets of blood. "Why? Why?"

Distracted by their fight, Saito jumped when a blast of spewed fire hit her shoulder and singed the sleeve of her robe. She yelped and patted at the burning silk, but the flames spread rapidly and Saito was forced to drop her weapons and tear the material out from under her *tosei dō gusoku.* The liquid fire fused the cloth of her robe to her skin. As she pulled at the layers of melted, burning silk, burned flesh ripped away with it.

Saito screamed from the pain.

Her scream caught Ichirō's attention. He turned toward her, taking his focus off Koken.

Saito watched in horror as Koken took full advantage of Ichirō's distraction.

Koken bucked his hips, jarring Ichirō from his perch on his chest. The pinned *kyuuketsuki* pulled his arm out from under Ichirō's one knee. In his hand was gripped his katana.

Ichirō snapped his attention back to Koken—too late—his glowing eyes wide as he watched Koken's weapon swing toward him—a powerful stroke—and the gleaming blade sliced cleanly through Ichirō's neck, sending a gushing spray of blood fanning outward. Ichirō's head tumbled away from his body. The glow of his open eyes slowly diminished until they went dark.

"NO!" Saito screamed and ran forward.

Koken shoved the headless corpse off. The body fell to the side and Koken leaped to his feet. He looked down at Ichirō. Headless and dead. Koken shrugged. "Like father, like son."

Saito rushed at him, tears streaming down her face. She slashed with her katana and tantō as she closed the gap between them. Her blades whooshed through the air.

"Saito-san..." Koken gasped, surprised.

Saito swung her katana. The blade sliced under his *mōgami dō,* cutting a horizontal wound across his lower stomach. Blood spilled, soaking his legs in red.

"Saito-san, please."

Saito didn't stop. She didn't listen. She rammed her tantō into his gut with such force she lifted Koken off his feet, burying the knife all the way to the hilt.

His *kyuuketsuki* eyes opened wide with shock and pain. Koken grabbed Saito's wrist and pulled it away.

Saito ignored the squeezing pain of his hold, maintaining her grip on her weapon, refusing to let go.

She slipped the tantō out of his stomach. Fresh, gleaming blood dripped from its curved steel.

For a moment that passed like an eternity, they stood, hateful eyes locked on each other. Then...

With lightning fast speed, Koken seized a fistful of Saito's hair. He yanked, forcing her head to the side, exposing her long, smooth neck, the slope of her throat. The hard pulsing jugular vein just under the surface beat visibly.

Strong.

Enticing.

Koken threw his head down at her neck.

His teeth pierced her flesh.

He sank his fangs deep into the throbbing vein...

And he drank.

Saito screamed.

Hungrily, savagely, Koken continued to tear into her neck, ripping with his teeth.

Blood spurted like an uncorked spring.

He held Saito in an iron grip.

Too weak to fight back, her arms dangled heavy and lifeless. Saito felt her blood spill over her neck and run down her chest, her wounded shoulder, and arm. Her vision faded. Darkness crowded her eyesight, as the surrounding fires dimmed and the burning buildings lost their brilliance. The sounds of fighting grew dull, muted, fading away. She was dying and she knew it.

Koken pulled back. His glowing eyes had lost some of their own brilliance, their bloodlust. His skin had regained some of its color, though the sight of fresh gleaming blood smeared over his chin and cheeks where it had coursed down his throat was still a horrific sight to behold.

"Saito-san, I am sorry. I never meant for…"

Saito stared up at him through half-closed eyes, her eyelashes fluttering as she struggled to stay alive. And for just a few seconds she did—long enough to drop her yumi from her shoulder.

With a final surge of her waning strength she thrust the bamboo end of the yumi upward as hard and as far as she could.

The intricately whittled tip of the bow broke through Koken's skin, pierced his rib cage, and punctured his *kyuuketsuki* heart.

Koken released her as he grabbed for the yumi protruding from his chest, but he was too late. As he fell, his face was a twisted mask of anger, shock, and, Saito thought, sadness. He hit the ground with his hands still clutching the yumi. His eyes were still open, but the red fire glow in them had been extinguished.

Saito managed to remain on her feet a moment longer—I'm the last one standing, she thought—and then she, too, fell dead, collapsed in a crumbled pile between Koken and Ichirō's dead bodies.

289

**A PALACE GUARD** pressed his hand to Saito Izumi's chest. He failed to feel a heartbeat. "This one, too, is dead."

The fighting was over. The *raijū*, the *itsumade*, the *oni*, and even the *gashadokuro* were all gone. And no wonder. The daimyō was dead. So too was his son, Ichirō, his only heir. The Katō clan had been brought to its end.

Yagyū Koken was also dead, and with him, his plans to rule Higo Province as daimyō. The shōgun Tokugawa Iemitsu would name a successor, a new daimyō, but that was politics for another day. This day would be for cleaning up, for tending to the wounded, and for mourning the dead.

Of which, Saito Izumi was one.

The palace guard shook her body one more time to be sure his pronouncement was accurate before moving on. Saito's eyes flew open and she convulsed violently as she tried to draw a breath.

Startled, the guard jumped back, but seeing Saito struggle, he leaned over her and pulled her up into a sitting position.

Saito gasped, trying to breathe, but she could pull no air into her lungs. Her face turned a ghastly shade of gray. The guard patted her back but had no real idea of how to help her. With a panicked expression he looked around the *nino maru*, desperate for help, but saw no one who could render any better aid than he.

"Are you all right?" he asked. "What is wrong?"

Stupid questions, Saito thought. It was obvious. *I can't breathe. I'm suffocating!*

She grasped at his *tosei dō gusoku*, clinging to him for help. The thick leather shoulder straps of his *mōgami dō* ripped away like rice paper. She and the guard both looked at the torn straps in stunned wonder. The strength it took to do such a thing...

Perhaps they'd already been damaged.

Saito dropped the *mōgami dō* and seized the guard's robe, pulling him closer, trying to speak. Her mouth opened and closed, but still she could not breathe: all she could do was make gasping, sucking sounds. She noticed the guard had been wounded. She saw the nasty burn mark on his upper arm. The flesh was blackened and rimmed with glistening, crusted blood.

His blood had leaked a trail down his arm, both caked and fresh.

Saito sniffed the air. Her belly rumbled. She gasped.

"Come closer."

The guard leaned in closer, off-balance.

"You're wounded." Saito made short, quick wheezing sounds.

Still panicked over her inability to breathe but now feeling something else, something more important than breathing, Saito realized she was hungry.

"Yes," the guard said. "If you are better, I must move on and look for more survivors."

A thumping sound assaulted Saito's ears, almost drowning out the guard's words. A pounding noise. Rhythmic. Her arms trembled. She was so hungry...no...she was starving!

The sound. It was a heartbeat. Not hers. His!

"Will you be all right?" the guard asked again.

Saito's mouth was dry, her lips parched. She tried twice to speak before her croaked words made any sense. "Yes, I'll be well...once I feed."

Saito Izumi's face lost all color. Her olive skin became a gray death mask, and her dark, brown eyes suddenly glowed red, burning bright as fire. Saito opened her mouth wide, revealing her new, gleaming white fangs.

The guard stared, too stunned to move or even scream.

Saito pulled him into her and sank her teeth into his neck. The guard struggled for a moment, then went limp in her arms as Saito fed.

No, not fed. She gorged until her hunger, her need, was sated. Until her transformation was complete. When she was done, she dropped the guard's drained dead body. Saito Izumi's coveted wish had come true.

She'd become what she wanted…she was *kyuuketsuki*.

If you enjoyed *Stone of Destiny*,
Be sure to check out the other books in the exciting Irish Cycle
series

And for exclusive content, information about upcoming new
releases and other deals,
please join our mailing list here:

https://www.subscribepage.com/irishcycleseries

# ALSO BY DAVID MILLER